Silver Mo...

HAVE A...
OF 92 GREAT NOVELS
OF
EROTIC DOMINATION

If you like one you will probably like the rest

A NEW TITLE EVERY MONTH

All titles in print are now available online at
http://www.onlinebookshop.com

Silver Moon Readers Service
109 A Roundhay Road
Leeds
LS8 5AJ
United Kingdom

http://www.adultbookshops.com

Silver Moon Books of Leeds and New York are in no way connected with
Silver Moon Books of London

If you like one of our books you will probably like them all!

Write for our free 20 page booklet of extracts from early books
- surely the most erotic feebie yet - and, if you wish to be on
our confidential mailing list, from forthcoming monthly titles
as they are published:-

Silver Moon Reader Services
109A Roundhay Road
Leeds
LS8 5AJ
United Kingdom

http://www.adultbookshops.com

or leave details on our 24hr UK answerphone
08700 10 90 60
International acces code then +44 08700 10 90 60

<u>New authors welcome</u>
Please send submissions to
Silver Moon Books Ltd.
PO Box 5663
Nottingham
NG3 6PJ
or
editor@electronicbookshops.com

SAVAGE JOURNEY first published 2002, copyright JOHN ARGUS
The right of JOHN ARGUS to be identified as the author of this book has been asserted in accordance with Section
77 and 78 of the Copyrights and Patents Act 1988

SAVAGE JOURNEY
by
JOHN ARGUS

The characters and situations in this book are
entirely imaginary and bear no relation to any
persons alive or deceased, or actual happening.

This is fiction - In real life always practise safe sex!

CHAPTER ONE

For all practical purposes, the life I led, the social and the formal educational side to which I had been exposed, both came to an end three weeks and four days after my nineteenth birthday. I recall worrying all the previous night over an upcoming assignment in Torts, attempting to memorize a variety of precedents to little success. It's odd to recall things like that, to remember with such clarity the foolish worries which were soon to be so vastly overshadowed by unforeseen events.

I was in my first year at university, studying law. I would like to say I had felt a calling to the profession, a desire to right great wrongs or see to the proper dispensation of justice, but in truth I was looking for little other than status and monetary success. Not, I suspect, unlike the majority of my fellows. All of us saw the law, and its clever manipulation as a venue to large houses outside the city, expensive cars and trips to the south of France during the holidays.

As it was my first year I was enjoying the freedom of being away from home, no longer being required to obey what I then considered the unreasonably strict rules set for me by my uncle and aunt (my parents having died a decade earlier). I had begun to experiment with both drugs and alcohol, partying long into the nights on weekends, and enjoying life.

Like most girls I had also begun experimenting with the shades of exposure different types of clothing and fabrics afforded me. My skirts had crept slowly upward as I grew more confident in my legs, and more daring in the length of them I might safely reveal without drawing censure from friends and acquaintances. My blouses occasionally grew quite tight or thin, and on my birthday I had worn my first really low cut dress to the party. That had been an evening which had left me slightly blushing and in a state of suppressed arousal. For to have my cleavage so well-displayed, to bare the tops of my softly rounded breasts in public, had been quite a daring act for me, and after my initial self-consciousness (my stomach had been filled with butterflies the first hour) and embarrassment I had felt a rather cocky sense of pride in my seductive appearance.

Boys, or rather, young men, I suppose one should say, were quite important at the time. I wasn't at all sure I understood them, or that I ever would. They were a constantly confusing group, now bright and pleasant, now sullen and angry. I knew I felt a small thrill along my spine when I was near some of them, when they touched me in a certain way, or even looked at me in a way which communicated the desires they felt for me. Of course I felt some of those desires myself, but being a young lady of good reputation I had to be quite careful about how I allowed those desires to be expressed, or how much I permitted the boys to get away with. I did not want people whispering unpleasant insinuations behind my back. Not only did I have a rather large measure of pride, but such things would hardly enhance my career prospects, nor help to build relationships based on respect among classmates who were, I thought, to become my future colleagues.

I would often afterwards consider the irony in that effort, in the hands I had fought off, the wrestling matches I had engaged in, and the sexual explorations I had not dared continue.

I should say that I was quite an attractive girl, or so everyone had been telling me up to that point in my life. My hair was a soft blonde, perhaps only slightly too pale for truest gold. I wore it straight, an inch or two past my shoulders, parted in the middle, with no bangs.

It was thick and rich, however, folding firmly and lightly along the contours of my oval face. My nose was smallish, and slightly upturned, and my eyes were, and still are, quite a bright shade of blue. I had pert lips and white teeth which drew many compliments to my smile.

I had been quite adequately, if not generously endowed, with rather nice breasts for my slender frame, and quite good legs, as well. They were never great round things to draw the eye, but they were quite high and firm, and filled out the pink string bikini I had begun to daringly wear quite nicely. Being just two inches short of six feet tall my legs were long and striking, and when I wore a short skirt the boys - and men as well - seemed to appreciate them.

I was, of course, aware of being attractive, and took pride in it, despite knowing how little of that was due to any actions on my part. I was flattered and pleased by the attention, but still quite nervous and even a little embarrassed about certain elements of it. Knowing, as I walked down a hall, or along the sidewalk, that men twice my age were examining my bottom, or my legs, and perhaps thinking quite lewd thoughts about me was still both exciting and disconcerting.

At nineteen, sex was still a foreign concept to me. Other girls my age had a great deal of experience in it, so in that respect my life experience was somewhat retarded. This was not due to any great moral decision on my part, but rather, indecision, uncertainty about when I should suffer my virginity to be taken, and to whom I should offer it. Circumstances had never quite seemed right. Either the gentleman in question was unworthy, or unreliable (I did not want tales of my deflowering to pass among my peers) or the setting was simply wrong. I had no intention, for example, of being deflowered in the back of a darkened automobile, or in a closet at a party.

Not that I had not experimented. I was no prude, after all. I had begun with the normal fumbling, allowing boys to grope at my breasts and bottom, then graduated into allowing their hands within my blouse, and begun the arduous task of learning how to please their members with my hands, and then with my mouth. I liked the latter more than the former, as it made me feel quite wicked.

I was relatively normal anyway, and had only a little less than the normal amount of exposure to sexual activities, while still retaining my virginity. I was intrigued by the idea of sex, even excited by it. But I was somewhat shy, and exposing my body completely - to a boy - was a daunting prospect.

And nothing less would do. I had too many fantasies to accept some dreary deflowering at the hands of a half drunken lout, a lout, moreover, who would thrust himself into my body, grunting like an animal, and then roll over and fall asleep. When I did give myself it would be to someone handsome and marvellous, and sober, in a bed, or perhaps before a blazing fireplace. He and I would both be passionate, and completely naked.

And it would, of course, be glorious.

I had discovered masturbation rather early on, but quite by accident. And through careful experimentation and very discreet conversations with girlfriends, I had come to realize that my responses to sexual touching were quite a deal more extreme than that of my peers.

My breasts were quite sensitive, especially the nipples, which would swell to fat, taut little buttons with my arousal. They would grow hotter and hotter, and become so sensitive that even the touch of a gentle breeze would send wicked pleasure flowing through them and my whole body. The touch of another's fingers could set them on fire, and the one time a boy had managed to get his mouth against one I had almost lost control of myself, so great was the wonder and passion.

Other girls reported little, if any, real pleasure from the fondling they received there. My breasts, however, would seem to swell up just like the nipples, the skin growing tight and straining, becoming more sensitive the longer they were touched. They would grow hot, and begin to throb, and after a time it seemed that every touch made me swoon and shudder with the sexual electricity flowing through them.

Things were even worse "down there". From my own touching, and the little bit of petting which boys had managed to inflict upon me there I knew that were a boy to get his fingers at my private parts for very long at all I would surely go mad and become little more than a quivering, wanton sexual animal. This was a great worry to me, for as I have already stated I did have a deal of pride. I wanted people's respect, and I knew full well this would be deeply eroded by gossip about my wantonness and lack of control.

However, any choice regarding this was to be taken from me from that day three weeks and four days after my nineteenth birthday. It's odd how one can live out such a day, carrying on the routine activities one is accustomed to, without any suspicions about what lies just ahead.

It was a Tuesday. I had Constitutional Law that morning. This allowed me to sleep in so that when I woke I was the only person home in the small flat I shared with two other students.

Nude, I slipped out of bed and padded to the dresser. I examined myself in the mirror, and felt a small tightness in my chest as I imagined Peter, a boy I had my eye on at school, seeing me then, imagined him lusting after me, his cock growing hard.

My first reaction, of course, when the door opened, was shock. I halted in mid-step, jaw dropping, unable to believe I was seeing a strange man standing in my doorway. An instant later I recalled my nudity, of course, and, I suppose, made some sort of scream or shriek as I tried to cover myself.

The man was extremely large, filling the doorway from top to bottom and side to side. He wore a pair of neatly pressed black trousers, and a black T-shirt which bulged against his massive chest. His bare arms rippled with muscles. He had a square jawed face, and his dark hair was cropped close to his head. He did not smile as he moved forward, and his eyes never left me.

He backed me against the dresser without touching me, and stood motionless, eyes cool as I stood there clutching a bed sheet against myself, stammering and blushing and filling with terror and anxiety.

When he finally moved it was to reach out and take hold of the sheet. I tried desperately to hang onto it but he yanked it free effortlessly, then seized my wrists and lifted them up above my head, pinning them together in one hand, then extending that arm so he could ease me back a bit and inspect me.

I was, of course, terrified as well as mortified. No man had ever seen me nude, at least, not in my memory, and here was this complete stranger, a grown man of at least thirty with his eyes taking in as much of my pale flesh as they desired while I was unable to do a thing to hinder him. I could almost feel his gaze moving over my breasts - jiggling slightly as my chest rose and fell furiously - my trim, flat belly, and my pale bush of pubic hair 'down there'.

"Let me go!"

I writhed helplessly, twisting and turning, but unable to change my position in any significant way.

"Please! Please!" I gasped, heart pounding. "What do you want!?

He did not speak a word. I begged, pleaded, cursed, made demands, and broke into tears, but he ignored it all. He looked at me in a sort of bored way and continued to hold my wrists up high until, I suppose, I finally wound down.

Then, shivering and trembling, my tears starting to subside, I felt his hands shifting, pulling my hands back behind my head, and there gripping my hair as well before pulling further down. With my hands forced back I was thus made to arch my back quite sharply. I knew, of course, that this was to accentuate my breasts, to thrust them out even more firmly for his inspection, and my skin burned with humiliation as his eyes roamed my body. He raised his other hand then and placed it on my stomach, sliding it slowly upwards as I shuddered and moaned.

I felt his large, work-roughened hand cup the underside of my right breast, then slide upwards to cover it. Even amidst my terror I could not but help note how delicious this felt. I sensed his fingers closing inwards, squeezing into my soft, malleable flesh, and moaned anew at such shocking and intimate contact with a complete stranger.

I could not see, for the pull of his hand on my hair forced my head upwards, yet I did not need eyes to follow the touch of his fingers as he moved them across the surface of my breast. I felt them seize my nipple, stroking and pinching it lightly, then tweaking it and rolling it between them. I could feel the nipple hardening and swelling, and my face burned with shame for fear he would think I somehow welcomed his touch.

I think it was this which drove me to kick out at him. It was quite foolish of me, for he was easily more than twice my weight, and many times stronger than I, but I felt I needed some signal that would indicate to him my outrage and displeasure.

My bare foot made contact with some part of his leg. The contact was not strong and probably caused me more pain than him. However, it drew an immediate response. He whipped me forward and sent me flying, staggering across the floor to sprawl face down across my table. I tried to rise, but a huge hand slapped down between my shoulder blades, pressing me into the desk hard enough that my breasts - pillowed out beneath me - ached.

"I shall be your first instructor, girl," he said to me in a low, throaty voice. "Those instructions shall be on the nature of your position from this time on. You will obey any order given, and will make no attempt to resist the wishes of those placed over you."

11

"I-I don't know what you mean!" I cried. "Let me go! Leave me alone!"

"You are not in any position to make demands," he said. "You will do as you are told or face the consequences of your misbehaviour."

He removed his hand from between my shoulder blades and I immediately tried to rise, only to be shoved down forcefully.

"Do not move!" he barked in a menacing voice.

Frightened, I obeyed, only whimpering when I saw him slide a thin, ugly looking belt from the loops of his trousers.

"Punishment for any resistance to your masters will be swift and painful," he said, speaking quite precisely. "You will be taught your place."

I screamed more in surprise than pain as the belt cut across my bottom. I felt shocked, even outraged, yet the fear was there, as well, and even as my buttocks began to sting, I made no attempt to rise again, or to twist away. Instead tears filled my eyes once more as the belt slashed in once more, this time harder. I cried out softly, laying my head on my hands, shuddering as the belt cracked loudly across my bared buttocks again and again, the pain building up like a growing fire. I felt a sense of disbelief to be experiencing such punishment from a stranger, to be naked as I was and so badly treated. I had no previous experience with such behaviour and was at a loss as to how to cope.

"P-please!" I cried out in a choked, tear-filled voice.

The pain was simply too much, each new crack of the belt sending a new wave of it searing through my burning skin and through my body.

The belt whipped down again, and again, and again, like his voice, very precisely laid, very carefully landed. I sobbed freely into the tabletop, knowing I could do nothing to stop him, that anything I tried would result only in further punishment.

He stopped, finally, and I felt a wonderful relief that the next blow had not landed. My legs were trembling and I could hardly see through my tears as his hand slipped down along the cleft between my buttocks, fingered my anal opening briefly, then dropped lower. He held my sex in the palm of his hand, squeezing it lightly, then pressing a finger against the tightness of my body. This would have shocked and horrified me previously, but at the time anything other than the belt was almost welcomed.

Naturally, from the moment I had seen him I had suspected to the point of certainty that he intended rape. I almost welcomed his touch, wanting him to get it over with and leave me alone to recover. Yet humiliation flowed through my veins as well, and hatred of him and my weakness before him.

I felt his big finger sliding up and down between my pubic lips, nudging against that hot little button at the top of my sex, then slipping lower and pressing into the small hole there. I closed my eyes, praying for him to hurry and finish, feeling his finger slowly working its way into my virginal body. It hurt a little, but the pain was nothing compared to my still burning bottom, and I simply stood there, sniffling and shaking as he eased it high enough to feel my hymen, then withdraw.

His big hands seized my wrists then, drawing them back behind me and pinning them together at the small of my back. A moment later I felt something, a strap of sorts, wrapped around them quite tightly, binding them together there. He pulled me upright, turned me, and then, much to my surprise, kissed me quite hard on the lips.

Both his big hands were up beneath my jaw as he kissed me, pressing upwards beneath my jaw to force me to my toes. I tried to keep my lips tightly closed, of course, but he would have none of that. His thumbs pressed in against the sides of my jaws until I cried out in pain.

"I said that you were to offer up no resistance. Did you not hear me, girl?"

I tried to nod, but his hands had such a tight grip of me that was impossible. My jaw was aching as his thumbs pressed against it, and my legs danced and twisted beneath me as his dark eyes bored into me.

Then he loosened his grip and I gulped in great lungsful of air as the pain diminished. He pulled me into him again and kissed me once more, his tongue sliding between my lips. He kissed me roughly, bruisingly, his tongue like a snake in my mouth, and I did not resist. I kept my lips slack, enduring the disgust I felt at his use of my mouth, too terrified to even think about resisting.

He eased back, and removed his hands from my throat.

"Kiss me," he ordered curtly.

Eyes wide, I leaned forward, forced to rise on my toes now and let my naked breasts flatten against his powerful chest in order to bring my lips against his. I kissed him uncertainly, then, as I felt his anger, more strongly, sliding my tongue into his mouth.

You cannot imagine how odd I felt, standing on my toes nude like that, face still wet from my own tears as I tried my best to kiss this man, tried more than I ever had with any boy I liked, He reached out then, gripping my hair behind my head. He pulled my head up and back, so that I cried out as my back was once again arched painfully hard. Then he pulled me forward again, and down, pressing my face into his chest, then his belly, then, forcing me to my knees, down against his groin. He rubbed my face against his groin for a long moment, then eased his hold on my hair so I could pull back.

There, on my knees, gasping for breath, sniffling fearfully, I watched him undo his trousers and shove them down, and my eyes widened at the sight of his manhood thrusting up and out from amidst a dark tangle of black hair. I looked away at once, or tried to, but he filled his hand with my hair again and jerked my face back until the head of his organ was mere inches from my nose.

"Get to work," he ordered.

My mental response was Oh No! Yet I knew the basics, despite being far from expert. I cried out lightly as his hand twisted my hair sharply, then before I could protest he had pulled me forward and thrust the head of it into my mouth.

It was soft, and almost spongy, warm and slick and yet hard at the same time. The pungent taste of it filled my mouth as I knelt there, and as it slid deeper, pushing against the inside of one cheek, then the roof of my mouth. I knew the helplessness of my sex, confronted by the power of the male animal, and whimpered softly.

A strange little shiver ran up my spine, however. For I had fantasised about this sort of thing many times before. I had imagined myself on my knees, hands tied, staring up at a powerful man who demanded my submission. And the memories of those fantasies, and the orgasms which had come with them seeped slowly through my flustered mind.

"Suck," he ordered.

And so I did. I closed my lips around the shaft, noting how much thicker it was than those of the boys I had hitherto been exposed to, and tried to please him.

It's odd the things which run through a young girl's mind at a time like that. I wanted him to come, hoping he would then finish, and yet I did not want him to think I was 'good' at it. There was, of course, no reason why I should care about his opinion of me but I still did not want him thinking I was a slut!

And I was beginning to feel like one, to be truthful. For my fear was slowly subsiding - though it was still strong, and so was my embarrassment. And this was, after all, one of my little fantasies. Here was an enormous, powerful, and, I admit, quite handsome man hulking over me, and there I was naked, absolutely NAKED at his feet, forced to please him. I began to feel a little erotic tingling between my legs which worried, and even rather appalled me.

I was distracted by, of all things, his instructions. For yes, he proceeded to instruct me in the 'art' of fellatio as I knelt there. His words were unforgiving, and curtly delivered, directing me to suck harder as I slid my lips backwards, to work my tongue more along the head, to caress his shaft with the insides of my mouth more, and to slide my lips down further, taking more of the shaft past my lips.

I found myself licking at the underside of his shaft, especially around the head, and bobbing my lips up and down to a certain rhythm while his fingers combed through my hair. I still felt embarrassed, and was deeply angered at what I was being forced to do even as fear continued to grip me. Yet the unquestionable arousal I could sense within my lower belly seemed to be having some effect on those feelings, and I felt a soft liquid heat spreading through my body and mind as my lips slid up and down his glistening shaft.

He began to push himself into me then, thrusting his organ deeper and deeper into my mouth. With my hands bound behind my back I could do nothing to restrain him even as the rounded head of his cock threatened to choke me. This was something new and frightening. I gagged repeatedly, and tried to twist away, but he held me remorselessly, and then he tilted my head back sharply so that I was looking up at him. He smiled, somewhat cruelly, I thought, and then spoke.

"Swallow."

I did not understand, or at least, not in time. He held my small head in his large hands, and suddenly, with practised ease, thrust forward and down, driving the head of his cock past my mouth and then straight down my throat.

My eyes bulged and I gagged terribly, but he simply kept pushing his thick cock forward, the gleaming shaft pushing past my helpless lips. I could no more scream than breathe, and he would not stop until my lips, parted so wide they ached, were pressed right in against his groin, my nose crushed against his hairy abdomen.

He held me like this as I trembled and shook violently, one hand with my hair wrapped completely around it, the other on the back of my neck. My chest burned and my mind fluttered like a trapped bird. My vision began to blur and I became light-headed. I slumped bonelessly, held up only by his strong hands as he eased his tool slowly back up the length of my throat, then out. I felt the head come free with an almost audible sound, and immediately retched and gasped desperately.

I drew in great, heaving, shuddering breaths of air, caring for nothing else but the sweetness of inflating my lungs.

"You will have to learn how to do this," he said, holding me steady. "It takes a little practice, but eventually you should even be able to relax your throat enough to breathe with one inside."

His cock was slick with my saliva, and he quite casually wiped it against my face as he held me by the hair. "You shall get a great deal of practice, so it's to your benefit that you learn to do it well."

And then, with my mouth as wide as a fish, he pushed the head into it again. I had just enough time to fill my lungs before he thrust himself forward and down, filling my throat with his shaft once again.

This time he held me against his groin for only a few seconds before pulling back. Yet he did not withdraw entirely. Instead he began to use my mouth and throat as though they were a vagina. His cock slid back and forth with growing force and speed, and if he cared at all for the terrible discomfort this produced in me it did not show in any manner at all.

I was again growing faint as he pulled free, and once more I was able to gulp in desperate breaths of air.

"Now if you'll make better use of your tongue we won't

need to do that again just yet," he said, sliding himself into my mouth again.

With such a promise I worked desperately, lapping furiously along the underside, bobbing my lips and sucking as best I could. There was no longer any room for resistance or hesitation. All I cared about was pleasing him. I was startled when he yanked himself out of me and held the head just before my face. Then he erupted, spurting thick white wads of his semen. It spattered, of course, across my face, on my lips, nose, and cheeks. He squeezed himself to force every drop out, then rubbed the head firmly over my face, smearing his semen into me.

I felt outrage, disgust at this, but there was relief as well, for, innocent that I was, I thought we might now be done. I was quickly to learn how much in error that was.

He produced a leather strap attached to a soft leather ball, and jammed the ball into my mouth, forcing my jaws painfully wide and filling my mouth to the point of overflowing. The attached strap went around my head and buckled behind. His hand on my arm lifted me roughly to my feet, and then he led me out into the hall. He paused at the stairs, turning me around, then bent forward and lifted me up across his shoulder, slapping my bottom as he pinned my legs against his chest.

He carried me through the kitchen and out the door into the alley which went behind our row of houses. There was nobody about to see as, still completely naked, he carried me to a small van, opened up the sliding side door, and pushed me inside. The door slid shut, and I was alone on the cold floor until he moved around and got in the drivers' side.

The realization that he was carrying me away came hard, another terrible shock to my mind. I just lay there as the van started up and made its way down the alley. Then I became almost frantic, trying to think of something to do, some way to escape. My hands pulled despairingly at the straps binding them behind me, and I sat up, looking around me.

"Lie down," he ordered without turning.

I obeyed, fearing to do otherwise, and for some time lay on the dirty floor, bouncing now and then as the van drove along. I tried to think of what he intended for me, tried to imagine some method of escaping. I feared, of course, that he was taking me somewhere to kill me, and as that built up in my mind almost any other fate would have been welcomed. The sky began to darken outside, but that was the only solid information I had about the passage of time. The van continued to move at a good clip, and the man in front said nothing to me.

Finally we stopped, and he got out, coming around to slide open the side door. He gripped my ankle and dragged me across the floor until my buttocks were at the edge and I could stand up on the ground outside. I felt grass and dirt beneath my toes, and in the dim light remaining could see we were at an isolated cottage somewhere on the coast. I could smell the sea, if not sight it, and wondered desperately what he intended.

The opening of the cottage door flooded the little area before it with yellow light. I blinked and squinted as two figures came out. I had a momentary hope of rescue, but the sight of one of the figures shaking hands with my captor dispelled that notion.

There were two people there, another man, large like the first one, and a woman, also quite tall, and quite beautiful. All three adults were in their thirties, and when they looked at me they smiled in a way that made my legs shake. My horrible embarrassment at being nude had faded, but now it flared powerfully with two new pair of eyes examining me, and my face turned scarlet as the two turned me from side to side, examining me from all angles.

"Very nice ass," the new man said.

"She'll bring a good price," the woman replied with a

19

nod.

She looked at me with a kind of contempt, then plucked one of my nipples, making me squeal silently through the gag in my mouth.

"Nice breasts," she said, actually squeezing one of them.

"Nice everything," the other man said.

"Let's get her inside," my captor responded.

A hand firmly on my upper arm, I was led up the walk and into the cottage. I had a brief sight of a comfortably furnished front room, then we were through into a kitchen, and then another room, a large one which at first resembled a garage. There were bare beams overhead, and brick walls with no furnishings.

"She's a virgin," I heard my original captor proclaim.

The others chuckled, and I felt a new source of shame, though why I did not quite know.

They unstrapped my wrists, and massaged them as they held me there between them. Then thick leather restraints were placed around each, and my arms were lifted up and out to either side, the restraints fastened by small chains to rings set in the sides of two vertical beams.

The rings were high enough up that the two men had to lift me right to my toes to clip me there. A moment later the woman pulled one of my feet to the side, sliding another leather restraint around it, and buckling it in place. My other foot was pulled wide, and I was literally hanging by my wrists, the leather digging into my flesh, my arms aching already. Soon both legs were chained apart to the beams, my toes an inch or two off the stone floor. My sex was lewdly exposed to their eyes, and I felt more shame.

Yet I was completely baffled by what they were doing. I was that naive.

They left me like that, closing the door and going into the other room. I felt relief, at first, alone at last away from the staring eyes of unkind strangers. My arms began to ache even more, and my shoulders soon followed. The pain travelled halfway down my sides, with my ribs feeling bruised by the tension, and my body writhed weakly as I sought to relieve the cramps and pain.

The thoughts and emotions which swirled around me were quite strong, of course. I was mortified at being naked and molested by these people, and terrified about what they had in store for me.

I simply could not comprehend why people, adults, (for I still thought of myself as a girl) would drag me out to God only knew where, and then hang me naked from my wrists.

It was desperately uncomfortable, of course. Every part of my body seemed to ache, and my hands quickly went numb. My arms were cramped and my shoulders felt ready to tear away. The nerves and muscles running down the sides of my chest were also somehow affected, for I found that simply hanging loose caused me considerable pain along my ribs.

My bottom was still stinging a bit, but for the rest of me, the sensation to my skin was quickly becoming cold and clammy, goose bumps standing out on my pale white flesh. My nipples were erect, as well, though not from any kind of sexual reaction.

At least I did not think so at first. Fear is an odd emotion, however. Like embarrassment, it has its limits in time beyond which one seems to grow anaesthetized. After that time was passed my fright began to dim somewhat. I tried to inspect my new surroundings, but little was visible in the bit of moonlight coming through a high window. It seemed a dark, bare room of concrete and wood. What objects I could see were mere shadows.

I could, however, make out my own body, seeming to glow almost white in that light, the leather straps around my wrists and ankles, and the gleaming chains which bound my arms and legs apart. I could see the beams and the floor, as well, but little beyond that.

I was resigned to rape, as I had since first spotting the man in my bedroom doorway, and my mind, now trying to put things into some kind of understandable perspective, imagined myself as a captive of pirates or some such.

This was probably a mistake, though of course, it really did not matter to my inevitable future. I had always found the idea of being a captive of pirates deliciously wicked and exciting. During my masturbatory sessions, in fact, I had often imagined myself bound to a stake or post while surrounded by leering, bearded ruffians. Of course, my wrists were together and I was standing on the deck of a ship, but there was enough resemblance to the fantasy to fuel the eroticism of my present position.

And that struck me almost like a blow. For all at once I realized why I was so bound, that it was for the arousal of my captors. Just as I had been aroused by the fantasy of being a helpless bound prisoner to the lusts of others, these people must have the opposite fantasy.

Oddly, this made me feel better, for at least I could now understand what their motivation was, why they were treating me so.

Now I could see how a naked girl, a beautiful naked girl, I thought objectively, hanging spreadeagled in such a fashion, could excite people. After all, such an image would have excited me in my fantasies.

Of course, were I to so fantasize I would not include the pain and discomfort, nor the humiliation of being so lewdly displayed before strangers, nor the fear of what was to come.

I looked down at my body, trying to see it as they saw it, imagine what they thought of my firm breasts and shapely thighs. Did they become aroused at looking at my pubic mound, my pussy opening? I had, as I mentioned earlier, become accustomed to people finding me attractive but being so displayed was a shocking new experience. And while it was terribly embarrassing, I still had the odd little flare of pride at being seen as attractive, even sexually desirable by adults.

But any real excitement I might have derived was easily overcome by my pain and fear as I hung there.

It was exhausting. Every breath became an effort, and my body was soon damp with sweat. The floor seemed so far, far below. And yet at the same time it was tauntingly close, just below my wriggling toes.

I wished someone would come in, have their way with me, and let me go. I wished, beyond everything, for it all to be over with.

CHAPTER TWO

I have no idea how long I hung there, but I was hardly aware of the woman's return at first, dazed as I had by then become.

My chin was on my chest and she lifted my head up by the simple expedient of grasping my loose blonde hair and yanking it back. I cried out at the pain, of course, but little sound emerged from the gag straining my jaw.

Though I was hanging by my wrists I was not raised up very high. My legs were spread apart so that I was actually somewhat lower than I would normally be standing. And so I was forced to look up into the eyes of this cold, haughty woman. I felt my mind stirring awake, and felt a fresh surge of embarrassment at being so utterly naked around another woman.

Of course, I wasn't just naked. I was naked and hanging from my wrists, my legs spread wide, my body utterly bare and vulnerable to this strange woman, in a way I knew was extremely lewd and sexually provocative. This made me feel vulnerable and weak, inferior, if you will, for I was utterly at her mercy.

Then again I would have felt intimidated by her even were I fully clothed and in a more equal situation. She was a powerful looking woman, with dark, intelligent eyes and a strong, handsome face. Her dark hair was cut short and swept back, and her every movement bespoke a strong will and confidence in herself. She wore very tight faded jeans below a white silk blouse, and a gold chain circled her slender throat. She was easily ten years my senior, and I felt little more than a girl alongside her.

Her hand moved against my body then, sliding down my back. I could feel the warmth of her skin along my cool flesh, and felt a startled tingling and then anxiety as she traced the length of my spine. Her fingers rubbed gently at the soft skin at the cleft of my buttocks, then her fingers spread wider,

24

and my eyes widened as she cupped my buttocks and squeezed.

"I want you to listen to me, little girl," she said, "for I'm going to explain some facts of life to you. Are you listening?"

I could do little else but nod.

Her hand moved off my buttocks, traced along my hip and then caressed my flat, taut belly as she resumed speaking.

"You have been taken for money."

I thought immediately that there had been a terrible mistake, for my uncle had no money. She smiled, as if able to read my mind through my eyes.

"No, little girl. We are not holding you for ransom. You're to be sold to a wealthy man who wants a pet."

Once again I failed to grasp her meaning.

"Do you know what a slave is?"

I nodded as much as I could, and she nodded as well.

"That is what you are now. You are a slave. We will train you so that you'll not give your new master any problems, and then sell you to him for a tidy amount of money."

I was astonished by this, of course. Slavery was something out of history. Innocent that I was, my mind was filled with the certainty that people did not buy and sell other people any more. I longed to tell her this, but she gave no sign of desiring my opinion.

"You will be trained to obey, to perform your duties as a good little slave girl, and to never talk back or even think about resisting your master's desires."

A slave? I? And yet it did correspond with my pirate fantasy, and so I began to understand her intent, at least to the small degree I was then capable.

Her hand slid up my body and cupped one of my breasts then, which unnerved me, she being a woman. Again, I was quite innocent. My first thought was not about being preyed upon by a woman with lesbian desires, but indignation that she should set her hands on me in such a way. Unlike a man,

25

after all, she was not motivated, or so I thought, by lust. I could understand men pawing at me, but another woman doing so could, I thought, only come from contempt and a desire to further humiliate me.

"You are raw meat," she said in a bold, certain, confident voice. "You are a plaything. A toy. A pet for others to use, to enjoy. Your body was designed to please the eye and the touch, and that is precisely what it will do. Your body will please any man - or woman - who wants to make use of it. And you will have no choice, no choice at all, but to participate, to cooperate, to obey and please those with power over you."

She eased her grip on my breast, letting her splayed fingers slide slowly along the skin until they came together just behind my cold, rigid nipple. Three fingers squeezed together against my nipple where it thrust out from the swollen areola, and began to stroke back and forth along it with just enough pressure to stretch my skin out slightly on each outward movement.

"Do you like that, little slave girl? Does your nipple enjoy the feel of warm skin against it?"

It did, in fact, and I was quite disconcerted about that. I could feel the warmth of her skin seeping into my nipple, could feel the gentle stroking beginning to send small rippling sensations of pleasure through my taut breasts.

"Have you dreamed of sexually exposing yourself, little girl?" she said, her voice almost a whisper, and strangely mesmerizing in that dark, silent room. "Have you dreamed of giving in to your impulses and being the sexual creature you so desire?"

She raised her other hand and caught at my other nipple, then began rolling both between thumbs and forefingers.

"You have lovely nipples. Has anyone ever told you that? No, of course not."

She smiled lightly, then let her fingers pinch together so that I jerked and gasped aloud into the gag. This drew another smile and she eased her grip, then spread her fingers out and slid them beneath my breasts to cup both and raise them lightly. She examined them, as I quivered helplessly in embarrassment and unwonted anticipation.

"Very lovely breasts as well," she said, looking down at them. "They could be larger. Many men like the really buxom girls, but yours are quite a good size, larger than your slim body, but not so large as to lose this youthful firmness."

Her fingers were gently kneading the soft flesh of my breasts as she spoke, and both were warming to her touch in a way which was tightening my chest and making it difficult to breathe. My mind was swirling with conflicting messages. I hated her, feared her, and deeply, deeply resented her presumption in speaking about my body in such familiar terms, much less daring to fondle my private parts as she was. Yet at the same time my body seemed to be gripped by a rising cloud of almost electrical tension, a quivering anticipation which seemed to pay no attention whatever to my embarrassment and anger.

Her hands moved abruptly, sliding behind me as she brought her body forward. I was startled as she pressed her body against my own, and I felt the softness and warmth of her breasts beneath her blouse. Her arms were gripping me now, her hands stroking along my back as a man would, and then they moved downwards to squeeze my bottom, each hand squeezing and kneading one buttock as she brought her lips an inch from my own gagged mouth.

"Do you dream of a man between your thighs, little slave girl?" she whispered, eyes boring into mine. "Do you dream of him thrusting himself into you again and again, of wrapping your legs around him and crying out in glorious pleasure?"

I turned my eyes away, unable to meet hers, and gasped as her head bent low and her lips trailed along the nape of my neck. I moaned through the gag as I felt the moisture of her open mouth and then the hardness of her teeth nibbling along my skin. Her tongue caressed my cool flesh, and my breasts were squeezed against her own chest as she squeezed me tightly against her, fingers digging in hard against the soft flesh of my buttocks.

Her lips moved up beneath my ears and her teeth nibbled on my earlobes, and my body trembled as my mind fluttered like a butterfly caught under a glass. I was completely flustered, not knowing what she was doing, or why. I felt her hands slide up then, going behind my head. She undid the strap holding the gag in place and then leaned back and gently pried the ball free of my mouth.

I cried out at the sharp stab of pain as my stiff, aching jaw was finally allowed to close, and for long seconds I could not do anything but cope with that pain. I moved my mouth ever so slightly, wincing, feeling the sore muscles and tendons begin to relax.

She leaned her body in again, kissing me lightly along my cheeks, then tracing her lips along my own. I again tried to turn away, but her lips followed, and her tongue darted forward.

"P-please!" I gasped.

She ignored me, and one of her hands slid up behind my head to hold it in place even as her soft tongue pushed deep into my mouth. My eyes widened in astonishment, and I tried once again to twist away, to no avail.

Her tongue danced along my own, and her lips pressed strongly against mine, and fear kept me from reacting with more violence. I dared do little else but moan my protests as her tongue ravished my mouth and her lips made free with me. My breasts throbbed against hers, and my nipples felt tight and hot, sparkling with tension each time her body moved against them.

She eased back finally, and I gasped aloud, gulping in breath as her hands moved down to my breasts and she seized my nipples in her fingers once more.

"Please untie me," I panted.

"No."

"But... but you must," I begged.

"You will call me mistress. Is that clear?"

I stared at her stupidly, and then cried out as her fingers pinched in against my nipples.

"Ow!"

"Is that clear?"

"Ow! Yes!" I cried.

Her fingers twisted my nipples harder, as she smiled at me like a scolding but tolerant schoolmistress.

"Yes, mistress!" I cried, squirming and straining against my bonds.

Her fingers eased their grip, but did not move off, resuming the gentle stroking she had engaged in previously.

"You will be a good little girl, won't you?" she asked.

"Y-yes, mistress," I panted.

"And a good, obedient slave."

I hesitated but agreed. "Yes, mistress."

"Say it then. Let me hear you say you are a slave."

I stared at her in confusion, but as her fingers tightened around my nipple I agreed.

"I am a slave!" I gasped, feeling a strange fluttering in my chest.

"Again."

"I am a slave."

"Again."

I repeated it again, and again, and continued to repeat the words under her forceful gaze and touch, and when she moved back and I faltered, a quick frown from her brought the words tumbling free of my mouth once more.

"I am a slave. I am a slave. I am a slave."

She moved out of my sight briefly, into the darkness behind me, and then light flooded the room, cold, harsh white light which had me blinking and squinting. She returned, rolling a small tray before her on which were a small bowl of water, scissors, a razor, and some cream.

"Continue," she ordered.

"I am a slave," I said, my voice faltering as she took the scissors into her hand and then reached between my legs.

"Continue," she ordered, raising her eyes to scowl.

I did so, staring in wonderment as she began to denude my pubic hair. She snipped quite close to the skin, not merely trimming, but cutting all the way to the centre of my mons. She moistened my sex and then spread a soapy cream over it before kneeling there and taking the razor to me.

I felt even more embarrassment than before, yet did not dare to question her. I continued to repeat the words she had ordered me to speak as the razor swept along my lower abdomen, then beneath my spread legs to shave my mound itself. I moaned and halted my words as her fingers pushed into my opening and gripped my labia, stretching it as she brought the razor along its edge.

"Continue," she ordered.

"I am a slave," I whispered.

She used a wet towel to clean off the remains of the soap or cream, and looking down, I saw to my amazement, that she had removed every trace of my pubic hair. I could not fathom the reasoning behind her actions, but my amazement was merely a background to the new sense of humiliation I felt. My sex had never been so open and visible, not since I was a young girl, and never before another person.

Even as I gaped at it my words halted, and my head was rocked back by a slap which stunned me.

"I did not say you could stop speaking," she said in a soft, chiding voice. "Continue."

I stared at her in shock, and another slap sent my head jerking back, my hair flying around me.

"Continue. You must learn to quickly obey orders you

are given, slave."

"I... but you..."

Another slap struck me, hitting me across the right cheek and flinging my head to my left. A moment later her other hand struck the left cheek and sent my head flying to the right. A third blow followed, and my jaw hung slack as she halted to grip my hair and hold my face steady.

"You must obey orders when they are given. You must always obey," she said, emphasising the last word.

She brought her face in close to mine, calm but stern. I was gasping and panting, my eyes watering, my cheeks aflame.

"Obey," she whispered, raising her eyebrows. "Say it."

"O-o-obey," I panted.

"Again."

"O-obey."

"Again."

"Obey."

"What must you do?"

"I... must obey," I gulped.

"Again."

"I must... obey."

She released my hair and eased her face back slightly.

"Why must you obey?"

"I... because I am a slave," I whispered.

She smiled benignly, then leaned in to kiss me gently. Her arms slid around my body and caressed me as once again her tongue pushed into my mouth. I felt a sense of gratification this time however, relief at having pleased her, at having given the proper response. I was still somewhat dazed from the hard slaps, and the memory of the sharp pain they had brought. I was desperate to please her that I receive no more such chastisements.

She pulled back, her hands sliding downward to cup and knead my breasts.

"Disobedience brings punishment, yet obedience can bring pleasure," she said. "Why must you obey?"

"Because I am a slave," I said.

"And because you are a slave what must you do?"

"I must obey."

"Repeat them until I tell you to stop."

And so I did. "I am a slave. I must obey," I said, as she eased down onto her knees before me and examined my naked sex.

"I am a slave. I must obey," I repeated as her fingers moved softly against my sensitive flesh.

I felt her fingers gently fold back the lips of my sex, and new heat came to my face as I continued my soft mantra. Her fingers stroked along my inner lips, and my mind knew intense embarrassment and shock, yet I continued speaking.

"I am a s...oh!"

Her finger had sought out that most intimate part of my body, that most sensitive slip of flesh, and my voice quavered as I resumed my chant.

"I am a slave. I must obey."

Her fingers began to caress my clitoris, moving in different directions. One long finger penetrated my body then, pushing upwards into my vagina, easing against my hymen and then drawing back to twist about within me. I stared down in amazement and fear and embarrassment, continuing to speak the words which I could no longer hear.

And then her lips pushed forward against my vulnerable opening, and I saw her soft pink tongue come out and...

"Oh!"

I had never felt anything like it, and could hardly credit I was seeing and feeling it now.

"Continue," she ordered.

"I am a slave," I panted. "I must obey."

Her tongue began to move along my inner lips, then circled my small hole before actually pushing inside. I could feel her mouth against me there as that amazing tongue flicked about within my body, deeper than I would have believed possible. My entire body was flooded with shock and alarm, and yet no pain followed. And as the shock and alarm faded I could feel the strangely pleasurable sensation of her soft, pumping tongue and the warmth of her skin against mine.

The pleasure grew rapidly, and nothing I could do seemed to hinder its strength. I could feel the flickering sexual electricity moving along my skin, through my nerves and veins and sinews as I hung helpless before her, and though I could not understand her behaviour my body did not seem to care. Amid the terrible discomfort it had felt over so many hours this hot, wonderful pleasure was a desperately needed distraction, and even were it not some dark part of me revelled in the sensations of lewd stimulation.

And then her attention moved upwards and I felt her lips over my clitoris. I lost all ability to speak then as her lips joined together and she began to gently suckle and lick. My body began to tremble and strain, to writhe in the bonds holding it as her tongue lapped more and more strongly against my clitoris. At first the sensations were simply too strong, and I was overwhelmed, then as my body adjusted the shocking pleasure cut through my body and mind like a maelstrom and I could only gurgle and moan in animalistic response.

I was on the edge of orgasm, of a powerful climax, my hips rolling and grinding against her. And then she stopped and moved away, getting to her feet and examining me as I hung there.

My movements eased, become twitches and spasms, and she raised my chin with her fingers.

"Do you see why I know you are a slut? Do you see why your place in life will be as a slave? You have a whore's body, and a whore's mind."

I could not deny it, even to myself. I was deeply shamed by my own response, and my sense of morality was revolted by the very idea of a woman putting her mouth on another's sex. Oh yes, I know it was done with boys, but this was so very different! The very idea was so foreign to me I could hardly accept it had happened.

And yet even amidst the shame I felt a deep yearning to feel her mouth against me once again.

"Did I tell you to stop speaking?" she asked patiently.

"N-no, mistress," I replied, voice filling with anxiety.

It was well placed, and I cringed as her open hand drew back to strike me, turning my head and closing my eyes as she swung.

Yet the blow did not land against my face. Instead I felt the sharp impact against the side of my left breast. I cried out in shock, my eyes snapping open, and then the sharp dagger of pain swept through me and my voice raised higher still.

"You must realize that whenever you fail to obey an order you will be punished," she said.

And with that she calmly struck my breast again, and then a third time. Each blow set it to jiggling and bouncing wildly, the heat of pain pushing aside the former glow of pleasure, and turning the pale skin an angry pink.

Again, amidst the pain, I felt a sense of shock and outrage that anyone would punish a woman in such a manner. It was yet another concept entirely foreign to my previous experience, or even imagination.

"As a slave, proper behaviour will be expected of you at all times," the woman said. "You will keep your eyes down, and respond to each command given you. Let me hear you say 'thank you mistress'."

I stared at her in confusion and she smiled for a moment and then slapped my breast again so that I cried out in pain.

"When you are given an instruction you are to obey it

without delay," she said in a calm voice. "Now let us try again. Thank me."

"Th-thank you, Mistress," I gasped.

"Thank you for punishing me mistress."

"Tha-thank you, Mistress, for punishing me," I gulped, voice shaking.

"You must understand that you are no longer a person. You are not even a human being. You are little more than an animal. You will do as you are told and like it, or you will be punished. Do you understand?"

I nodded mutely and let my head roll as her hand cracked against my cheek.

"You will respond verbally," she said. "Do you understand?"

"Y-yes, M-mistress," I whimpered, my eyes watering now as her violence began to overwhelm my ability to cope.

"Will you be a good little slave?"

"Y-yes, Mistress."

"Would you like to be let down?"

"Yes, mistress!"

Again I was slapped, tasting blood in my mouth as my head was thrown back. I began to cry now, in my misery and helplessness, feeling desperately hard done by and in distress at the unfairness of it all.

"Your wishes are not important, slave. Nothing you want is important. Only what pleases me is important. You will be let down if it pleases me, and only if it pleases me. Do you understand?"

"Yes, M-m-mistress," I sobbed, voice breaking.

"Your tears will avail you nothing here, slave," she said. "No one cares how a slave is feeling. No one cares if she is unhappy. Your body is all we need."

She seized my hair in both hands then, jerking my head back as she crushed her lips against mine. Startled, I could only tremble as her tongue pushed deep into my mouth and her mouth ravished mine. Her fingers pulled and twisted at my long hair heedless of my pain, and I whimpered softly into her mouth.

She drew back, looking smug and self satisfied, and I felt a surge of hate and envy for her.

"What are you?" she demanded.

"A-A slave," I gulped, sniffling.

"And what must a slave do?"

"Obey," I said in misery.

She leaned in again. "Kiss me," she ordered.

I stared her, aghast for some reason, then the need to avoid further pain sent my lips forward and I kissed her awkwardly.

She laughed in much amusement.

"That was not a kiss," she said. "Kiss me as you would your boyfriend, your lover, as you would the man you wished to give your virginity to."

She pressed her lips forward again and, cringing inwardly, I did my best to kiss her, sliding my lips against her own and easing my tongue through them. Her tongue rose to respond and I felt a mild wave of pleasure and relief as she kissed back. She held the kiss for long, long seconds, and I, of course, was too fearful to draw back before her.

Then she did withdraw and I drew in a deep breath.

"Now then, do you want to be let down?" she asked.

This was a question I dared not answer at first, but then realized I would be struck if I did not. I arrived at the answer just as her hand rose to deliver another blow.

"If it pleases you, Mistress!"

She smiled and stroked my hair.

"Good girl," she said.

I felt great relief at having satisfied her.

She released the chains from my ankle restraints and I was able to bring my feet together and reach the floor with my toes. This released the strain from my arms, wrists and shoulders, and nearly made me swoon with relief. She released the chains from my wrist restraints then, and let me sag to my knees.

"Kneel there for a moment."

She moved to a corner cabinet and drew forth a length of narrow chain and a long slender flexible looking crop. She returned to me and showed me the loop in the chain, then slipped my head through it. It was a choke-chain, of the kind used with large dogs to keep them from straining at the leash.

"Now, onto all fours. At once," she said briskly.

I fell forward, pulled by the chain, and knelt on hands and knees.

"This is one of the most natural positions for a slave," she said, observing me from above. "She demonstrates her submission and positions herself to please from either end. She can use her mouth or be mounted from behind."

She tapped my bare mons with the crop and I winced and jerked slightly.

"Raise your bottom and spread your legs apart," she ordered.

Cringing mentally, I obeyed, and at a small snap of the crop, raised my bottom still further, opening myself like a dog to be mounted.

"You will be taken in this position many times," she said.

As she spoke she let the crop slide between the lips of my sex and then stroke gently up and down.

"And you will learn to love it. Of that I have no doubt. A bitch in heat is your natural mental disposition."

She drew the crop back and tugged lightly on the chain.

"You will crawl at my heels like a good dog. You will keep your head at my heels, no further back, no further forward. Do you understand?"

She was mad, I thought frantically. That was all there was to it.

"Yes, Miss," I gulped.

I cried out as the crop whipped down against my buttocks, but the cry was choked off as she reached down and yanked on my hair.

"Mistress," she corrected.

"M-Mistress," I moaned in a shaky voice.

"Get on all fours. At once."

My hesitation earned another blow from the crop, and again I cried out, rubbing at my inner thigh.

"On all fours, miserable slave!" her voice snapped.

I moaned and sobbed, then rolled onto my belly and weakly pushed myself to all fours.

"You will have to be punished for your disobedience," she said. "A slave must be disciplined, and it is quite apparent you lack that gift. You will place your face on the floor and spread your arms out straight to either side. Keep your bottom raised high, but bring your knees together."

Still panting and sobbing, I obeyed, my breasts pillowing against the cold, gritty stone as I positioned myself to her satisfaction.

"You will remain in this position. Is that clear?" Her voice sharpened and chilled.

"Y-yes, mistress," I replied in a frightened sob.

For I was frightened. Violence was entirely foreign to me, and never before in my life had anyone treated me with such cold brutality. I was terribly afraid she would not hesitate to choke the life out of me if I behaved poorly enough.

"If you move, your punishment will be doubled," she warned.

With that she moved behind me, and I realized her intent. I moaned softly and felt the tears fill my eyes once more at the unfairness of it all.

Then the crop hissed through the air and struck my upraised bottom. The weight of the blow was not heavy, yet an instant later a jagged dagger of pain ripped through me and I cried out. I could feel my buttocks glowing with heat where she had struck, and even as that terrible sudden pain faded from my mind another blow landed, and another, and I burst into tears as the pain mounted. Yet I dared not move.

I knelt, trembling and moaning, crying out through my tears as the crop landed with short, careful, measured strokes. I Almost broke my position. Only the certainty that the pain given me would be worse if I did held me in place.

Finally the blows stopped and I shuddered in relief, my bottom on fire with pain by then and my eyes blurry with tears.

"Thank me for punishing you," she ordered primly.

"Th-thank y-you for... for pu-punishing me, M-mistress," I stuttered.

"Back on all fours. At once."

I moaned and, still trembling, pushed myself upwards.

"Good slave," she said. "Now crawl."

She began to walk, and I followed unsteadily, eyes blinking rapidly, panting very much like an overheated dog. She led me along the wall, then into the corner for a turn, along the next wall, then the third. We walked around the room, or rather, I crawled along at her heels. My breasts felt heavy and cold as they dangled below me, and my knees ached as they met the hard stone. She led me for several circuits around the room, tapping at my buttocks whenever I was too slow, tugging on the choke chain if I was too fast.

Finally she led me into the centre and paused.

"I want you to spread your legs more and raise your bottom invitingly. Pretend there's a man behind and you wish to be mounted."

I obeyed miserably, feeling broken.

"You are a slut, girl. You have a slut's body, and we shall soon free a slut's mind to become what it desires. Do you see these boots, slut?"

I looked at the black boots she wore and almost nodded.

"Yes, Mistress," I said, remembering in time.

"They're dirty. I want them cleaned."

"Yes, Mistress," I said, confused.

"With your tongue, slave," she said. "Immediately."

I was startled and, even through my pain, indignant. A quick slash across my back woke me from that and I bent, moaning at the pain and swiping my tongue across the dusty top of her boot. Tears filled my eyes again and I silently wailed at such things being done to me. It was so unfair!

I tasted the grit of dust and sand as my tongue licked at the woman's boot. She snapped the crop down whenever I slowed, forcing me to slide my tongue all around the sides, and then even down by the floor. She raised one foot on its spiked heel then and directed my attention to the bottom. I blinked my eyes dazedly, but obeyed, sliding my tongue, now dry and tasting of dirt, along the underside of her boot as she looked down from above.

"The duty of a slave is to please her master in any way her master wishes," she said. "You are a slave, and you had best start learning how to please those who own you."

I did not believe I was a slave, but rather, that she was mad. Yet the pain was very real, and I continued to lick even as my tongue grew numb. And as I did so I began to feel a nasty, wicked heat. The situation was so preposterous, so wildly divergent from every experience I had ever had or anything I had ever really imagined, that it felt almost like a dream. Yet it was a wicked, wanton dream, where I was a slave girl, a creature of sex and sexuality, tormented and abused because of her beauty. I had not previously noted any great streak of masochism within me, but as I knelt there being so cruelly treated, something deep within me responded, further shaming me.

She finally pulled back and led me for another crawl around the room, pausing, directing my tongue at dirty spots on the floor, or into small cracks near the wall. Each hesitation brought another blow, until I was sure my entire back was striped and I was exhausted both physically and emotionally. Yet as I crawled, my breasts swinging beneath me, my buttocks raised, and the air chill on my bare sex, I felt a strange kind of animal sexuality surrounding my mind. It was not strong enough yet to override the fear, shame, outrage and pain swirling through my mind, but it did give me a deal of self awareness about how exotically sexual my movements were.

She reached down then and gripped my now bedraggled, tangled hair, taking a fistful and using it to pull me upwards, before pulling my wrists up behind me and then chaining them once more to two vertical beams on either side of the room.

"Think on obedience," she ordered. "On the obedience a slave owes her mistress and master, and the need to please them."

The door closed behind her and I was left alone once more. This was a great relief, of course, for I was simply drained, my mind numb, body sore all over. Yet standing there was hardly restful. An hour passed, then another. Or so I assumed from the passing of the moon overhead. I had no other way to measure time as my legs cramped and my body ached. I cried from time to time, angry and resentful, miserable and frightened, and wondering what new humiliations the horrible woman would inflict upon me when next she entered.

I was an intelligent woman, on her way to becoming a solicitor, and this simply was not fair! That notion continued to twine its way through my thinking processes. I was an independent minded girl proud of my academic success, proud of my intelligence. To be treated like a wanton slut who was of value only for her naked flesh was counter to every scrap of dignity I had learned over the past many years.

Could it be true, as the woman claimed, that I was destined to remain a prisoner for a long time to come? That I was to be a sexual slave to cruel and perverse people? Such a thing was almost unimaginable, and difficult to reconcile, yet a small but growing part of me was beginning to realize that this was indeed my likely fate.

CHAPTER THREE

The door opened and light flooded the room. I felt relief warring with alarm as my head rose and turned to the door. Then embarrassment flooded through me as my squinting eyes saw the man closing the door behind him and coming towards me. It was not the one who had kidnapped me, but the other whom I had seen on arrival. And my hands jerked feebly against the leather bindings as I instinctively sought to cover my nudity.

Like the other man he was in his late thirties. He had short brown hair and a set look to him, as though he were about to begin a job and was determined to do it properly.

"Slave," he said, stopping before me and inspecting my body.

I said nothing, dropping my eyes in humiliation.

"When your master enters the room you should greet him," he said.

I had barely heard him speak earlier, and now discerned from his accent that he was an American.

I raised my chin anxiously and saw his scowl.

"H-hello, master," I said, voice quavering, further humiliated by the words.

"Better."

Yes, they were all surely insane.

His hands made free with my body for a few moments, caressing and fondling me, plucking at my nipples and squeezing my breasts. He seemed to take pleasure in my discomfort, frequently caressing my shoulders or sides or hips, only to quickly slide his hands between my legs or over my breasts, causing me to flinch in instinctive protest. He pinched my small nipples until they ached, pulling them and stretching them out so that even my breasts were distended.

Then he moved behind me and I turned my head aside, warily following him as he moved to a small cupboard and rummaged about there. He returned with what I first took to be a small sack in one hand. As he brought it closer I saw it was a dark leather hood.

Without speaking he placed it atop my head, then pulled it downwards. It was tight against my skin, and I gasped as it ground across my nose, then pulled down over my mouth and chin. There were no eyeholes with which to see, though my mouth seemed free enough. I felt the material pull in beneath my jaw, then around my throat, where his fingers worked for a moment before I heard a small click, as if a lock had been closed.

"What are you doing!?"

"Slaves are told only what their masters want them to know."

For a long moment I was alone in silence, then strong fingers pressed in against the sides of my jaw as something was pushed against my mouth. I moaned, my mouth opening, and felt something resembling the ball gag forced in. This one was not so wide, but longer, and I coughed instinctively as it threatened to enter my throat. The strap was much thicker and wider, and I could feel it completely covering the flesh around my mouth, so that, I thought, not an inch of my face might now be visible.

I next felt his hands behind me, on my hips. He slapped my bottom sharply.

"Spread your legs."

I obeyed, blinking my eyes beneath the dark hood and breathing more heavily as fear and anxiety began to rise higher within me. I felt his hands at my bottom, then his finger pressing insistently against my anal opening. This shocked me, and my legs came together, my body half twisting as I tried to dislodge him. Another sharp blow against my sore bottom halted my resistance, and I spread my legs once more.

My mind continued to squirm however, for I was appalled

at what he was doing. It was another way in which these people demonstrated their perversity, and I simply could not understand it.

His finger pushed inside me, riding a slippery substance of some sort as it wriggled deeper and deeper. Blinded, I imagined I could sense its movements even more closely, and all my attention focused on it.

And then I felt something else, something before me, at my groin. Again my legs tried to twist, but strong hands held them in place, and I quickly recognized the feel of a mouth against my sex. New embarrassment flooded me, along with frustration. What did they want of me?

The finger in my bottom pushed in to the knuckle, then began to slowly rotate. Meanwhile the soft tongue lapping at my sex was riding higher along my slit and approaching my clitoris. I followed its movements with a desperate anticipation, frightened of the thought of my body betraying me once more, yet feeling a dark eagerness to experience again that delicious immersion in sensual pleasure.

I felt hands I thought must be the woman's squeezing my buttocks even as the face pushed in harder against my groin. At the same time the finger pulled out of my bottom and strong hands slipped around me from behind to fondle my breasts.

They were using me as a slut, just as she had warned, and so the shock was less than it otherwise might have been. But I felt resentment nonetheless, along with a myriad of other emotions. My body, however, felt only the pleasure rising up from my groin as that delicious tongue lapped up against my clitoris and began to set it thrumming with wicked, quivering excitement.

I wanted to cry out to them, to demand they stop, but of course, even could I speak, such a plea would have been pointless. They had already made it clear that my wishes were of no importance to them, that I was to be a slave for their enjoyment.

I recalled my nineteenth birthday party, and the low-cut dress I had worn then. Late in the evening I had been in the garden with Dennis Pierce, and he had caught me from behind, chewing on the nape of my neck as his hands came around me. I had known, of course, that it was wrong, but I could find little strength to push him off as his hands slipped up and down my bare sides, then, shocking me, eased in beneath the sides of my gown to cup my bare breasts.

My hands had gone to my breasts at once, only to find his hands within the cups of my dress. And the shocking lust which had swelled within my chest had prevented me from doing more than standing still and moaning as his fingers had deftly squeezed and kneaded my flesh, and his lips had chewed and sucked at the nape of my neck.

I could feel his groin pressed against my bottom, could feel his erection as he ground himself into me, and knew that I was rapidly losing control of myself. But my breasts were on fire and my groin was so hot, so voraciously needful that my hips were grinding, my left knee bent, foot up as I rubbed my thighs together. The sensations passing through my nipples were so intense they almost hurt and then...

I was brought back to the present as I felt a pressure at my bottom. It was his erection. I could feel it lying between the cheeks of my buttocks, long and thick and quite warm to the touch against my chilled flesh. Then it slid downwards and pushed against my anal opening, and I moaned and trembled as I began to realize his intent. I tried to squirm away once more, twisting my hips to one side, straining at the bonds holding my wrists up and back. I felt his hands slide down from my breasts, then grip my thighs and force them apart and back. Another pair of hands joined them and I was held in place, begging into the gag, demanding they release me.

Yet it was hopeless. I could feel the warm head forcing a

path deeper and higher inside me, now halting, easing back, now pushing forward once again, thrusting aside my tight flesh, forcing my anus wide before it. My insides soon ached with the pressure inside me, and my legs continued to strain against their hold. My hips bucked and jerked feebly, and my back arched as I sought to pull myself forward and away from him.

They held me easily in place as more and more of his thick erection was forced upwards into my body. I could feel cramps deep within my abdomen now as the head of his organ pushed up against I knew not what. And still he thrust forward in short, hard little strokes, grinding his pelvis in a slow, circular motion.

The woman began licking and sucking at my clitoris once more, and shortly afterwards I felt the man's pubic hair against the soft underside of my buttocks. The cramps grew worse, but my cries were ignored as he was determined to force the last of his cock into my body. I felt like a rag doll being torn apart by a pair of eager dogs, and my struggles eased as I resigned myself to my fate.

I was horrified at the feel of him inside my anus, at the knowledge that his cock was actually up inside my body. I wanted to scream at them. "Get it out! Get it out!"

His hands continued to grip my inner thighs, forcing my legs open, but even could I close them I knew it would not dislodge him. I felt impaled, and each time he ground his pelvis against my backside I could feel his cock twisting around inside me like something alive, like a snake.

His hands returned to my breasts, and for long minutes it seemed we remained like that, the woman licking softly at my sex, the man grinding his pelvis against my buttocks as he kneaded my breasts. The sense of revulsion began to fade, and in truth, once that and the cramps were gone, he really did not feel at all bad there inside me. In fact, it was a mildly pleasant sensation, and made me wonder what it would feel like to have a man's organ inside my vagina.

As if he could sense my thoughts he drew back, and I could feel his cock fighting the squeezing walls of my rectum as it slid down. Then he pushed up again, grinding his pelvis into me before once again withdrawing. He began to pump in slow, even movements, using short strokes.

More of my attention had been diverted to my pussy now, as that insistent tongue licked and twisted and caressed me all along my sex, and now I felt myself pierced by her fingers, slipping in and out in a rhythmic motion which melded with the pumping of the cock in my rectum. I felt the flickering sexual tension within my lower belly rising once more, spreading through my body. I felt a surge of guilt and self-hatred at this, but I did not truly wish to turn it aside. I was tired, and too badly abused, at least in my mind, and any source of pleasure was a sought-after diversion.

And so I raptly followed the movement of her mouth against me, and made no further attempt to close my legs. And the intrusive thrusting of the man's cock into my nether hole grew slowly more powerful in counterpoint to her more gentle lapping mouth. Yet as it grew it held its own feel of seductive carnal pleasure. I was a virgin, of course, and had never felt such a thrusting within me, only imagined it. Now I was being fucked, and I use the word with deliberation. I had used it before, of course, for it was in common use, but as his speed and tempo picked up I began to appreciate it the more. Making love was a sharing of movement and purpose, but we were not making love. I was being fucked. And no doubt it would feel similar when they eventually took my virginity from me.

The jarring of his hips against my body sent shudders through my groin, and seemed to add weight to the gentle stroking and licking of my clitoris. I felt the sexual tension building up within me, building to the point it never had during all my bouts of masturbation, to the point I only rarely experienced, and then only at the hands of others. My chest was tight, my belly fluttering, and my body trembling lightly with the intensity of the sensations flowing through my nervous system.

Whore!

Yes, I was a whore, or so I told myself, for only a whore would give herself to such lewd and disgusting practices willingly. Of course, I was not there willingly, and the bonds around my wrists proved it. Yet at the same time I could not lie to myself about my own body's response, nor pretend I did not welcome the pleasure, did not fling wide my arms to welcome it with wanton abandon.

I grunted softly into the gag now, as his strokes were becoming deeper and more violent. He was thrusting almost straight up into my body, and I rose onto the balls of my feet, and even to my toes as he drove himself up with greater strength. I could feel the long length of his organ now each time it slid out of my body, almost all leaving me entirely, and each time it paused before thrusting forward once more I felt a desperate eagerness and anticipation. Then I would groan aloud as I felt the long length slicing back up into my body, wishing that the sensation of penetration would last forever.

Of course, it could not, and soon came the harsh impact of his pelvis against my buttocks as he sheathed the last of himself within me, and I would grunt with the force of the blow, rising to the balls of my feet.

Again and again, faster and faster, but never too fast, never so fast I could not savour the long, deep sliding penetration. And soon I began to feel a strange kind of dark, sensual fulfilment each time I knew the entirety of his cock was inside me. It was a strange mixture of masochistic pleasure and sluttish erotic satisfaction to imagine how deep inside me he was, to think about the long length jammed high inside my belly.

My nipples ached against the palms of his hands now, and I was finding it difficult to breathe through the small nose holes of my hood as my breath grew ragged and sharp. I was no longer chilled, but warm, my skin beginning to sweat as the sexual pressure continued unabated.

The woman was avoiding my clitoris now, her tongue dancing along my inner lips, coasting up and down my furrow, pumping lightly against my vaginal opening, and tauntingly circling my clitoris. Yet she avoided direct contact, and I was held in helpless thrall, gripped by the full power of my body's wanton sexual desires, but without being able to reach the climax I so desperately sought.

And throughout came that harsh, strong, thrusting up into my anus, a thrusting that had my body quivering and shaking even as his lips and tongue and teeth began to move along my shoulder and his hands pinched and plucked at my aching nipples.

I had never experienced such a high degree of sexual need for such a length of time. I was growing exhausted and breathless, my legs turning rubbery and my insides going numb.

And then the woman began to stroke her tongue directly across my clitoris. At the same time the man withdrew himself completely from my anus. I moaned helplessly into the gag, a maelstrom of sensations twisting inside me. I felt the pleasure rise higher still, and knew its limit had almost been reached. I hovered on the edge of a powerful orgasm.

I felt the head of the man's cock against my bottom, again, and then he entered me, and the penetration was like an explosion within my mind and body. I came with a power I had never imagined, the pleasure exploding within my body. I could not breathe, nor think, nor move. I hung there, quivering violently as my insides howled with the most powerful climax of my life.

The man using me thrust himself up hard and fast, my

body bucking and jerking from the force of his strokes even as the woman held my thighs wide and licked hungrily across my throbbing, swollen clitoris. I felt myself spiralling upwards into realms of pleasure I had never before experienced, and exultantly clung to the ecstasy as it flowed over, through and around me.

I was so wicked, and terrible! Yet it was too wonderful to not grasp with every fibre of my being. I came and came and came, until I thought that I would surely pass out from lack of oxygen - and did not care.

After my orgasms faded the two left me. I felt a gloom and guilt and shame at my own behaviour, and a sense of disgust at the realization the man had spent himself in my anus. And then I simply felt exhaustion and discomfort as more and more time passed without event.

I stood there, sometimes raising one leg or the other to bend them and ease their stiffness, shifting my weight from one leg to another, and trying to twist my lower torso from side to side. Yet for the most part I must remain in position, and exhaustion took its toll, as did thirst, and also hunger.

Several times I lost consciousness, only to be yanked back to wakefulness as my legs collapsed or my body swayed too far forward and all my weight came down upon my arms and wrists.

Finally I felt a touch, and knew I was no longer alone. I felt a deep sense of thanks, and tried to stir my sluggish mind into comprehending the words spoken to me.

A slap to the face brought me more awake and I blinked tired eyes within the hood as the woman spoke once again.

"...onto your knees and we'll go for a walk, little slave."

My wrist restraints were released from the chains and I all but fell to my knees with a groan. I clasped my arms together over my chest and luxuriated in being able to bend my spine, my arms and my legs all at once, at having the weight off my feet and being free too move.

I felt a sharp little blow, as from the crop, at my shoulder, and her voice lashed out as well.

"Onto all fours, slave. At once."

I had to obey, yet even so I felt a great delight at being bent, so, after so long with my body held straight. I felt the chain slipped around my neck, and the pressure drew me forward. I crawled at her direction, turning as she ordered, moving at the pace she set, though aching arms and legs protested. I felt us leave the room when my fingers came down on carpeting, and felt a thankfulness for my bare knees.

We continued forward for some metres, then turned once more and halted.

"Now you are going to learn to follow orders at once. Do you understand, slave? Nod."

I obediently nodded.

"If you follow orders with alacrity, you will be given food and water. If not, you will be returned to the position you recently left, and kept there for the rest of the day."

My mouth was already salivating at the thought of water, and I determined to obey her every command, however lewd, as quickly as I could.

"Sit on your heels."

I obeyed at once.

"Keep your back straight and your knees well apart."

I quickly positioned myself according to her orders.

"Clasp your hands behind your back."

I did so.

Over the following minutes I was positioned and repositioned. I had to rise to my full height - on my knees, to place my hands behind my neck and arch my back, to lay upon my belly and spread my legs, to place my head and shoulders on the floor, while raising my bottom and spreading my legs, to lay upon my back and draw my knees back tightly against my body, and take an assortment of other positions according to her whims and orders.

Occasionally I could hear one of the men speak, but neither of them gave me further orders, so their presence served as little more than an additional source of embarrassment.

And then I was ordered to lie on my back, spread my legs, and place my feet flat on the floor.

"Now, slave, what I want to see you do is simple. It's something you've done often. I and my friends here want you to masturbate while we watch."

I believe it was the word itself which struck me so. Masturbation, after all, was that most intimate of actions, something one was always embarrassed about, and which one discussed with no one. The full force of the word took my breath away as I realized what she required of me, and my mind instantly balked. To even discuss masturbation would have once been too humiliating to even contemplate, and yet I was expected to demonstrate it before others!

Of course they had already seen me naked for some time, and already degraded, demeaned and humiliated me, yet this seemed a thing I could simply not do. The very notion made my mind quail.

"Now, slave. We know you've done it before. We want to watch you."

I'm quite certain now that her words were deliberately chosen, made to goad a girl only a day in captivity into recalling what her own cultural conditioning had taught her of self abuse. For now I realize how they had already so quickly taught me to obey, had already humiliated and violated me, and taught me a small measure of pain. But there were other lessons I had to learn, and they were intent on teaching me quickly.

And when I did not obey I was forced to crawl back the way I had come, to feel the hard, cold stone beneath my feet and knees once more, and was raised up into my former position. This time, however, I was raised higher, so that even with my feet together the tips of my toes merely brushed the floor. All my weight now hung from my wrists, and I moaned in pain and discomfort, not realizing that this would soon be but a minor part of my punishment.

"You're going to experience what happens to a slave who disobeys her master," the woman said calmly. "You are going to be flogged."

My mind shied away from the meaning of her words. I had thus far been punished in manners with which I was at least somewhat familiar. I had been slapped, pinched, and strapped (or cropped) on the buttocks. Having my breasts slapped was outrageous but still, it was not something from a lost work of fiction, not something from the dark ages. I was not entirely certain what she even meant, for flogging brought to mind the bare backed crews of Nelson's navy being whipped with braided strips of leather. And surely that was absurd.

And yet that was almost exactly what she meant. The flog she used was, I have since come to know, a mild variety of the assortment available to a master who wishes to punish a recalcitrant slave. The leather strips were light, and with no knots. Yet still, when I felt the impact against my back I was shocked.

The strips in themselves were of light weight, but there were many of them, and each stung quite severely as it struck. The overall effect was quite painful, and I screamed in muffled horror as I felt the pain stab into me from a dozen spots along my back.

My body shook and jerked violently, my legs kicking uselessly as my body reacted to the pain. And then another blow landed, higher against my back, and another dozen stinging aches made me scream as a terrible warmth grew across my flesh.

I'm being whipped!

Even in the midst of the pain I knew an amazement, a wonder. People simply did not do such things today! She could not do such a thing to me! And yet another blow landed, and I screamed silently, writhing and twisting and kicking helplessly as the leather slashed in against my lower back.

Another blow landed, and another, and my eyes were wet with tears, my throat rasping from screams which did not penetrate my gag. My back was on fire and my wrists threatening to break from the pressure of my thrashing body. Another blow landed, and another, the long strips arching down and around to snap at my right hip. My initial horror and the rush of adrenaline which had given me strength began to run dry, and my movements became less violent in the face of hopelessness.

Another blow landed across my rump, then another, then the flog moved upwards, striking my lower back, then my upper back.

This is not happening! This cannot be happening!

I felt dreadfully sorry for myself in between the cries of pain and yet - and yet there was something else there in the background of my mind. The image of a girl being hung naked from her wrists and then - shocking, outrageous - being whipped, was casting a strange, dark, seductive glow about my mind. My entire back was a throbbing mass of heat now, and so each new blow was denied the full force of pain. A curtain of pain already present masked the severity of the blows and though there was certainly pain it was not beyond my ability to cope.

I'm hanging by my wrists naked and being whipped.

There was a measure of wonder in my thoughts, and I felt a dark little shudder of excitement at being the recipient of such a wanton, barbaric, forbidden action. So cruel, they were, so cruel and heartless to me. Ahhh, and another blow landed, and I groaned and twisted weakly, a poor, whipped girl, naked and abused.

My pussy began to thrum weakly, but with rapidly growing strength, and I felt a sudden flare of electricity run along my body. Another blow and another, and as my back arched I could feel the flesh pulling tight across my breasts, could feel the stiffness of my nipples, and the tension in them.

I heard a shuffling movement, and then cried out in new pain and shock as the flog lashed across my chest. My breasts burned and I thrashed wildly, tears spilling from my eyes once again.

They daren't! They can't!

Another blow landed, this time more squarely upon my breasts, and both my throbbing orbs screamed in protest even as my nipples burned hotter. The next blow landed just below them, across my lower chest. Then the flog snapped down over my taut, straining belly.

They're whipping me! They're whipping me! They're whipping me!

I could not think of anything but my shock at what was happening, the wonder and horror, pain and despair, and even so the heady sensual thrill of being subjected to such a cruel beating. The flog snapped against my abdomen, then my stomach again, and thence onto my lower chest. I braced myself, but screamed even so as the many leather strips bit into the soft flesh of my breasts, one even scoring a glancing blow against one nipple.

My breasts were whipped again and again, as the flog concentrated on them for a dozen blows, and dark pain and heat flowed through my body and mind. As with my back, however, a curtain of throbbing heat rose around my chest to shield me from the worst of each new blow. And even as the flogging continued I felt that dark part of my mind exulting in the cruelty being visited upon them, wished that I could stand aside and observe the indecent cruelty being forced upon me.

I could hear voices now, giving orders, their voices loud

in my ear, yet it was difficult, given my flustered, dazed, shocked state of mind, to comprehend them. Fingers pinched at my inner thighs as inspiration, and finally I was able to understand.

"Open your legs wide. Open them."

I was exhausted and weak, yet I sought to obey, groaning with effort as I parted my legs and drew them out as widely as I could. I did not think at all upon the consequences of such actions, for already obedience was becoming instinctive. And when the flog lashed in and struck my sex directly the pain drove all other thoughts from my mind.

"Open your legs. Wide. Spread your legs."

I sobbed within the hood, yet the words were commanding, angry, and I did not dare to disobey. I raised my legs apart and again the flog struck, wrenching a scream from my already aching throat.

"Open your legs."

They could, of course, have simply raised my legs themselves at any time, yet they persisted, shouting, pinching, convincing my dazed mind to obey their wishes. And each time I spread my legs apart the cruel flog lashed in, the strips slicing into that most tender flesh at the joining of my thighs. One blow landed directly across my swollen clitoris, and I almost leaped in my shackles, screaming at the force of the sensation ripping through me.

And then strong hands gripped my buttocks and the woman's tongue slipped up into my sex once more, and after mere moments of light dancing across my wounded clitoris my body began to spasm and shake with a powerful climax.

CHAPTER FOUR

There is little to be said of what happened soon after, for my mind was in such a state I remember little of it. I was allowed to rest, but only briefly, for having my mind in a rested state was no part of their plan. I was forced to crawl about the room once more, then returned to the front part of the cottage, and once again presented with the orders to position and reposition my now well-striped body. Afterwards I was ordered to masturbate, and did so to the best of my ability. I did not expect to feel any pleasure from caressing my body, and was surprised at what small sexual heat I was able to raise. However, I went through the motions, and upon further orders did my best to pretend that I was enjoying and even climaxing from masturbating.

Following this the gag was removed from my mouth, and I was permitted to drink a small amount of water which was placed in a bowl on the floor before me. I was not permitted to use my hands for this action, but must drink in the manner of animals. Following this I performed fellatio on both men, and then was introduced to cunnilingus, performing on the woman who had used her own mouth on me earlier to such powerful effect. And once again was shocked at how excited I became as I imagined being able to watch myself performing such lewd and submissive acts.

I was given a small amount of somewhat tasteless food to eat, and again must eat without the use of hands, as though I were an animal. Following this was an exercise in verbal self-abuse where I repeated numerous foul statements regarding my morality and sexual proclivities and confessed to uncountable perversions. The slightest hesitation in movement or statement drew a blow, sometimes quite sharp, and so I learned to obey without thinking.

The hood was not removed for several days, and this time I spent in absolute helplessness, subject to blows at any time without even the ability to see their approach. For hours on end I was stood in the middle of the front room, wrists locked together above my head, and at any time, without notice, a harsh blow from hand or crop would land somewhere upon my body. It kept me in a state of constant wariness and anxiety mingled with that strange, dark pleasure, which, I suppose now, was the intent.

When I was not bound in that way I was further degraded by being forced to remain on my hands and knees like an animal. To this end my ankles were lifted back and strapped tightly to the backs of my thighs, and my wrists were pulled back and bound to my upper arms just below the shoulders. Thus, hooded and blind, I was forced to hobble about on my elbows and knees, eating and drinking from bowls set before me and using my tongue on whatever parts of the floor, wall or other people's bodies I was directed to.

Any use of my voice, on the occasions in which I was not gagged, drew instant repercussions, normally a quick blow with either hand or crop. I was permitted to answer questions or make statements as directed, but I was not allowed to ask for anything, be it food, freedom, or mercy. On one occasion, as if to remind me of my animal-like appearance and status I was ordered to bark like a dog.

At night, or what I took, in my blindness, to be night, I was bound more tightly, often to the point where I could not move so much as an inch. I was constantly hungry and thirsty, and in a state of some disorientation due to my blindness. To take advantage of this a pair of headphones was firmly placed against my ears each night, and the woman's soft voice would croon to me for hours on end.

"I am a slave," she would whisper, her voice sometimes so low it was difficult to hear. "I am a whore. I am a slave. I must obey. I will be hurt if I do not obey. I must serve my master. I love my master. I must always obey. I am a slave. I am made to give pleasure. I must obey. My purpose in life is to bring pleasure. My body was made to be used. I am a slave..."

On and on it would go, whispering, crooning, hour after hour after hour until it all became almost a background noise, hardly even recognized.

By morning I would groan with relief and gratitude as I was released from my rigid immobility to perform sexual acts upon one or the other of my captors. And I would hardly think about the words spoken in my ear all night long. Yet that night they would return, hindering what little sleep I might find.

Finally, after long congratulation regarding my behaviour, and many warnings that a single instance of disobedience could set me back to the beginning, the hood was removed and I was once again permitted to see. I cannot adequately express the relief I felt at once again being able to look on the world around me, even if that world consisted of nothing but a small room and three not very friendly people. I was surprised to find my body relatively unmarked. It had, of course, been several days since I had been flogged, yet I had expected to see long red weals criss-crossing my pale skin, and there were but a few very light lines to recall the event.

I was permitted to crawl into the bathroom then, and kneel on all fours in the bathtub as Mistress (for I had no names for any of them) bathed me and shampooed my hair. This felt glorious, for I was quite filthy by then. After this was done she removed her own clothes and slid into the tub alongside me, pulling me around so I lay on my back, and kissing me lightly.

I responded at once, and gladly, for you will understand that after the harsh treatment to which I had been subjected I was not only desperate to avoid more, not only eager to please my cruel captors, but also, as a young girl is wont, desperate for any measure of affection and gentleness. And as my Mistress held me in her arms and gently caressed my soapy flesh I returned her kisses with no hesitation whatever, our lips moving together in soft, but growing passion.

She brought one of my hands to her breast, and I squeezed it carefully, marvelling at the feel of it against my fingers, at the soft, tactile pleasure as my fingertips sank into the warm flesh and grazed the bump of her nipple. Our tongues slid lazily together as our lips made soft love, and my hands began to move over her body, mirroring her own upon mine. It was the lovemaking I had never known, and my mind soared in wonder and delight as we rolled slowly there in the water, half in, half out.

I lapped at her nipples, large and brown, but swollen with lust. I closed my mouth around one, tasting some soap, but not caring, suckling like a babe as she sighed and caressed my head and breast. I moved from one breast to the other, eager to pleasure her, my fingers gently kneading her breasts as she stroked my head like a faithful dog.

She eased herself up out of the water, sitting on the edge of the tub, in the corner, and spreading her long legs out along the top. I needed no urging, nor was I at all reluctant as I slid forward in the water and brought my lips against her sex. I made careful love to her, using all that she had taught me, feeling a mounting excitement as she moaned in pleasure and began to slowly roll her hips against me.

"Darling little slut," she groaned, caressing my head. "Filthy little slave. Yes, darling! Use your tongue there. Ahhh, filthy little girl. Nasty, wicked little slave! You're so baaaaad."

I teased her clitoris with my tongue, circling it slowly, then reversing my direction before lapping directly across it. I brought my lips against it, now suckling rhythmically, now massaging it by rubbing my lips in opposite directions. I drew back and blew a stream of warm air across it, then pushed forward, licking hard, varying my actions according to her responses. My hands caressed her moist thighs, sliding up along her dripping body to gently knead her breasts, and she sighed and moaned encouragement, telling me again how sluttish and cheap I was, and what a good slave girl I had become, one worthy of her affection.

I brought her to climax, and she shuddered as she clutched my head, jamming my face into her sex. Then she groaned in relief and slid back into the water, pulling me into her arms and hugging me tightly.

I was on my best behaviour thereafter, and each day would bring more testing, more training. I was put through my paces like a dog, rapidly changing the positions of my naked body as required, performing whatever menial thing was demanded of me, stating whatever wicked thing I was ordered to, all without hesitation or thought. And, of course, I was used as a sexual pleasure toy by all three of them, sometimes one at a time, sometimes all together.

One night I was permitted to actually sleep in a bed, rather than bound into a tight state of discomfort on the floor or in a closet. On this occasion Mistress was out, and the two Masters took me to a large bed early in the evening. We made love for many hours, each taking me in turn, or on occasion, together. Often I would fellate one as the other sodomized me. And afterwards I was permitted to stay in bed with one of the men, the American, with no bondage but a chain locked to my collar and the headboard of the bed.

A day after this I was ordered to position myself on my feet in the centre of their front room. I stood straight, my hands behind my neck, unbound, yet locked into place by their orders. All three were present, and I looked nervously upon a small tray the woman rolled before me. On it were medicinal bottles of some sort, together with a group of very sharp little instruments.

"You will hold your position, and not move. Do you understand, slave?" she said.

"Yes, mistress," I replied, anxiety filling me due to uncertain, and the coldness of her voice.

"Your nipples are going to be pierced," she said. "This is not much different to when you were younger and had your ears pierced and I do not want you to act like a silly baby. If you move your position you will be punished."

That, of course, I had already known. I was less anxious after her words, though gripped by a wonderment and a little quiver of excitement. To have my nipples pierced was a shocking idea. I was attempting to consider how and why this might be accomplished when one of the men gripped my wrists behind my head and jerked back roughly, forcing me to arch my back even more, and look up towards the ceiling. He then let go, forcing me to self-discipline - which to my mind was considerably more difficult.

I gasped as I felt a harsh sensation against my left nipple, but after a moment recognized it as an ice cube. They had taunted and teased me with ice cubes at various times over the previous few days, even slipping them into my anus and pussy, so I adjusted quickly. The ice cube was rolled back and forth across my nipple, forcing it to swell and pucker and thrust out to meet its fate. I was attempting to discipline my breathing, which was becoming harsher due to my anxiety, when I felt something pinch my nipple just at its base.

"Don't move," she ordered.

The pain was not inconsiderable. I had, of course, adjusted somewhat to pain over the course of my captivity, and was less shocked by it than I had once been. Nevertheless, the harshness and sharpness of the pain biting into my nipple made me tremble and shake, and the air began to raggedly puff in and out of my chest as tears filled my eyes. I moaned softly, but did not dare to move, interlinking my fingers and clenching my teeth against the pain as it became more biting, more sharp, and then began to fade.

Perspiration stood out on my chest and forehead by then, and I felt a continuing source of pain in my nipple as her fingers twisted it lightly. Then she drew back slightly and I felt the ice cube rolling against my other nipple. I whimpered slightly, but braced myself both body and mind to a repeat of the pain I had already experienced.

One of the men behind me pushed his foot between my ankles and forced my legs further apart, then jerked back on my wrists. My arched back had eased somewhat and he clearly required me to draw back further. Again I felt a terribly sharp pain against my nipple, causing me to grind my teeth and close my eyes, forcing my body to tremble and shake with the need to escape. Almost did I give way and throw myself back. Yet I knew this would not avail me, for they would simply hold me in place to repeat the necessary piercing and then beat me.

The pain faded, though both nipples felt somewhat heavy now, and throbbed hotly, and I started to straighten, wanting to examine them.

"Don't move!" she snapped harshly.

I froze in place, arching my back further still.

"We are not finished. Spread your legs further."

I obeyed, wondering what else they intended, my insides quivering and fluttering with alarm, pain and anxiety.

"We're going to pierce your clitoris."

I thought that surely this was mistaken, that I had either misheard or she was making an idle threat. But strong hands gripped both my ankles then, holding them in place, and my wrists and hair were gripped behind my neck, held tightly.

I felt her fingers spreading open the soft lips of my sex, then easing the hood back to expose my clitoris. Yet even then I did not believe she had spoken truly. I was staring up at the ceiling, gaping really, I suppose, shocked and wondering, alarm rising higher and higher inside me as the ice cube played over my clitoris.

"Please," I whispered.

I felt my clitoris pinched, and my ankles jerked instinctively against the hands holding them in place.

"Don't move," I was ordered.

The pain which came next was shocking in its intensity, and its effect on my body. My limbs all spasmed and jerked violently and my body began to sway and pull against the hands holding it in place. I felt a terrible pain accompanied by a sense of nausea and cried out as both grew stronger.

Then they both subsided somewhat, and, trembling and weak-kneed, my flesh glistening with perspiration, I was released. I staggered a step or so, and immediately cupped my groin with both palms, bending dizzyingly over to see what had been done to me.

My clitoris had indeed been pierced, and a small gold ring had been inserted through the hole. Furthermore, as I bent, I could not but help notice both my nipples were similarly pierced by identical gold rings, each quite thin, but large enough to fit around my thumb.

"Try not to touch any of them. We don't want you getting infected," Mistress said.

I thought that they actually did look quite pretty, in an odd, but deeply erotic sort of way, but the pain still throbbing within my nipples and clitoris prevented me from welcoming these new additions to my body. However, for the next few days my captors were careful about the way they handled and fondled me, and this at least was some relief.

My training continued unabated, however. Long periods of time were spent on my knees, instantly twisting and contorting my body to the orders one or another would snap out to me, or immediately responding orally to statements or questions.

"What are you?"

"A worthless slave, master."

"What must you do?"

"Obey, master."

"What is your purpose?"

"To give pleasure with my body, master."

Any hesitation whatever would draw a blow, which inspired me, of course, to very quick obedience.

Mistress then taught me how to strip and dance, and we spent considerable hours rolling our hips and moving our bodies to various songs coming over the radio. She instructed me on how to make my face appear seductive, or coy, or shy, depending on what persona she wished me to take on. I was also taught to speak in a subservient manner, always with a tone of respect if not admiration for my masters and mistress.

Of course, I was alone quite often, usually bound, and had a considerable amount of time to consider my situation. Although I was being trained, and learning to obey instantly, I cannot say that I was an eager student. I resented my captivity and abuse and longed for freedom and the peace it would bring. My values had changed, of course, for outrage, indignation and humiliation at being naked and sexually abused could not continue indefinitely. Even sodomy soon came to be routine, and hardly caused me any trauma or unhappiness.

Yet I continued to feel my situation was most unfair and that despite what they said, and despite the frequent betrayal of my body, I was not the subhuman creature they continued to insist I was. My awe and fright of them began to ease, and my opinion reformed accordingly. The men were arrogant, but so far as I could see, had little cause for such a sense of superiority.

The woman however was different. She seemed to take sex and all that went with it as a matter of great and natural pleasure. She was insatiable in that area, and I sensed that she found little guilt in treating me the way she did because she considered such treatment not only natural but desirable. Rather than the arrogance I sensed in the men she had a seemingly limitless degree of lust and passion, triggered always by her subjugation of and use of me as her slave.

In truth I found that excitement contagious, and her

obvious delight at the beauty of my bound, naked body gave me a feeling of pride and attractiveness, a sense that people would be intensely eager to taste the softness of my flesh and feast their eyes on the beauty of my helpless, bound form. At times, as she positioned me to be used, binding me down, I felt my loins throbbing and heating with excitement as the leather or rope tightened around my wrists and ankles, and my body would welcome her every touch as she forced it to experience the thrill and pleasure she felt herself.

It was with considerable shock and dismay that I found myself, one day, sent away from her. I did not miss the two men, but I had grown strangely fond of Mistress, and feared the unknown to which I was now to be subjected.

I was given a thin silk shift to wear. It was much like a poncho in nature, being a long strip of square material with a round hole through which my head protruded. It fell to just below my groin and buttocks, front and back, but was open at the sides. A slim gold chain went around the middle to hold the two sides in place, but the lower part continued to flap widely whenever I moved, so the cover was slight.

My wrists were shackled together behind my back, and my ankles were also shackled, with a chain of sufficient length to permit me to move by quick shuffling, but not to give any hope of fleeing. I was gagged, and collared, and the man to whom I was given led me by a leash out of the house and across the yard to a van similar in nature to the one which had brought me there. I was placed in the back and strapped in place on the floor, and as the door slid shut I saw my kidnappers for the last time.

We drove for some time, and the man spoke to me not at all. I dosed a little, for I had not had any real length of sleep since my capture, but anxiety kept my sleep light and troubled.

It was night by the time the van stopped, and I waited warily for my fate to be unveiled. Away from the cottage, at last, I began to think again about escape, about finding some way to call outside attention to my plight. Yet I saw no opportunity, and the discipline to which I had been subjected made me quite wary of drawing more.

The man unstrapped me and helped me sit, then pulled me free of the van. I found we were on a wide, darkened dock next to a large ocean-going ship of some kind, a freighter. The man, holding my arm now, instead of my leash, led me to a gangplank which led up to the dock. I looked around in vain for someone to whom I could signal for help, but the only people in sight were my captor and two dirty, smirking individuals standing at the foot of the gangplank.

Both looked at me with hungry eyes, lust and contempt equally clear in their minds, and I felt deeply grateful for even the slight modesty the little white shift afforded me. For though I had become accustomed to nudity around Mistress and the two masters, still my face heated at these new eyes and minds ravishing my body. I also felt a rising indignation. I wanted to shout that I was a solicitor, or would be, that I was far more intelligent than they, and better educated.

Yet they cared nothing for that. They cared only for my breasts, for my sex and buttocks, for my legs and lips. I was an object of desire for them.

The man led me up the gangplank, then down into the bowels of the ship. The air was damp and chilly, and the dark steel corridors dirty and unappealing. After descending several stairwells, stairwells so steep my captor was forced to unchain my ankles, we paused before a narrow steel hatch. My captor unlocked the hatch and flung it inward, then pushed me into the small cabin.

There were three bunks along the walls, and girls sat upon two of them. Each girl seemed approximately my age, with one being a big busted brunette, and the other being a blonde with waist-length hair. Both were nude, and their arms were

68

apparently bound behind their backs.

"You will cause no trouble. There is water there on the table, and the toilet is in the corner. You will be fed when it is time and you will be permitted up on deck for air after dark. Obey."

Obey.

The word sent a strange little shiver through me, and my eyes blinked helplessly as he pushed me forward.

The man glared around at each of us, then left, closing the door behind. We all heard the solid snick of the bolt being shot, and were alone with each other.

The brunette had a round, sad face, and a cute, pageboy haircut and looked quite miserable as she sat on the edge of her bunk. The other blonde girl looked angry, sullen, glaring at me and the brunette, then at the porthole, then at the hatch.

None of us spoke, however. I had become accustomed to not speaking unless I was spoken to, and not once since I had been captured had doing so failed to bring a blow. I supposed the other two had been similarly taught.

After a few minutes the blonde girl lay down, stretching long legs along the bunk and looking up at the ceiling. The brunette looked at me miserably, wide brown eyes looking much like those of a puppy I had once owned.

"Do you know where we're going?" I ventured at last.

The brunette's eyes widened and she gasped in fear, turning quickly to look at the hatch. The blonde girl turned her head and glared at me. Neither replied for a few minutes.

"We're whores," the blonde girl said finally.

"But I'm a virgin."

She looked at me in disgust.

"I want to go home," the brunette whimpered.

"Shut up, you cow," the blonde snapped.

"I wonder if we're going to Arabia or something," I gulped.

"Maybe," the blonde said. "Somewhere we can be nicely

abused without any of the authorities intervening."

"You have nice eyes," the brunette said, rather oddly.

I frowned at her. "Thank you," I said uncertainly.

The blonde looked at me slowly. "Yes, you do have nice eyes. You look kind of... delicate. You'll fetch a nice price, you and big tits here."

"I still don't understand how people can sell us!" I exclaimed.

"We're girl meat," she replied bitterly. "That's what they told me. Nothing but girl meat, toys for the boys."

The ship shuddered briefly, then with a growing quiver as it moved away from the dock. Before long we were out to sea, moving slowly and rolling slightly from side to side. We lay back and tried to get some sleep in the dark, but were all too fearful.

We spoke very softly, all having acquaintance with beatings for speaking anything approaching a protest, commiserating warily with one eye on the door. The other blonde was named Sara, and the brunette was Penny. Both had been taken, much as I had, though by different people, used, beaten, and repeatedly taught their place in the world was that of a slave.

It was a shocking thing to learn those who had captured me were not unique, that there were possibly whole legions of such people about, kidnapping helpless girls, abusing them, and then selling them abroad. I could hardly believe such a thing could happen once, let alone with such apparent regularity.

Sara spoke with an upper class accent. She had been at university, in her third year, studying art history, of all things. Her parents were wealthy and she had grown up amidst the privilege of the public schools and proper society. It was clear her present circumstances infuriated her.

Penny was a shop girl, having worked in her parents' grocery store. While Sara's intelligence was obvious Penny was quite clearly not generously endowed with intelligence. She seemed sad and bewildered more than anything else.

We had no sense of time in our little steel box. A long while passed, however, before the hatch opened. A man came in, all shifty eyes and eager leers, carrying a tray of food. He set bowls of food and water on the floor, then turned to look warily behind him before darting forward.

He gripped Penny's hair and bent over her as he forced her head back, grasping one of her breasts crudely and squeezing it quite hard. His mouth moved to her nipple, chewing and suckling in a frenzy as his fingers twisted and mauled her breast. Penny took this action with feigned pleasure, moaning and begging him for more, spreading her legs wide so that he could grope and fondle her there.

But then the man turned and hurried out, slamming the hatch behind him, and her face turned sad once more.

The three of us moved off the bunks and examined our food and water, then attempted to eat a little and drink - in the manner we had been taught, bent over on our knees, lapping like animals.

More time passed, and we lay back on our bunks, talking softly, wondering where we were bound, and what chances of escape might come.

The door opened suddenly and a strange man stood there. He examined us all shrewdly, then snapped his fingers at the floor before him. Sara, for all her bitterness and rebellious attitude, grasped his intent first, but Penny and I were but an instant behind in throwing ourselves to our knees before him.

He looked us over, then reached out to Sara, grasping her hair to pull her to her feet and press her body against him. She returned his kisses with an apparent eagerness that was embarrassing to see, for I knew the depths of her anger and resentment. She preened before him, rubbing her naked body against his chest and moaning in pleasure as she slid her tongue into his mouth.

71

He bent and hefted her over one shoulder, then motioned Penny and me back, and left, locking the hatch behind. After a few seconds we heard the sound of applause from somewhere not very far away, the sound of men's jeers and approval. It softened as we lay back on our bunks, but now and then we could hear a cheer or a shout from some man or other.

The sky darkened and the door opened once again. A new man appeared, bald, foreign seeming, and with a goatee. He looked at us dourly, then motioned us out. "I will take you on deck for some air," he said with a discernable accent. "Do not do anything foolish. I am not nearly so kind and gentle and forgiving as your earlier masters."

We were led down a narrow corridor to a steep staircase, then up it to another level above. We could hear the men much more clearly now, and as we turned to take the stairs to the next level passed an open hatchway.

There were perhaps a dozen men inside. They were a rough and ragged looking group, unshaven and crude. And Sara was with them. She was straddling one rough looking man who sat in a chair, his cock was thick and seemed to gleam in the light as it pierced her shaven sex. I could quite clearly see the tautness of her labia as they spread around it, and watched them pushed inward as she slid down to take the thing deep within her.

She moaned in apparent pleasure, then pulled herself up, only to sink down once more, riding him with great enthusiasm. She was showing none of the anger or rebelliousness she had below. Her eyes were alight, a look of lust and pleasure on her face as she rode the man's shaft with wild abandon, the muscles in her thighs moving strongly as she impaled herself repeatedly on the upright prong. Another man stood just to her right, and her head was twisted so that she could take him into her mouth. She was bobbing her lips excitedly - or pretending to at any rate, as the room full of men looked on with sneers and obscene comments on their lips.

A man moved behind her, an erection pushing against her backside, and she drew her lips off the cock beside her long enough to shout in delight. "Yes! Oh God! Fuck my asshole! Fuck my filthy asshole! I love being fucked in the asshole and cunt at the same time! Fill me with your wonderful cocks!"

Her voice was emotional, yet I heard the edge of hysteria in it even as a rough hand jerked her mouth back and it was filled with cock once again. I felt ashamed at having watched the performance and at the arousal it had caused in my own treacherous body.

"Move," the goateed man ordered.

I turned away and climbed the next narrow staircase to the deck above, then walked out to stare at the sea, followed by Penny.

"Nothing in sight," the man said in satisfaction. "You are far from home. You go to a new life in a new world."

"Yes, master," we said softly.

"That girl below, she still thinks of herself as better than she is. That is why I give her to the crew and my men. They will use her the entire voyage, an unaccustomed treat for them. When we are done I will clean her body just as their use will clean her mind."

He smiled cruelly and reached out to squeeze one of Penny's big breasts. "It is too bad you are not blonde," he said to her. "For you are a biddable girl with large teats. You would be more valuable as a blonde."

"I'm sorry, master," she said weakly.

Without warning he gripped my hair from behind and yanked me back hard, so my back slammed into the side of the cabin, then bent my head back over the top to arch my back.

He undid the little gold belt, then tugged the poncho-like

shift up and over my head, throwing it over the side of the ship.

"No clothing, not to cover up your nakedness," he said, running his hand over my body.

He turned to Penny and yanked her down onto her knees.

"Eat her," he ordered.

I felt Penny moving between my legs, and a moment later her tongue pressed against my sex. I could not move if I wanted to, and I did not dare to want to. I stood there, legs apart, head pressed back onto the top of the low cabin, staring at the night sky as Penny's tongue lapped at my clitoris.

"The girl below pretends," the man said, his face close against mine, so close his bad breath was warm against my skin. "She pretends, she thinks she can fool me. She waits for her chance, when she thinks to escape, to return to her old life. Foolish girl. She will go on acting the part until, without even realizing it has happened, the part will become real."

My loins were throbbing lightly as Penny's tongue lapped at my clitty. I felt the man's free hand cupping one of my breasts, pinching my nipple lightly, and my breasts throbbed in response.

"She is a blonde girl. Do you know why we prefer blondes?" he asked softly. "Nothing is more a natural whore than a blonde girl. They try to pretend otherwise, but this is a proven fact. Peel away her manners and her education and her sophistication and the girl down there is nothing but a raw animal whore. As are you."

I shuddered softly, wanting to deny it, but not daring to. And as Penny's tongue worked its magic on me my insides flowed like liquid metal, burning away at what pride still remained to me, and I began to grind myself against her.

"Whore," he whispered in slick, oily satisfaction. "You do not pretend like the other blonde girl. You know what you are."

I was breathing in short puffs and pants, eyes closed as my body burned, and I whimpered softly as he rolled my nipple between his thumb and forefinger.

"You are a sexual animal, a creature made to bring pleasure to men. This is why you will fetch so much on the block. Because you have the mind and heart and soul of a slave."

I came, my hips bucking helplessly into Penny's mouth as the man sneered down at me.

We were many days at sea, and saw little of Sara during that time. Late in the evenings she was half dragged back to our cabin and tossed onto her bed. Even from across the room with the porthole wide we could smell the raw sex, the sweat and semen that coated her bruised body. She lay dazed and exhausted, hair a tangled mass, plastered against her face and forehead by sweat and bodily fluids. Her legs were spread wide, and remained so as she stared silently up at the ceiling.

She never spoke, nor replied to our half-hearted attempts at conversations, and early in the mornings as the crew wakened, she was dragged off to please them once again. Later we discovered she spent her days on hands and knees with a scrubbing brush, washing the decks - and being mounted by any man who had a fleeting interest in her.

In the evenings she was in that room, the centrepiece of the men's partying and celebration.

We were marched off the ship in the dark. By then she had been cleaned up but I saw little sign of defiance or anger in her eyes as we walked, single file, along an abandoned dock and into a low car. The air was warm, but I did not know where we were. It was a small, anonymous dock surrounded by hulking shadows.

The car drove us to a warehouse, and after a brief hesitation, drove into the opened door to park amongst a number of others there.

The warehouse was dark. There were two rows of benches in a square about ten feet wide. Two dozen people, almost all men, sat on the benches looking at the girl standing in the middle of the square. What light there was came from a spotlight above, trained only on the girl.

She was older than the three of us, and dark of hair, her skin showing a Mediterranean origin. She was nude, and in chains, slowly walking about the square, displaying her body for the men. There was something terribly cruel in the sight. She was so young and beautiful, her body sleek and glossy, and yet she was naked and helpless before a collection of what appeared to my eyes to consist largely of fat, older men, few of whom seemed very attractive or athletic.

She had a petite face, her eyes brown and downcast. Several times she stopped as a man to one side spoke rapidly - praising her body and lack of spirit, her desire to please and the value of her sexual abilities. Several times she stopped and turned, her young, athletic body assuming poses for the benefit of those men looking on. Now she was on her toes, legs apart, displaying her bottom. Now her hands were behind her head, pushing her breasts out proudly. Now her mouth was wide, showing her teeth.

I was embarrassed for her, and fearful, knowing this awaited me as well. My mind screamed at the cruelty and indignity of it all.

She was sold, apparently, to a fat man with a white moustache. He stepped forward and slapped a collar around her throat, tugging it sharply, then led her off to one side. Our car door opened and the man with the goatee motioned Penny out. She gave me a final, terrified look, then hurriedly obeyed, following him to the benches, and stepping through an opening to take her place under the bright, cold light.

Again the auctioneer called out, describing her value. As had the girl before her she was made to pose for the watching men.

"Show them your tits, whore," Mr. Goatee ordered. "That's it. Now spread your legs more. Raise your ass better. Good. Now get down on all fours."

She crawled along before the benches, her big breasts jiggling as the men examined her. One called out a question and Mr. Goatee ordered her to crawl before him. He examined her, bending to squeeze her breasts, perhaps assuring himself they were real.

"Mooo," he said.

The other men around him chuckled or laughed.

"Moo like a cow, slut," Mr. Goatee ordered.

"Moooooo," Penny said in her high quivering voice. "Mooooo."

More of the men laughed, and the men before her slapped her on the backside and called something out. There were more calls from the surrounding men, and I realized they were making bids on her.

She looked so pathetic there, so terrified, and so ill-used. I felt a rising sense of outrage on her behalf. This poor, frightened girl who had harmed none, and did not deserve to be treated so... so cruelly, so barbarically, as a slave, an animal.

And yet even as my outrage glowed hotly that dark, wicked side of me was awakened, and I felt a sense of dark lust at her abuse, at the cruelty. In a sense, somewhere in my mind I had developed a link between wickedly sexual acts and arousal. The more outrageous the act the more forbidden... and the more forbidden the more wickedly exciting. And so as I watched poor Penny crawling about, this sweet young girl, being stared at and inspected and sneered at by these men, most of them old enough to be her father. I felt my mingled outrage and dark heat suffusing my body and mind, and knew a breathlessness as I realized I would soon be subject to the same cruel inspection.

She was sold, and led off on all fours with a collar around her throat. The car door opened and Mr. Goatee motioned me outside.

I stepped onto the rough stone gingerly, my heart pounding frantically as he took my arm and led me towards the other men. I felt my skin redden as I was led out into the square beneath the light, and fought to keep from visibly trembling. I blinked rapidly in the bright light, dropping my eyes down as I stood in place. I found myself wishing my wrists were still bound, for then I would have something to do with my hands, which kept trying to instinctively cover myself.

"Straighten your back," Mr. Goatee ordered.

I straightened up at once, but that meant raising my head, and I blushed furiously, feeling my skin crawl as I stood there under those piercing eyes.

"Start walking around, slut. Let them see your tits and ass."

I shuffled forward, feeling almost light-headed as I moved before the seated audience. It was all so very unreal, walking around naked in front of all these people. I could hardly believe it wasn't some ghastly nightmare. One of the men reached out as I passed him and I halted at once, inhaling sharply as his fingers rubbed at my sparse pubic hair. It had been permitted to grow back in somewhat so that purchasers could be assured that I was a true blonde, yet it was far too short to offer any real protection to the eyes examining me.

He pulled his hand back and I resumed my slow walk as the man, the auctioneer, I suppose, called out what I supposed were things about me, but I heard the words as though from a great distance, with an odd echoing sensation, and can not now relate them. I recall the stir among the men, however, as my virginity was announced, and another man reached out to halt me. This time his finger pushed roughly into my pussy.

"Spread your legs, slut," Goatee ordered.

I opened my legs more as the man, a squinty eyed little black man, pushed his finger up my pussy to feel my hymen.

He pulled it back and I shuffled forward again. Another man stopped me, a tall, thin Asian man, who looked extremely dignified in a tailored suit. He also slipped a long finger into me to check on my cherry, then turned me around with a hand on the hip and squeezed my bottom. He nodded and slapped me there, sending me on.

"Move to the middle of the square and stand with your hands behind your head," Goatee ordered.

I obeyed, and then turned slowly in a circle at another command, my feet well apart. I bent over at the waist, showing those behind me a view of my bottom and pussy, and then to my horror, Goatee ordered me to dance.

There was no music, of course, but I knew there was no command I could not obey, and knew that if I failed to do as he wished in front of all these men I would be severely punished. I frantically thought of the dance Mistress had said I did best, and tried to play the music in my mind.

I rolled my hips slowly and seductively, sliding my hands slowly up my body and then through my hair. I let my hands rise as my hips rolled and my head began to turn as my eyes slitted.

All those people watching!

Unable to breathe, I turned slowly, straightening my right leg, half jumping forward onto my right foot and twirling, then letting my body undulate.

"Enough," Goatee ordered.

I halted, dazed. I stood still as the men bid for me, aware of the moisture on my face and forehead and between my breasts. The lights sparkled before my eyes, and for a long moment I wondered if I would faint.

The bidding went on for longer than it had for the previous girls, and I noted the last two involved were an older man holding a cane, and a young man, perhaps not so very much older than I. The older man had dark, flinty eyes which bespoke a cruel spirit. Yet the younger man seemed little

79

better, eager and cocksure. Oddly, a woman sat beside him, an arm linked possessively, or perhaps, for protection, in his. She wore a large hat which hid her face in shadows, but she seemed young and attractive.

The young man won, and pumped his fist in the air in victory. The woman kissed him on the cheek and I saw bright, penetrating blue eyes turned upon me from beneath the hat. The man rose and went to the auctioneer, dealing out a large number of bills of unknown denomination. Then, face flushed, he came into the square. He grinned at me, but more as a man happily examining his newest toy.

He pulled my wrists together behind my back and shackled them in place. Then he pulled from his suit pocket a short chain. I realized almost at once that it was parted near one end into two slightly thinner strands. Each strand ended in a clip and the man attached each one to one of my gold nipple rings.

He moved back and tugged on the chain, pulling painfully hard against my nipples. My breasts stretched out and I gasped in pain, leaping forward to ease the pull as he laughed in delight. He led me out of the square, holding the leash high so that my nipples strained upwards, forcing me almost to walk on the tips of my toes, gasping and moaning in pain.

The woman rose and followed, appearing to be as happy as the man in their new possession, and giggled each time the man forced the chains to pull upwards and my body reacted.

"God, she's cute," the woman said in delight, her voice American.

"We're gonna have a helluva time with this little slut," the man boasted gladly.

They led me to a Mercedes, and the man unlocked the trunk. He forced a thick ball-gag into my mouth, then pushed me in, pulling my ankles up behind my back and fastening them, with a strap, to the shackles about my wrists. A moment later the hood was slammed down and I was in darkness.

I cannot say I was well pleased or impressed with my new master. He seemed brash, uncouth and entirely too shallow and self-absorbed, a great contrast to the confidence my earlier captors had displayed. Still, I consoled myself that if he were in fact, as inexperienced as he seemed, then perhaps I would have greater opportunity for escape.

CHAPTER FIVE

I could hear the growing sounds of traffic around us; car and truck engines, honking horns, and the babble of voices. Both my new master and my new mistress (or so I supposed her to be) had American accents, and I wondered if we were now in America. But I had no way, of course, to discover this from the boot of the car. After some time we turned in somewhere, the car slowed, and the sounds faded, to be replaced by the kind of echo one hears inside concrete garages.

We stopped briefly, then continued on, turned sharply, and stopped once again. Now I felt the car sway and the car doors slammed shut, and braced myself for what might come next.

The lid was lifted, and I looked up at the two of them, both beaming happily at their new possession. The man reached in and unfastened my ankles, then he pulled me out, setting my bare feet down upon the cold stone. We were indeed inside a garage, but in a small, private section separated from the greater garage by a metal door, the last foot of which came down even as I watched. The smaller inside garage held only a few sports cars, including the Mercedes.

"I should take the little slut right here," the man said cockily.

The woman, or perhaps, given her temperament, I should say 'girl', giggled, eyeing me with bright, excited eyes.

"Do it, Chad! Give it to her right here! She's supposed to be a virgin. Won't this be a great place to lose it, in a dirty fucking garage?!"

She squealed with laughter, and the man snickered as well, giving me a smug, arrogant look.

"Yeah. Let's go for it," he said.

He took off his suit jacket and began to undo his tie, and

the woman gave another little squeal of inspiration and jumped forward, grasping at the chain still dangling from my nipples and catching it up.

"Oh let me try this!"

She pulled back on the chain, backing away, and I, of course, followed forward. She laughed in delight and moved back faster, then quickly raised her hand high, twining the chain around her wrist and forcing me up onto my toes. My nipples ached and burned as my breasts began to stretch out and up from the pressure. I moaned and let out a soft cry of pain, but she was far from sympathetic. She let out a whoop of cruel delight and lowered the chain abruptly, forcing me to bend, then drop to my knees, then, bent over and holding the chain low, she backed away, and I was forced to awkwardly crawl along on my knees, wincing and crying out as she tugged on the chain.

"Enough of that. Let's pump this pussy," the man said, grabbing me by the hair and lifting me up to my feet.

"Yeah! Pop her!"

I was pulled backwards by the hair, protesting weakly, and then forced down first to my knees, then onto my back on the cold stone floor of the garage. Chad was naked now, and had a fine, athletic body, obviously well cared-for. He taunted me as he fondled his erection.

"This is for you, slave," he said with a sneer. "You're going to love it too."

He was older than I had supposed, probably around thirty. Perhaps it was an inherent immaturity which caused me to believe him younger. Certainly he was a handsome man, but his air, his manner, was that of much younger man, without the sense of decorum or dignity I had come to expect in men of his actual age.

"Fuck her!" the girl squealed, eyes bright and sparkling with anticipation as she moved forward to kneel at my head.

Unlike Chad she was more my own age, but there was

something distinctly odd about her. She had shoulder length brown hair, but it was completely unkempt, and with her glinting, eager eyes and wide, grinning mouth served to give her a feral appearance.

"Calm down, Kristine. She belongs to us. We can take our time with her."

"Not like those other sluts," the girl said, giving me a predatory look.

Chad had carefully placed a folded over blanket on the floor, and knelt upon it as he grasped my ankles and yanked them far apart. He ran his hands up my thighs, and over my body with possessive pride, and squeezed my nipples before discarding the chain. The girl giggled, roughly squeezing and kneading one of my breasts and plucking at the ring piercing my nipple.

I felt embarrassed anew as the two strangers ravished my body with their eyes and hands, feeling a sense of being rushed, of time moving faster than I could cope. My previous captors had been slow and deliberate, mature and careful. I felt as though I were in the hands of children, spoiled, malicious children.

"You ready to be fucked, slave?" the man demanded, leering proudly down at me.

"Yes, master," I gasped anxiously.

The girl squealed in delight again.

"Say it again, slut!"

"Yes, master," I felt shamed at their gleeful response, knowing to what level I had been reduced, yet could hardly imagine denying them.

"I like the sound of that," Chad said smugly.

He pressed himself against my pussy as the girl knelt beside me. She leaned forward, roughly pulling and twisting my hair, then slapping and squeezing my breasts.

"You ready, slave girl?" she taunted, bringing her face down close to mine. "He's gonna fuck away your virginhood now. He's gonna ram his cock up you so far it comes out your mouth!"

I felt Chad's cock being forced into me, and grunted with pain as the lips of my sex were forced wide. His spongy cockhead pushed deeper, then withdrew.

"Moisten me up, baby," he demanded.

"Why should I?" Kristine demanded. "Let the slut do it!"

"There's an idea."

He moved forward, straddling my chest, sliding his cock toward my mouth, then reaching beneath my head to lift it upwards.

"Get me nice and wet, slave," he ordered, forcing himself into my mouth.

I obeyed as best I could. Of course my wrists were still bound behind me, and was in little position to move my head either. He pushed deeper into me, to the point of almost choking me on his fat cock, then pulled back.

"Shove it down her throat!" the girl demanded eagerly.

"Later."

He moved back carefully, favouring his knees, which had apparently become sore against the bare pavement, and settled himself onto the blanket.

Then he pushed himself into me again, forcing his now somewhat lubricated cock deeper.

The girl was sitting back on her heels, watching excitedly. She was biting her lower lip, eyes wild. She fell forward, laying on her side, and pressed her face in close against mine.

"Does that feel good, slave girl? Do you like that? Mmmm. Feels good, doesn't it? I bet you'll like being fucked a lot."

"Like you don't," Chad sneered.

"Shut up," she said in annoyance, turning to glare at him. She turned back to me and her lips drew back in a leer.

"You want him to fuck your cunt, slave girl?"

"Y-yes, mistress," I panted, face hot at the response I knew I must make.

"Mistress!?" she exclaimed. She laughed in delight and turned to Chad. "She called me mistress!"

"I told you, she's a slave."

"Fuck!"

Chad ignored her, jamming himself deeper inside me. I felt myself stretching and straining, the ache within me growing as his erection was forced higher. It reached what seemed to be the obstruction within me which signified my virginity, and drew back, then pushed forward once more. I felt a sense of straining and stretching within my pussy, a growing sense of pain as he jabbed his hardness against the obstruction.

I felt an odd sense of anger at this, at the prospect of losing my virginity in such a place to such a man, and this pushed aside whatever excitement or even curiosity I might have otherwise had at finally being penetrated there.

He was grunting and straining, his face a sweaty mask of glee, and then I felt a final tearing sensation within me, a sharp, but easily bearable pain, and his cock surged forward, forcing aside the soft, hitherto closed portion of my sex as he crowed in triumph.

I felt only a strange sense of relief, and the oddity of feeling movement where I never had before. The sensation was not unnatural, nor even painful, though I did feel strained by his sudden, rough penetration.

"Took out her cherry," he said with a leer.

"No more virgin," the girl cooed. "Just another slut now."

I felt very full down inside my lower belly, my insides spread quite wide in a not unpleasant way, despite the sense of strain. I did not feel any shame at losing my virginity, for I had resigned myself to it, and was rather relieved it had finally been accomplished.

My abuser groaned above me, apparently quite delighted

at his conquest, and at the physical sensation of my tightness around his erection. He ground his pelvis in jerky, circular motions so that his cock turned and twisted about within me.

She pushed her tongue out and licked slowly up along my cheeks as Chad continued to grind himself against me.

"Yeah!" he cried, much like an enthusiastic boy.

The girl ran her hand over my breasts, tugging and twisting the rings cruelly, pulling each until I cried out in pain then doing the same to the other. Her hand moved down between my legs and fingered my clitty. She appeared surprised for a moment.

"Fuck! I forgot her clit was pierced too!" she exclaimed. "Oh man! This is so wild!"

Chad's strong fingers dug deep into the soft flesh of my thighs as he forced my legs back sharply against the pavement, and my insides throbbed and ached as he began to yank himself in and out with crude enthusiasm. I was startled at how deeply his cock slid inside me. I had had no idea how long my vagina was or how deep it travelled. The head of his organ felt like it was lodged deep within my belly each time he jammed himself down.

"Fuck her! Fuck her harder!" the girl was demanding, eagerly watching his cock driving into my sex.

The two of them slapped and groped and pinched and squeezed and fondled my body as Chad continued my deflowerment. I was disappointed at how banal their assault was, at how lacking in imagination or passion was their behaviour. Oh there was a cruel, lustful eagerness, but cheap and tawdry in its nature. I found myself comparing them to Mistress and my earlier two masters, and the two did not fare well under such a comparison.

Yet even so, so deeply had the conditioning set that I began to feel a sense of eroticism in my deflowerment, a sense of martyred masochistic pleasure. Kristine was tugging repeatedly at the ring set into my clitoris, and the sharp little stinging pains were combining with the hard, deep thrusting of his erection to draw me into a mood of eager participation. I was being used for the first time there, and so long had I anticipated it that I now wished to bask in the sensation of being fully pierced.

Despite their crudeness my mind was beginning to attune itself to their mood of sexual excitement and arousal, and my body began to throb with sexual pleasure. The fast, heavy impact of his thighs and hips against me there was a new and exotic sensation which was deliciously nasty and long dreamed of. Again and again my mind followed the full, hard thrust of his cock, followed the plunge of the head through the soft flesh of my body, down into that centre which seemed to grow so warm and alive.

I hardly watched them at all, my mind turned inward, a little startled, a little gleeful, a little anxious, but for the most part fascinated with this new experience and sensation. I had, after all, come to be convinced I was a creature made for sex, and now I was finally experiencing it fully, finally being used properly.

Yes, there was a degradation there at my crude ravishment, yet even degradation had come to be twisted in the dark recesses of my mind, twisted into that sense of masochistic excitement which now gripped me. And so as his hard cock thrust into me my mind half floated, basking in the experience and feeling the pleasure grow.

Kristine began to tug and twist on my nipple rings, even while continuing to tug and twist my clit ring, and new stings rippled through my mind. Yet the pain and the cruelty which drove it only added to my dark pleasure. My nipples were fully engorged, and my breasts swollen with heat, and every touch of the girl's fingers made them throb and crackle with a raw heat.

It was all sensations now, as I fell more fully into the

hunger. The painful pressure of his thumbs against my thighs, the cold stone beneath my back and buttocks, the heat of my breasts, the stings from the girl's cruel twisting and pulling, the pounding of his hips against my groin, and above all that hard, deep stabbing cock being driven into the depths of my belly. I found myself urging him on, glorying in the deepest penetrations, anticipating them as he jerked himself back, gasping in pleasure as he thrust himself in.

The sense of penetration was something I felt certain I was going to grow addicted to. I found myself thinking Yes! each time he reached the end of his withdrawal and thrust himself into me. Each deep penetration sent a hot surge of delicious sensory heat through my body, washing up through my lower belly as a liquid wave. I began to savour that inwards thrust, that sensation of being penetrated, pierced. The deepest point of his penetration was cause for both delight and loss. For while I found myself feeling a deep sense of carnal arousal at feeling him so deeply within my body it was, at the same time, the end of that delicious inward movement of his organ, and precipitated its sudden withdrawal.

I knew I was going to climax powerfully, and thought of how right Mistress had been in calling me a whore, in knowing I was made for this.

And then he finished, with hardly any slowing, with no warning. He gave a gasp and finished, and slowed to a halt, breathing heavily. My eyes flickered, and I knew a sense of shocked disappointment and denial as I lay there. I could feel his manhood sagging, growing smaller within me, and then he pulled back with a satisfied smirk.

"Let's bring her upstairs. I want to play with her now," Kristine demanded.

Chad dressed as I lay there mourning the loss of that wonderful new sensation of penetration and use, then he and the girl raised me to my feet and led me to the doors of an elevator which had been standing open for some minutes. It was small, and apparently private, for neither seemed to have any fear of being discovered. Of course, unlike myself, they were not nude, but I assumed they would not want strangers intruding, and perhaps summoning the police. The walls were mirrored, and I examined myself in the glass, looking to see if there was any visible difference now that I was no longer a virgin.

Kristine fondled me as the elevator shot upwards, often leaning in close against me to promise me how she was going to fuck me once we were upstairs. I found her less than threatening. Compared to Mistress she was merely a garish little girl.

The elevator door opened at last, and I thought we must be quite high indeed for the journey to have taken so long at the speed we had seemed to travel. The two led me out into an enormous apartment, the likes of which I had only ever seen before in movies and television shows. Beyond an enormous glass wall gigantic skyscrapers towered, their lights a kaleidoscope of colours against the night sky. Only one city I knew of could possibly be so immense, with so many sparkling towers. New York. I was indeed far from home.

"I need a drink," Chad said.

"Me too," Kristine said, "And get me some blow. I want to really enjoy our new slave."

Chad moved in one direction, and Kristine took me in the other, leading me down a wide, marble hall, and thence into an enormous bedroom - a bedroom larger than any I had yet been inside. The four-poster bed looked large enough for a dozen to sleep in, and there was a full set of sofas and overstuffed chairs alongside tables, a desk, and a number of dressers. Christine pulled me to the bed and then flung me down onto my knees beside it.

She quickly stripped off her clothes, showing me a slender, tanned body, with smallish breasts and a small diamond in her naval.

"Have you ever done it with a girl, slave?" she demanded.

"Yes, mistress," I replied.

Stupid girl, I thought.

She seemed disappointed for a moment as she stroked her sex.

"We'll see how good you are," she said finally. "And if you don't make me come I'll take a whip to you!"

"Yes, mistress," I said.

The words seemed to excite her further, and she spread her legs, pulling on my hair and guiding me in between them.

Chad issued a strange yell of sorts, but neither of us understood it.

"Hurry up," Kristine yelled back. "I want to be high when I come."

"Maybe I can arrange that."

The voice was male, and quite deep, and certainly did not belong to Chad.

Kristine turned her head and gave a cry of alarm and shock, then leapt away from me.

The man at the door was enormous, but not in nearly so muscular a way as my first captor. He was black, with a bushy beard around his grinning face. Kristine leapt for the bed and yanked a bed-sheet before her. I was shocked, as well, and blushed under the man's eyes, but of course, could do nothing to hide my nude body.

"W-what are you doing here?" she demanded, all her arrogant superiority gone. "How did you get in?"

"I got tired of getting busy signals and paid your doorman fifty bucks to let us by."

He stepped inside, and a moment later two more black men shoved Chad in. He stumbled to one knee before picking himself up and turning to face them.

"So where's my money, Chad?" the large man demanded.

"Phil, baby, you know I'm good for it," Chad said, spreading his arms wide and grinning.

"No, as a matter of fact I don't. I heard your daddy cut you off."

"He does that all the time," Chad said dismissively. "He'll come around again."

"I heard he found out you were dealing drugs and cut you off for good."

"Hey, give me a few days to work on him and he'll be eating out of my hands."

"Where's my money, Chad?" the man demanded, his voice hardening.

Chad smiled nervously. "I uh, I don't have all of it right now. I mean, I was counting on that money from my father and..."

"How much do you have?"

Chad washed his hands together uncomfortably. "Well, not enough and I..."

"How much?"

"Uh, seventy thousand."

The big man shook his head sadly.

"You disappoint me, Chad," he said.

"I'm good for the money, man!"

The man moved forward and gazed down at me, then gave me a little smile. I smiled back nervously, embarrassed anew under his eyes, and the eyes of the two other black men.

"Cute little games you white folk play," he said, running his fingers through my hair.

"Hey, look, Phil, you can borrow her till I get you the money."

The man raised his eyebrows.

"Get this man," Chad said eagerly. "She's a slave, a real actual slave. I just bought her! She's quality stuff, man; you can't just find something like her on a street corner. She's all trained and everything."

The black men stared at me, and I saw hunger in the eyes

of the other two, but Phil only looked angry.

"And how much did you pay for her?" he demanded.

"Uh..." Chad looked hesitant.

"How much of my money did you spend on this bitch?" the man demanded angrily.

I winced as his voice rose.

"Only uh, about a hundred thousand."

Phil rolled his eyes and motioned to one of the other men.

"I'm gonna get plenty of more money, Phil!" Chad said desperately.

One of the men hit him, knocking him to the floor, and the other kicked him brutally. Kristine screamed, and was yanked forward and thrown onto the floor at Phil's feet, minus her bed-sheet. He reached down and dragged her to her feet, then smoothly pulled her arms together behind her back and pinned them there, one large hand gripping both arms at the elbows. Kristine seemed considerably less enthusiastic about being helpless and naked than she had about me being in that position, and her face burned red as she squirmed in embarrassment and fear.

I stayed where I was, breathless and frightened, hoping none of the anger these men apparently felt for Chad would attach itself to me.

"You spent my money on this bitch?" he demanded, pointing at me.

Chad coughed and groaned, and one of the men kicked him again, then both yanked him to his feet and held him.

"Who did you give my money to?" Phil demanded.

"Man I... I can call my dad and..."

One of the men punched him in the stomach and he gurgled and half collapsed.

"I want my money now, Chad," Phil said.

"I... I can get it," Chad gasped.

"Tonight."

"I... but I need time," he moaned desperately. "Take the

girl and have fun with her. You know I'll come and get her."

"I got all the whores I need, boy. I don't need another one."

I flinched at such casual dismissal of my worth, such contempt in my character.

He leered at Kristine then, reaching up to run his hands over her body. "Maybe I'll take your girlfriend, though. She might be a little fun for a while."

Kristine squeaked and shook her head frantically.

"Yeah, sure!" Chad exclaimed eagerly. "You know I'll get the money to you then!"

"Chad!" Kristine screamed in shock.

"She's great in bed, man. Really! You won't..."

Another punch in the stomach dropped him to his knees and he coughed and gasped for breath as the two men yanked him up again.

"You're pathetic, man. You're gonna tell me who you gave my money to," Phil said. "And I'm gonna get it back."

"B-but they won't refund it!" Chad exclaimed, clearly frightened. "I mean, she's uh... she's damaged goods now."

"What the fuck does that mean? She looks like fine stuff to me." Phil grinned at me again.

"She uh, was a virgin."

"You're kidding? So? You just got in the fuckin' door. When did you have time to do anything about it?"

"Downstairs in the garage."

Phil cursed and rolled his eyes. "That's your problem, boy, you got no patience. You can never wait a little bit to enjoy yourself. You gotta have everything right away. Now you're gonna tell me where my money is, or you and this slut girlfriend of yours are gonna take swan dives off the balcony."

I inhaled sharply, only slightly comforted by the fact he had not mentioned me.

Two more black men appeared in the doorway, and the

room began to seem much smaller than it was. Their eyes were drawn immediately to Kristine, and then to me, and I saw grins and leers appear on their faces. The anxiety and embarrassment within me rose still higher, and I dropped my eyes.

"Take this asshole out and find out where he spent my money," Phil ordered them. "And don't bring him back without it."

Two of the men took Chad out, and Phil shoved Kristine towards one of the other men.

"Tie that bitch up," he said, settling into a large, plushly upholstered chair.

One of the men grabbed her, and amused himself by groping and fondling her as she yelped and squirmed and protested feebly. Phil turned his eyes to me and I quailed in fear.

"So you're a slave, huh?"

"Yes, master," I replied.

He blinked in surprise, then grinned widely as the other two men laughed.

"Come here, slave."

I rose to my feet, walked forward, then dropped to my knees before his chair, trembling slightly.

"You got a nice, fuckin' body, slave."

"Thank you, master," I replied.

I was embarrassed, yet encouraged that he found something in me to his liking. He seemed quite a dangerous man, perhaps more dangerous than any I had ever encountered, and I was eager to convince him of my value.

"What's your name?"

"I am a slave, master," I said almost automatically.

He snorted in amusement.

"What's your name?" he repeated, more loudly, as if to a simpleton.

"I was told I had no name any longer, master," I said

uncertainly.

"Weird," one of the other men said.

"You got no name?"

"I will only have a name when I am given one by my master, master."

He looked oddly at me, stroking his chin consideringly.

"Ain't that cool," he said. "So what can you do, slave girl?"

"Anything you tell me to, master," I replied, trying to keep the tension and anxiety from my voice.

A slow grin spread across his face, and he made an impatient gesture at the other two men, who made obscene suggestions.

"Play with that bitch over there and leave us be," he ordered them, not taking his eyes off me.

I heard a squeal from Kristine, and laughter from the two men, followed by sounds of a struggle, but I continued to look up as calmly as I could at the large man in the chair before me.

"Come here," he said, motioning me forward.

I smiled and slid forward, rising on my knees. He took my arms, effortlessly dragging me up and sitting me across his lap. I continued to smile as his hands explored my body, and then, remembering how Mistress had trained me, made signs of pleasure, sighing and smiling more broadly, arching my back and spreading my legs somewhat.

"Damn," he said, sounding intrigued. I leaned my head forward, licking at his fingers, then taking one long finger into my mouth, giving him a seductive look as I slid my lips slowly down its length and licked at it.

"You're really somethin' else," he said admiringly.

He began to slide his finger in and out of my mouth, adding a second, and I kept my lips pursed, licking at them and moaning softly. He pulled his fingers free, sliding them down between my legs and stroking them along the line of

96

my sex, and I felt a little shudder, spreading my legs wider.

"So you're a virgin, huh?"

"Except for once, master," I said weakly.

"Then you're a virgin, cause Chad don't count."

He grinned and stood up, lifting me in his arms as though I weighed nothing. I could see Kristine now, still struggling weakly against the other two black men.

"Don't! Don't touch me! No! Ungh!" she gasped, as she was pinned back into a large chair. One of the men forced her legs up and back, yanking them up so that she was laying more on her back than her bottom, jamming her knees back over the arms of the chair. Grinning, the other man helped hold her there, and Kristine's body thrashed and jerked more desperately. Then the first man leaned in against her, positioning his cock at the centre of her sex and thrust into her.

She let out a curse and then a wail of anger and despair, thrashing even more violently, but as the man jammed himself deeper and then began to pump, her struggles weakened and her head dropped back.

Phil carried me to the large bed and climbed onto it, setting me down on my back. My arms were still bound behind me but he seemed to either not notice or not care. He stripped off his shirt, then as I spread my legs, posed his heavy body atop me. His elbows took much of his weight, but I still felt overwhelmed by the size of him as he lay upon me, his flesh soft against my breasts and belly.

He began to kiss me, and I, of course, kissed back eagerly, despite my fear, embarrassment and anxiety. His hands moved over my body, squeezing and fondling my breasts and groin. Then he jerked down his loose pants and drew out a thick black erection, panting somewhat now as he positioned it against my pussy. I felt my lips being spread apart for the second time that day and braced myself for further pain, but he did not force himself in, instead he jabbed lightly, all the while continuing to kiss and fondle me.

Across from us, Kristine was grunting now as the man thrust with growing savagery. Her shoulders were jammed against the seat back where it met the seat, forcing her chin forward on her chest, and her legs were splayed widely, the man using her gripping both behind the knees and jamming them down over the arms of the chair to spread her sex wide. His black bottom was a blur as he slammed down furiously, the sound of flesh meeting flesh growing quite loud in the room.

My own pussy began to ache now, for Phil's erection was thicker than Chad's had been. Yet he was thrusting in more slowly, grinding his hips as he did so. Several times he removed his cock and rubbed the moist head back and forth along my slit, causing my pierced clitoris to twitch and quiver in response. He mouthed my nipples, rings and all, sucking and chewing slowly but forcefully, and I felt them begin to throb and harden.

My pussy seemed to loosen under his careful attack, and soon, though it strained and ached, the soft, elastic walls were being pushed aside by the long thickness of him, my taut lips squeezed tightly around his intruding member. I groaned and panted for breath as he chewed on the nape of my neck. Then he buried himself within me with a sudden thrust that caused me to cry out.

"Yeah. Tight," he whispered, squeezing my breasts as he chewed on my throat.

His hips moved in a grinding motion and his organ twisted about within the confines of my abdomen.

Across from us the first man finished with Kristine and slapped the palm of the second, who took his place. Kristine made a feeble effort to resist, but soon he was thrusting into her as forcefully as the other had. "Not so hard," she begged, her voice breaking.

In response he thrust harder still, and the two men

98

laughed.

"You like that baby?" Phil whispered.

"Yes, master," I replied, putting as much enthusiasm into my voice as I could manage.

"Hot little bitch, ain't you."

"Fuck me, master," I replied.

His teeth gleamed and he began to do so, his hips continuing to grind and roll from side to side as he began to stroke. It ached, at first, but my insides very quickly came to accept this movement, and the pain faded. I was thus able to examine the sensation of being fucked for the first time, for I had not been capable during my initial deflowering. I decided it felt rather nice, much like being sodomized but... better, more natural.

The long length of Phil's erection stroked back and forth between my taut pubic lips, and I began to feel that for the first time I was truly being used as a slave by a master. Yet there was far less sorrow in that than I would have expected. Instead, I felt oddly complete. And as the sensations in my breasts and lower belly began to turn to pleasure my anxieties faded and I began to actually enjoy my ravishment.

Phil eased back from off of me, still stroking, but doing it from a kneeling position. He gathered up my legs, lifting them onto his shoulders, then leaned into them, pressing them back over my own head as he thrust into me. He did not use me as forcefully as Kristine was being used, at least at first, but the long length of his cock thrust deeply down into my belly with each stroke, and the speed and force of those strokes was growing alongside my own excitement.

Yes, excitement. For Chad's eager, if graceless use had already prepared my body, given me the hint of what I was made for, a taste of the sensation a slave could receive from a full and powerful use. Now both my body and mind were relishing the sensation of a real man inside and above me. Still, I was glad the other two were distracted somewhat by

Kristine, for embarrassment still gripped me at such carnal behaviour in front of strangers.

Although that too was strangely altering shape. One of the other men had his back to us as he fucked Kristine, but the other stood alongside the chair, and each time I felt his eyes turn towards us I felt a simultaneous rise in shame and excitement. The excitement was an odd, wicked kind; a lewd exhibitionism I had not quite known I possessed.

Yes, I was a beautiful, sexy slave girl. I was hot. I was exciting to look upon and to touch. Men desired me. I was seductive and erotic and...

Or so I had come to realize over the past days. Perhaps I was merely a thing, a toy to use, but I was a greatly desired toy which could make men's eyes widen and their cocks harden and their hearts beat faster. So each time I felt the man turn to watch me being used I felt a tightening in my chest, a breathlessness as he watched the thick, gleaming black cock thrusting down into my body. I felt wicked and lewd and sluttish, and daring for being all of that.

"You like that, baby? You like that?" Phil panted.

"Yes, master! Fuck me, master! I love your cock!" I groaned.

This was not entirely a falsehood. I was growing more and more excited by the steady plunge of his thick cock deep into my body, by the steady downward thrust of my knees, forced back by his powerful chest, by the way my body was being bounced up and down on the mattress, and the heavy weight of his hips as they slammed against my upraised buttocks.

"That's some kinda slut," the man across from us said admiringly.

I felt a little shudder of excitement at the words.

Abruptly, Phil eased back onto his heels, and then yanked me up so that I straddled his body, impaled upon his thick cock. I shuddered and groaned, laying my head against his shoulder as he chewed on my neck and kneaded my buttocks. Abruptly, he grasped at the shackles binding my wrists, and then pulled my head back.

"How do I unlock this shit?" he demanded.

"I don't know, master," I said.

He fumbled at the shackles, then looked across to Kristine.

"How do I unlock these handcuffs?" he demanded.

She did not answer until the man using her halted and slapped her face lightly.

"Where's the keys to the handcuffs, bitch?" he asked.

"I don't know," she groaned miserably.

He slapped her again and she whimpered. "Chad had them."

"Shit," Phil grumbled. "Go check his coat," he told the other man.

He resumed kneading my buttocks now, and leaned his head in and down to mouth and chew against my nipples. His powerful arms began to raise me up and down on his cock, and I worked my knees in tighter against him then began to help, riding up as best I could, sighing in genuine relish each time I sank back upon his mighty cock and took it deep into my body.

A moment or so later the other man returned, bent over behind me and unlocked the shackles binding my wrists. I immediately brought my hands forward and slid them over Phil's shoulders, now able to ride him more easily, grinding my breasts into his face.

"Yeah. Ride that cock, slave girl," the other man said admiringly.

He had an erection again, and Phil turned my head, firmly, but not unkindly directing my lips forward. I leaned slightly towards my left, still using arms and legs to ride up and down on Phil's cock, and took the other man between my lips, moaning around his tool as he pushed deeper. I licked at the head and bobbed my lips at first, but soon he was pumping and I need only hold my head still while riding atop Phil.

My entire body was thrumming with sexual excitement now, and I could feel a glow between my legs, a glow which began to inflame my mind and body to the point where nothing else mattered. I reached out to the other man suddenly, feeling a masochistic desire to be truly impaled, grasped at his buttocks and pulled him nearer even as I leaned further to my left. The head of his cock popped through into my throat and slid down inside me as my lips moved all the way to the base of his organ.

"Oh fuck!" he groaned.

I felt a shudder of elation and pride, and then as Phil chewed on my nipple and I rode his cock, my orgasm arrived. My body stiffened, then quivered violently as the ecstasy rode through my nervous system, and I felt truly wanton, truly a sexual animal, a wild, hedonistic creature fully in her element.

I almost blacked out, so great was the disorientation and pleasure, that I forgot completely about the cock filling my mouth, the cock pumping excitedly up and down inside my throat, blocking my breath. Then the man pulled back of his own accord, gripping my hair and rubbing his wet cock across my face, over my lips and cheeks as I gasped for breath.

I recovered somewhat, but still felt wild and wanton, and, remembering my sight of the blonde riding the man on the ship as others looked on, turned, gasping and moaning, and begged him to sodomize me even as I sat impaled upon Phil.

He cursed, and Phil laughed, and a moment later I was held between them, knees spread wide, leaning in against Phil as he lay further back, and feeling the other man's stiffness pushing into my anus. The pressure mounted, and I felt my wrinkled anal opening slowly being forced in and back, my mind burning with masochistic arousal now as the head of his cock began to force its way up into my body.

I groaned aloud, groaned into Phil's mouth, then groaned

louder still as he pulled his lips free and fastened them around my nipple, chewing and biting. I could feel the cock jabbing at me from behind, could feel the ache as it forced my anus open inch by inch, driving higher into my belly alongside Phil's mighty shaft. The flesh between the two thick cocks seemed so slight and so flimsy that I imagined it tearing so that the two great male organs could join together inside me.

"Oh God!" I gasped explosively.

My abdomen felt so full, so cramped and aching with the two thick male organs within, and then as they began to move I felt as though my insides were being stirred and twisted, as though my inner organs would be turned to a hot, steaming stew around their hard, thick erections.

I felt a new ache now, a cramping deep within my belly as the cock within my anus climbed uncomfortably high. Yet that cramping, that ache, only fed the dark hunger inside me, and as I felt his pelvis press in against my soft buttocks and force my hips in against Phil I let out a long shudder of bliss at how deeply penetrated I was.

For a moment they held still, their cocks buried within my belly, their hands moving over my body. Then they began to grind against me, and Phil's hands eased down to my hips to push me upwards and drop me down. Moments later the cock in my rectum began to pump as well, using short strokes at first, loosening up my sphincter.

Their hard, heavy male bodies ground me between them, their hands and teeth mauling me as they threw their hips in against me, and I rolled bonelessly between them, glorying in my own use, in my own subjugation, in being a wild, sluttish sexual toy for their play. The cock behind me pumped faster, harder, and Phil began to growl, to rock my body up and down against him. They were tearing me apart, and I gloried in it.

I climaxed again, crying out in wanton delight, bucking my lower body between the two stiff cocks, shuddering and convulsing as the pleasure rose to unbearable limits and threatened to swamp my mind utterly. Oh how shocked my friends would have been to see me like that! How utterly wicked and wanton I was! A sluttish slave girl!

Phil, gasping for breath, spent himself within me, and moments later the other man did the same, jamming himself deep into my anus as the two squeezed me between them, and within seconds we were all on our sides, gasping for breath, hot and panting and satisfied.

CHAPTER SIX

Afterwards, I danced for the three men, as Mistress had showed me. I was embarrassed at being the centre of attention, and would have been even if I were fully clothed. Naked, the sensation of being under their eyes as I danced was... indescribable. Yet amid the embarrassment came a dark and wicked pride and excitement as their eyes feasted on my body's lewd movements. They seemed to find me and my dancing very exciting, even arousing. Phil had me perform on him as he sat on one of the chairs, kneeling between his spread legs and taking his thickness deep into my throat. As I did, first one, then the other of the men knelt behind me and used me quickly, their hands mauling my breasts as their hips beat a tattoo against my raised buttocks.

Phil then ordered Kristine to perform cunnilingus on me, pinching and slapping at the sullen, whimpering girl's breasts until she obeyed. I tried to feel sorry for her but could not. And as I sat in the chair, legs spread wide and draped over the arms, the centre of attention again, I began to feel another powerful orgasm rising within me. I stroked Kristine's head and hair, groaning and rolling my hips up to meet her lapping tongue.

I closed my eyes, arching my back, my breathing coming faster and faster, yet even so I could not forget for a second that three pairs of eager eyes watched me, ravishing me, and when I climaxed I writhed and thrashed in some exaggeration that they might grow even more excited.

Shortly afterwards the other two men returned, without Chad. Phil spoke softly with them, appearing unhappy.

"Well how am I supposed to get my money now?" he demanded.

His gaze turned to Kristine and me, and he stroked his chin thoughtfully.

Shortly afterwards we left the luxurious apartment,

105

travelling downward in Chad's private elevator. Both Kristine and I remained nude, and my wrists had been shackled once more. We were placed in the back seat of a large black car with tinted windows, and then driven away. Phil sat between us, occasionally groping or stroking our bodies, but talking little.

"Where are we going?" she asked after a time, looking about nervously.

"I'm going to drop off the slave girl."

"What about me?" she asked anxiously.

He turned and looked at her coolly. "Your boyfriend still owes me money. You're going to pay it."

"Me?!" she gasped. "But I don't have any money."

He smiled and slipped his hand between her thighs, cupping her sex.

"You got something worth its weight in gold. You might be a snotty bitch, but there's nothing wrong with this body. It can earn a whole lot for me."

She gaped at him, her mouth opening and closing soundlessly.

"I... I won't!" she gasped at last.

He simply smiled, and she dropped her eyes, trembling.

"Hundred bucks a pop, ten, twelve times a night, and you'll have me paid off in no time," he said. "Maybe five, six months, tops."

The men in the front seat snickered, and Kristine looked at them in despair.

I did not dare inquire as to my own future, for fear that I too was destined to be a prostitute, for such was obviously to be her fate. Yet he had implied something different was in my own future, and I looked out the window nervously.

The signs I could read on the shops we passed began to change, turning from English to Asian lettering. The people I could see through the tinted glass were more and more likely to be Asians now, as well, and I decided we were in

106

New York's Chinatown area. Then the car turned into a dark alley and stopped. One of the men who appeared to work for Phil opened the door and he pushed me out ahead of him.

He took my arm and led me through a small doorway, then down a short flight of stairs and along a narrow corridor. The contrast with Chad's apartment could not have been more obvious, for here my feet padded across age darkened linoleum instead of marble, and overhead, bare pipes and wires were tangled together along the ceiling.

We turned into another corridor, then went through a door framed between two Asian men wearing suits. I felt another little wave of embarrassment accompanied by excitement as their eyes examined me, feeling lewd and wicked for being so exposed before strangers.

We entered a small, dim room. The floor was covered by a thick, soft Persian rug, and a middle aged Asian man sat behind an antique desk of walnut. The door closed behind us and the man stood up, coming around the desk to examine me.

"Mr. Wu," Phil said respectfully.

"What is it you bring me, Mr. Smith?" the man asked.

"A gift. A sign of my respect for you," Phil said.

"A captive girl?" Mr Wu raised his eyes in question.

"This is a slave girl," Phil said proudly. "She was just trained, but the first man who purchased her came to some uh, trouble. So she became my property. Of course, keeping slaves is illegal in this country and I wouldn't want to break the law."

Mr. Wu smiled faintly.

"What is your name, girl?" he asked.

"I am a slave, master," I said, for the first time feeling a little flutter of excitement in my belly at saying the words. "I have no name unless I am given one."

He arched an eyebrow and slipped a narrow finger into one of my nipple rings, raising it slightly and stretching my nipple.

"So you are a slave."

"Yes, master."

"And what might you be good for?"

I blinked uncertainly. "I am a slave, master. I am made to give pleasure."

He smiled, but seemed intrigued. "And how do you do that?"

"Whatever way I am told master."

"A western woman who knows her place," Mr. Wu mused.

"I thought, well, you have friends in China..." Phil's voice trailed off and Mr. Wu smiled again.

"Where blonde women are an endless fascination? Yes, I do indeed. And there are more than a few men I can think of who would be... much pleased with such a gift."

"I thought you might put her to good use, Mr. Wu," Phil said, beaming.

"Indeed. I thank you for this gift, Mr. Smith. I am in your debt."

Phil gave an awkward little bow, and then began to back away. One of the Asian men had come in unnoticed by me, and now opened the door and let him out. At a signal from Wu he exited himself, leaving us alone.

"So you are a slave."

"Yes, master," I said, somewhat breathless now.

"Your voice. You are from England?"

"Yes, Master."

"The English once ruled parts of China. Do you know this?"

"Yes, master."

"We have long memories. There will be men who will delight in owning a blonde English slave. Powerful men, especially in the inland provinces where westerners are seldom seen."

"Yes, master," I said uncertainly.

My insides were twisting at the thought of being sent to the Orient, and yet there was also a strange dark thrill in my chest at the idea of me, a poor English girl, kidnapped and sent to the far east to be ravished by cruel Orientals.

I saw little of America beyond a small, windowless room. The next day, clad in a beautiful, ankle length Chinese robe of blue and black silk, and wearing light sandals, I was driven between two large Asian men to a small airport, and placed aboard a private jet. Neither man touched me or made any indecent gesture, but they were clearly guards to ensure my cooperation. I was not bound except by fear of their reaction should I attempt to draw any undue attention to myself.

An Asian woman wearing a short uniform style dress presented me with food, after a time, eyeing me strangely. I wondered if she were aware I was a sex slave, a helpless English girl being taken to my imprisonment in her country so as to be ravished.

My lower belly quivered at such thoughts, filled with both anxiety and excitement, with fear and a dark sexual pride.

The aircraft landed after several hours, but I was not taken off. Instead several Asian men boarded, taking seats nearby. The seats on this aircraft, unlike most, did not face forward, but into the aisle between them, so that the passengers might converse unhindered. All of the men eyed me with interest, and spoke to the two men guarding me. I did not, of course, understand as they all spoke in what I assumed to be Chinese.

Some time after the aircraft was in flight once more, one of the men, an older man, spoke earnestly to the two guards, grinning towards me and making gestures. The guard seemed uncertain, then nodded as if in agreement and turned to me. "You are to dance for them," he said. "These are important men, friends of Mr. Wu."

"Dance? In this?" I asked uncertainly.

"Without," he said.

109

"Yes, master," I gulped, face flushing.

I had been seen naked by many people only at the time of my sale, and had been in a state of shock then. I found that my acceptance of such public nudity had improved only marginally, and was red faced as I stood and all their eyes gazed eagerly upon me.

The girl I took to be the stewardess entered as if summoned, and was spoken to by the man who seemed in charge. She bobbed her head rapidly in agreement, gave me another odd look, then hurried forward. Moments later music filled the cabin, a soft oriental rhythm.

Ten men looked at me expectantly, and I felt my blush deepen. Yet I could do nothing but obey. My heart pounded and my chest was so tight I could barely draw breath as my fingers moved to the belt about my waist and unbound it. The long silken gown parted and the men on both sides of the aisle leaned forward eagerly as I drew it back over my shoulders and let it fall back onto my seat.

There were gasps and whispered exclamations, and I knew another wicked excitement at being so admired, even as my insides twisted in humiliation. I drew in a deep, shaky breath, then stepped forward so I was in the midst of them all. I began to let my body sway in time to the rhythm of the music, slowly relaxing my stiff frame, rolling my hips and letting my arms move 'like swaying palms' as Mistress had taught me.

My legs began to move as well, and as the worst of my embarrassment faded I began to dance more naturally, my head rolling, a seductive expression taking form on my face, my hips undulating sensually. I let my head pull sharply from side to side every so often, intrigued by their fascination with my blonde hair, making it sweep across my face and back as I moved more quickly.

One man, quite old, reached forth and laid a hand against my backside, rubbing it very lightly and gently before drawing his hand back. The two guards looked at him nervously, but no one else moved to touch me.

I sank to my knees in the middle of the floor, aware now of the stewardess staring from just inside a curtained area in the front of the cabin. My legs spread wide as I sat back on my heels, and I let my body roll and sway, my hands sliding up over my breasts, up through my hair, combing it back. I threw my head back, letting my hair fly back, and arched so sharply it swept against the floor below.

I rose shakily, feeling the heat between my legs now, feeling the stiffness and tension in my nipples. I wondered if all ten would take me, and felt a wild thrill crackling through the fear which accompanied the thought. I changed the rhythm of my dance as the music altered, and then as it stopped I froze in position, and then stood straight.

The men applauded, and again made numerous comments which I could not understand. One of the guards quickly motioned me back towards my seat, holding up the robe to me, and I carefully wrapped it around myself and sat back, feeling robbed of the ravishment I had been contemplating.

Apparently I was not to be touched, for Mr. Wu had promised me to someone in China, someone powerful. Yet the men were mesmerized by me, and their excitement had been roused. And while they dared not go against the wishes of Mr. Wu or insult the powerful man who was to be my new master, they sought an outlet for this lust.

The unfortunate beneficiary was to be the young stewardess. After a half hour or so of drinking and joking, she was called forward by one of the men, who made obvious demands on her. Just as obviously she was shocked by their demands, and extremely reluctant and embarrassed about them. Her head shook frantically as her wide eyes regarded first one then another. The voices of the men were alternately harsh and seductive, menacing and brusque.

With growing desperation she seemed to plead with them

but then at a sudden harsh string of words from one of the men her shoulders seemed to slump hopelessly, and began to strip.

She removed her white blouse, then her skirt, and seemed frightened and mortified as the men eagerly feasted their eyes on her body. Her face was stricken, her eyes downcast. After several harsh orders her trembling fingers undid her bra, then slipped her panties down. She stood nude, head bowed, as the men chortled and laughed, their voices low and sneering as they commented on her body. She had a small, thin, neat frame, with small, high breasts and a round little bottom. Her long black hair covered her face as she stood with head bowed, and I sympathised with her plight even while recognizing that the humiliation she appeared to be feeling was now beyond me - at least for such simple things as being exposed to the eyes of others.

One of the more powerful men then reached forward and grasped her wrist, yanking her towards him. She stumbled and fell to her knees, and he held her there by the neck, undoing his trousers.

She resisted, her face a mask of denial, but he firmly guided her lips to his erection, and after a final gasp of pain as her hair was twisted her mouth was forced onto the rounded bulging head of his cock. Soon her mouth was wrapped around his manhood, bobbing up and down, and another of the man was behind her, forcing her legs apart, fondling her sex and buttocks, then taking out his own erection and forcing himself into her pussy with unrestrained glee. This aroused both my sympathies and jealousy, for I felt I should be in that position, feeling the hardness of male erections thrusting into my body. Yet though the men looked upon me often none made a move to touch me.

Instead they each waited their turn, and the girl was taken again and again by eight of the ten men there. Only the two guards remained aloof. And when each of the others had taken her, either in the mouth or the sex, they started again, drinking heavily and enjoying themselves as the girl was passed between them. I grew more and more aroused as I watched the girl's abuse, and felt guilt over that. Yet it was difficult to feel sympathy for a girl experiencing what I wished to experience myself. And I licked my lips as I watched, my hands together between my legs, grinding against myself as unobtrusively as possible.

Eventually the men, very drunk, wore themselves out on her. A few fell asleep in their seats. The girl, face dazed, crawled to her scattered clothing, fumbled awkwardly in her attempts to pick them up, then staggered to her feet and away from the cabin, closing the curtain up front behind her.

This availed her little. For after some time the men began calling out for her once more, and she returned, fully dressed, carrying a tray of drinks. The men chortled to see her dressed, and after taking their drinks demanded she remove her clothing. She cringed but did so, and one of the men took her clothing that she might not dress again, ordering, or so it seemed, that she remain nude for the remainder of the flight.

She stumbled off, face pale, but soon returned to service a few more of the men who had grown excited once again. Over the following hours she continued to provide food and beverage service, to fetch pillows and blankets when night fell, and to sexually service any of the men who required it of her. Eventually her reluctance seemed to fade under the continuing demands and she even started instigating some of them, which fuelled my jealousy. If only I were free to express my newfound wantonness. But at last I fell asleep in my seat, but no one moved to molest me, and woke, yawning and feeling stiff, to see the girl on her knees a few feet away, gasping and whimpering, her cheek pressed against the floor and both arms held firmly together behind her back by one of the men.

She had already been fucked repeatedly, so I wondered

113

briefly as to the cause of her distress, then realized she was being sodomized. Perhaps this was a new thing for her. There were tears in her eyes and her face was a mask of misery as she clenched her jaw together. The man's hips slapped repeatedly against her small upraised bottom as he drove himself into her. He used her fully and completely, apparently in no hurry, and then finally completed his task with a grunt of relief and eased back, allowing the girl to slowly crawl away.

I was in a state of some excitement when the plane finally landed. I looked out the cabin window in fascination, eager to see China.

We were at a small airport, exceedingly quaint by British standards, with only a small wooden building for a terminal. The plane drew up near it and the girl, now permitted to dress, opened the door and drew back, looking down at her feet as the men descended the stairs quickly rolled in place.

The two guards and I descended, and they led me across to a black automobile parked nearby. Its driver opened the rear door and all three of us got in. To my disappointment, I was required to sit between the two men, and thus my view of the surroundings was not what I might have hoped. I saw many Asians, however, some pushing strange looking wooden wheelbarrows, or dragging them behind. Others carried large packages atop their shoulders or on their backs. While many young children ran about.

I did not know where we were, but there appeared to be no great city nearby, nor even a town of any size. We drove for some time along a quite narrow paved road, with heavy, leafy bushes and trees to either side. Occasionally we passed a village, its homes usually made of rough, unpainted wood, the streets unpaved. The heat was tremendous, and seemed to grow greater with each passing minute, and the humidity was worse. I felt as if I could open my mouth wide and drink the air in. I was soon perspiring heavily, despite wearing nothing but the thin silk robe, and my hair stuck to my forehead no matter how often I brushed it back.

Eventually, we ran out of paved road and continued on a reasonably smooth dirt road for a time. The brush opened out around us and I gasped at the sight of enormous green covered mountains rising high to left and right. We drove through a quite narrow valley between them, and thence on upwards to our right, climbing one of the mountains. Greenery was everywhere, from massive trees to small, scrubby bushes and long leafy grass, all of it glistening in the intense sunlight.

We stopped at a small gate, and two Asian men holding guns peered in at us, speaking to the driver for a moment before waving us on. We continued our drive, the road steadily climbing for almost another hour before meeting a similar little gate. As before, the men looked in at us, spoke briefly and then permitted us to continue.

We moved down over the mountain, and a city was spread out before us. It was a low rising city with a great deal of greenery. The buildings were an odd mixture of cold, blockish concrete and beautiful sculpted stone and clay. The latter were clearly much older, perhaps hundreds of years old, while the former were already decrepit looking. We passed through narrow streets, and large crowds of people on foot and bicycles parted before us. I observed them with great fascination but no hope whatever of assistance from any of them.

We passed through the gate of a tall, sculpted iron fence to stop before a large, beautiful, ancient stone building. Ivy climbed one part of the building, and the corners, windows and doorframes were beautifully sculpted, with stylised figures of animals and birds. The ground before the building was covered in well-maintained lawns, beautiful flowering bushes, and bright fountains of clear water.

115

Our car passed around to the side of the building and stopped before a door. We stepped out and immediately went inside, leaving me little opportunity to feel the soil of China beneath my feet.

The corridors were bright and clean, and quite beautiful, with more sculptures, and paintings adorning walls, doorframes and floors. Most of the open doorways we passed gave onto lovely rooms with tall ceilings, and I thought that we were surely in some wealthy man's private home rather than, as I had first thought, an office building of some sort.

Yet we passed several people along the hall, men and women both dressed in those drab Mao suits I had seen on the television. All seemed intent on some task, and while all let their eyes stare at me until they passed, none seemed willing to question the two men accompanying me as to their purpose.

Finally we stopped, one of the guards knocked on a door, then pushed it open. We entered a small room which appeared to contain dirty laundry, buckets, large tubs for cleaning, and the smell of soap. Two squat Asian women, both in their forties or fifties, turned to bow, and one of the men spoke to them. The women bowed repeatedly, and after a long moment the two men left.

The women looked at me with a mixture of curiosity and disapproval, but one moved forward at once, undoing the belt of my robe, and pulling the garment free of my body. I felt a slight flush of embarrassment, but made no effort to hinder her as she carried the garment away. The second woman, speaking perhaps to herself (for I certainly could not understand her) took my hand and led me across the room to a corner where there sat a large tub. She turned on a faucet and motioned me to stand in the tub. Quickly understanding, I obeyed and she then had me kneel so that she could more easily wash my body.

She fingered the gold rings at my nipples curiously, and

seemed quite fascinated by them, then set to work with a sponge and wet cloth, soaking me and then soaping me up. After a few moments the other woman returned, and she knelt beside the first, seizing my head and pulling it back sharply, then pouring water over it. As the first cleaned my body, the second woman began to soap up my hair.

They spoke to each other at times, obviously concerning me, and I wondered what they thought of me and what they were saying. I blushed somewhat as one of the women scrubbed my pubic area, then thrust soapy fingers quite casually up within my vagina. Then, still covered with soap, I was pulled from the tub and made to lie along a narrow bench with my head hanging over one end, my hair dangling, and my legs spread wide apart.

As my hair was shampooed and rinsed the pubic hair which had begun to appear around my sex was carefully shaved off. My teeth were brushed for me, and I was then given a douche, much to my embarrassment. I was then required to bend forward and spread my legs somewhat, and then quite mortified as one of the women gave me an enema.

After that I was washed a final time, then rinsed off. My hair was dried and brushed out until it shone and sparkled, and perfume was applied to my body. I was clad in another long silk robe, this one a beautiful bright red with a white flower across the back.

One of the men who had accompanied me to China then arrived and led me away. We walked some further distance along corridors before coming to a great doorway guarded by two men. They nodded and opened the two doors, and I was led into an immense office. It was perhaps one hundred feet wide, and the largest desk I had ever imagined occupied a space beneath twenty foot high windows across a vast expanse of red carpet.

The man walked me across the room, and I stared about me in fascination, observing the many obvious antiques, their wood glistening and polished, and the sculptures and paintings decorating the walls. I had come a very long way from my small flat in England.

We paused before the immense desk, and a slightly plump Chinese man in his middle years examined us. The man accompanying me bowed his head low and did not speak as a full minute passed. Finally the man behind the desk spoke, and he responded, then backed away before turning and leaving the room. I looked at the man before me, then worrying about giving offence, bowed my head as well.

"You are a beautiful young woman," he said finally.

"Thank you, master," I replied, still looking down.

"Remove your robe."

"Yes, master."

I undid the belt and then, remembering Mistress' teaching, allowed it to part gently, so that he could catch glimpses of my flesh. I ran my fingertips up and down along the edges for a few moments, then gently eased them further open, drawing my shoulders back as I raised my arms, and letting the soft silk slide over my shoulders then gently waft down to the floor behind me.

I stood straight, as I had been taught, with my head bowed. I felt a certain pride in my appearance, for by now I was well acquainted with the lust it inspired in men, but still felt quite anxious before this man, a foreign man of unknown tastes but with obvious power, a man who could, I was sure, do whatever he chose with me or my body.

"You are English, I am told."

"Yes, master," I replied meekly.

"The English have always been an arrogant people."

I bowed, but did not reply.

"I do not like the English."

"I'm sorry, Master," I said, feeling my fear grow.

And yet with it was a sense of indignation, that an ignorant heathen from backwards China should dare to believe himself superior to the people of Britain.

"Come around the desk."

I obeyed at once, pausing before his chair.

"Are you an obedient girl?" he demanded.

"Yes, master!" I said automatically.

"English girls are weak and fragile. Chinese girls are strong and sturdy."

He reached between my legs and cupped my sex, then squeezed hard. I winced and braced myself, but did not move, and yet as he applied more pressure the pain within me grew almost unbearable. His strong fingers dug into the soft, sensitive flesh of my groin, and he looked up at me in expectant contempt as my legs began to tremble.

"Do you think you can please me, English girl?"

"I-I will obey your wishes, master," I gasped, panting for breath through my pain.

He eased his grip and then pushed his chair back completely and spread his legs.

"Do so then," He ordered curtly.

I sank to my knees gratefully, then crawled between his legs. My fingers went to the belt about his waist but he slapped them off, indicating I should only undo his zipper. I did so as he stroked my hair and let it slide between his fingers, then brought his surprisingly long and thick cock out and into my hand. I began to lap at the head, using long, slow licks, rubbing his cock in my hand as I sought to excite him. I licked down the shaft, pushing his zipper opening wider that I might draw out his testicles and mouth them.

I took each one into my mouth as my hands massaged his staff, using my tongue to massage them against the insides of my cheeks as I gently suckled. Then I lapped at the head of his cock, rubbing it against the soft skin of my lips and cheeks as it began to harden. Finally, it was erect, and I took it into my mouth, sliding my lips up and down as my fingers massaged his testicles.

There was a knock at the door, and I heard his voice call out. Moments later a man's voice spoke from the other side of the desk. I could see some movement out of the corner of my eye but did not look up, concentrating on my task. I felt some new embarrassment, but not as much as I would have once.

I continued to bob my head up and down on the man's cock, then, bracing myself mentally, forced myself down fully upon it, feeling the head thrusting up into my throat. I heard a soft grunt of surprise, and knew a moment's pleasure, then as my lips pressed against his groin I felt his hands come down hard against the back of my head to hold me in place.

My tongue licked at the underside of his shaft as he ground my face into his groin, and my mind quivered with anxiety as my chest grew hotter and tighter. I wondered how long he would hold me in place, and whether he even cared if I stopped breathing. I tried to avoid struggling, even as my vision began to grow faint, but pushed up only slightly, even as my desperation grew.

Finally his hands moved back and I quickly slid my lips up and off, gasping for breath as he smirked at me in satisfaction. I gulped in breaths of air as I rubbed his cock around my cheeks, using my hands to massage and caress the long, moist, gleaming length of it until I could once more take it into my mouth.

He barked an order of some kind, but I could not then understand. He pushed me back, then gripped me forcefully by the arm and hair, lifting me and pushing me towards his desk. His chair was pushed in against it, and he bent me across the top so that my bottom was elevated even as he spread my legs. I lay down, my breasts squeezed beneath me against the hard wood, and awaited his attentions with some eagerness.

I had only just come to appreciate the pleasure of being penetrated, and yet the experiences had been only enough to whet my appetite. The excitement of watching the pretty girl being so fully used on the aircraft had left me with a sense of longing to be similarly taken, to be mobbed by lustful men, and yet none had touched me until now.

"We will see how much discipline you possess," he said.

I had expected to be penetrated by his rigid erection, and yet instead, even as it bobbed strongly before him, he opened a drawer in a cabinet behind the desk and drew forth a long, thin crop of some kind.

He moved to stand behind and to one side, then lay the crop along my upraised bottom.

"Be silent," he ordered.

I swallowed anxiously as I felt the crop slide back and forth along my curved bottom, then gasped as he drew back his arm and brought it down sharply against my hitherto unmarked flesh. I did my best to keep silent against the stinging pain which rippled through my flesh, and to hold my position as he once again let the leather surface of the crop caress my now throbbing flesh.

He brought back his arm once more and again brought the crop slashing down upon my bottom. A second source of stinging pain erupted, and then a third, and a fourth. My fingers were white as they dug into the palms of my hands, and perspiration began to bead my forehead and chest as the pain mounted.

And yet... and yet there was still arousal. My naked, vulnerable position, the excitement of being a prisoner of this obviously powerful man here in the exotic Orient, and the outrageousness of his attack upon my soft flesh all combined to make me quiver somewhat with sexual hunger even as I winced and gasped to the stinging kiss of the thin crop.

And between each blow now he began to let the rough leather tip slip between my trembling thighs and rise up to stroke along my sex, stroking precisely along my neatly

121

shaven slit as he spoke soft words in, I presumed, Chinese. I found myself, oddly, wishing I were bound so that I could more fully fall into the masochistic excitement of being the helpless white prisoner being tormented by the evil Oriental.

With my bottom flaring with heat he halted, stepping forward. Without a word or any warning he roughly gripped my thighs to force them wider, and positioned himself at the entrance to my body. Then drove himself into me with a hard, yet smooth stroke that had me shuddering in both pleasure and pain.

He was thick and long and I luxuriated in the sensation of being fully pierced even as my buttocks stung from the feel of his rough trousers pressed against them.

He drew back, then began to pump, quite casually, at first, as his hands roamed familiarly across my body. He reached beneath me to fondle my breasts, pinching and twisting my nipples, then released them, his hands dropping calmly onto my back as his hips moved in and out.

I, of course, remained unmoving, breathing unsteadily as I felt his hips strike firmly against my bottom and his cock pump back and forth within me. The pain began to fade and the pleasure and inner heat grow. The distraction of my stinging bottom eased, and I felt myself growing ever more moist as he pumped more firmly, more powerfully. I spread my arms, allowing my chest to come down more firmly on his desk so that my movements would grind my breasts beneath me.

I gave myself into his use, abandoning myself utterly to his desires as I focused all my attentions on the sensory pleasure now rising through my body.

And then he stopped. He pulled back without word or notice, and moved away. I peeked behind me and saw him carefully replacing the crop. His hand moved indecisively across a number of other instruments in the shadowy interior, then fastened upon one and pulled back. It was, I saw, heart pounding, a flog, a short one. I turned my head quickly away as he returned to me, then gasped as I felt his hand grip my hair and force me to stand.

"Pull your hair up and place your hands upon your head," he ordered.

My eyes blinking uncertainly, anxiety returned to me, I obeyed, lifting my hair to bare my back and standing before him as he moved back. I knew better than to turn my head with him watching, and yet I felt a nearly unbearable desire to do so as I awaited what he would do.

"Do not move. Do not speak."

I attempted to brace myself, and he made no objection as I shifted my bare feet apart on the floor. And then I sensed, as much as saw his arm swinging, and the strips of the flog cracked across the centre of my upper back.

I shifted a half foot forward, a soft cry leaving my mouth as the pain, like a dozen needles, rippled across my back. Yet I resumed my position quickly as the flog whipped down once again, moving only a little lower.

It was light in weight, and each strip lighter still. Its impact was certainly not sufficient to drive me forward. Yet the sharpness of the pain almost was. Each strip snapped down against the surface of my skin like a bee sting, the pain crackling across my nervous system like an electrical shock. My body twisted and jerked and trembled, my hips twisting this way and that, my back arching and then bowing. Yet I managed to hold, more or less steady as the flog snapped in again, and again and again, the strips biting at my shoulder blades and the sides of my chest, at my lower back and upper buttocks, setting my entire back afire with sharp, bruising pain.

He halted without warning. I was near dazed and hardly aware of his touch until he had me bent over once again and was thrusting himself into me. As before he used me casually, but deeply, his cock pumping firmly and fully into my exposed sex as my cheek lay pressed against the desk and I stared dazedly at nothing

I felt his fingers reach in to pinch at my inner thighs next to my sex, felt the tips actually gripping my outer lips and forcing them up and apart as he used long, slow, deep strokes, muttering to himself as he forced himself to the hilt inside my panting, now reddened body.

My back ached, and it was difficult to focus on anything else for a time, difficult to feel once again that seductive sense of being used fully as I was meant, yet slowly it began to come once again, as his use continued, and I began to hope that he might ride me to the climax I deserved for his mistreatment.

And yet again he halted, and a sudden anxiety gripped me as he forced me to stand once again. The flog was still in his hand as he turned me to face him, and though his face was without expression I had little doubt as to his intent as he raised it and pressed it up against the underside of my right breast.

I had, obedient to his last words, left my hands on the back of my neck, pinning my hair in place. Now he kicked my legs apart and reached behind to pull on my hair, forcing my head back further, forcing my back to arch and my breasts to thrust out.

"Stand so," he ordered.

Almost I begged him, yet I knew it would avail me nothing. And I recalled his contempt for the lack of discipline and strength in English girls and a small part of me continued to feel some indignation over this, continued to feel the desire to prove him wrong. I tried to brace myself for the feel of the flog, and yet when it came was unprepared. For it did not fall upon my breasts as I had expected but upon the taut, smooth surface of my belly.

I let out a gasp of pain and lost my position, if momentarily, and he barked out a curse, reaching for me, jerking my hair back even more harshly. His voice rose in an angry string of words which I could not understand, and he stepped back.

I could not see him now, for I was looking up towards the ceiling. I felt the movement of his arm, however, and groaned as the flog snapped across my belly once more. It fell again, harder, and then again, still harder, the strips snapping and biting at my belly and abdomen as I stood shakily, gasping and moaning.

And then as I began to adapt to the infliction of this pain the flog snapped down across my breasts. This drove me back, even while I held my position, for the pain was quite intense. The next blow was more forceful, the pain greater still, and again I staggered back, my buttocks now pressed up against the desk as he moved forward to follow.

The flog landed more quickly, blow following blow as he whipped first one breast, then the other. I found that my eyes were blurry and my cheeks wet as tears streamed down my face. My breasts burned and ached, and each fresh blow brought the level of pain closer and closer to the point where I knew I would be unable to maintain my position.

The urge to twist away and cover my breasts with my hands was almost overwhelming. Only the certainty from my experiences with Mistress that the pain would be redoubled should I do so kept me from moving.

And then he roughly twisted me about and forced me over the seat of the chair once more, thrusting himself into my gasping, exhausted body as he had before. He rode me harder than before, either through excitement or anger, his hips slamming painfully into my bottom so that I grunted weakly. I thought that surely he would finish with me now, for there was no longer a part of my body left for him to whip.

Suddenly, there was another knock at the office door, and he called out. The door opened and a thin, middle-aged man in a suit came in. The man hesitated at the sight of me, then moved forward, looking nervous and uncomfortable. His discomfort raised the same sensation in myself, and I felt some embarrassment as he stood before the desk, apparently trying very hard not to notice me there.

The two men spoke, and the man read from a paper of some kind, his voice hesitant, as if he were having difficulty concentrating. The man using me, my new master, apparently found this to be quite amusing, and used longer strokes, deliberately spreading my legs and thrusting into me with long, deep, fast strokes, then withdrawing slowly. His hand gripped my hair and forced my head up and back. I groaned in pain as he pulled harder, and my chest was forced to arch, raising it up off the desk.

He reached beneath to grope at my aching breasts, speaking in a casual voice to the man before the desk. I saw the man had an erection now, and he had turned his hips slightly to one side in a desperate effort to hide his arousal. He seemed very eager to be off, and twice turned to leave, only to be barked at and turn swiftly back.

Finally he was permitted to leave, and almost ran from the room as my master chortled in amusement.

He pushed me back down on the desk then, and slapped my bottom.

"Spread your legs more, slut," he barked.

I obeyed, raising my bottom as he began to pound himself into me with greater speed and fury. I ached a little inside, but even so felt a strong sense of lust and excitement as I was so rudely and cruelly used.

"We will see how much discipline you have," he said, grunting each word as he finished with a final series of thrusts.

127

CHAPTER SEVEN

I was taken by a blank-faced young woman up several flights of stairs and then down corridors which became progressively more palatial. The rear of the building gave onto a view of extensive gardens and fountains, and despite my uncertain situation I could not help admiring them as we passed by floor to ceiling windows.

I suppose I had feared, and almost expected her to take me to a cell-like room where I might be locked in like any prisoner. But there was no need for that here. For there was nowhere for me to go. We left the broad, thickly carpeted corridors for a narrow wooden hall, and then paused at one of the doors. She opened it, gave me a curious look, then turned away and left me.

The room was considerably larger than any I had ever had before, larger than any of those of my friends or acquaintances either. The centre of the room was taken up by a very low, but comfortable looking bed. There were no posts to this bed, for it rested directly on the floor, little more than a gigantic mattress framed by polished redwood. The matching tables beside it were of a similar type, and both no more than a foot off the floor.

On the left side of the room, beyond the white carpeting, was a tiled floor, and in the midst of it a large, sunken marble tub. There was a fireplace, a small bathroom, and several chests and dressers. A small window looked out on the garden, and I opened it to let some of the hot, stuffy air out.

"I am Kira."

I whirled around to see a dignified looking Chinese woman in her late thirties standing just inside the door. She wore a long robe, like me, but hers was considerably heavier than the thin silk caressing my own naked flesh. She was a diminutive woman, with her hair done up in formal style, and seemed to fairly glide forward, clad in dignity and

128

confidence as her eyes inspected me with open doubt.

Her face was extremely beautiful, oval and golden, with the softest eyes and the smallest, most dainty nose.

"You may call me mistress Kira," she said softly. "While you are here you will act on my word and bring all questions to me. It is given me to teach you civilized behaviour and a civilized tongue. You will be expected to work very hard at learning both. You will not be forgiven for failure. Do you understand?"

"Yes, Mistress," I said.

"Speak more softly, with more humility, and lower your head as you speak."

"Yes, mistress," I said, my voice barely above a whisper.

"Sit," she ordered, then sank to the floor.

I sat down awkwardly, only to be ordered to rise again. Again and again we practised sitting on the floor, sinking down in a slow and stately manner amid our gowns. My legs quickly grew weary, and Kira informed me that I would have to exercise in order to strengthen my 'soft' body.

"Remove your robe," she said, voice still very soft.

I slipped off my robe, and she did the same. Her body was quite thin, her breasts small, but very firm.

"Position your body as mine is," she ordered.

Sitting on our crossed legs, we practised the very basics of Mandarin until my legs were cramped and my bottom sore. I wanted to ask her to at least move over to the bed, but her attitude was not open to such suggestions.

We began by moving through some of the same positions I had with my original mistress. Kira would speak a word or phrase in Mandarin, and I would kneel or lie back and spread my legs, or stand, or turn.

But there was more, for I had also to learn the words for a variety of foods and drinks that my master might require, so that if he wished I could bring it to him. And also for other services he might desire, such as my help in bathing or clothing him. Sex, it seemed, was merely a part of the duties of a good Chinese slave.

Kira herself was Japanese, and had been owned by Chow Lei, the provincial governor, since she was a young girl. She had long ago resigned herself to her life, and advised me to do the same with all speed. No defiance or resistance of any kind would be tolerated by Master Lei, and punishment would be swift and painful.

At last, Mistress Kira rose, as smoothly and gracefully as if she had not been sitting on crossed legs for hours, and I, groaning and stretching, rose, as well, awkward and feeling clumsy under her disapproving eyes.

"Come," she said, turning her back on me.

She donned her robe, but as I reached for mine she shook her head and I reluctantly dropped it. We went to the door and then out into the hall, and I felt my shoulders turning inwards as I hesitantly followed. I crossed an arm over my breasts and let my hand dangle before my groin as we walked down the small hall and into one of the broader, far more brightly lit corridors.

"Do not hide your body," she said, frowning.

"I'm not used to... being naked in a big... public place," I said awkwardly.

"If you behave as if you are shamed then you will be," she replied shortly.

We passed into a shower room. Walls and floor were of simple brown tiles, and a row of faucets projected from the right side. On the left were sinks and mirrors, and in the middle a number of long, thin, padded tables. There were several naked men beneath the showers, and one at the sinks, and my heart skipped a beat as they turned to stare at me.

Kira led me over to one of the padded tables, then called out in her singsong voice. Several of the men responded, and she selected one who was beneath the showers with a small nod. Dripping naked, but not the least ashamed, he walked across to us, his penis dangling between his legs, then with an appreciative look at my breasts, sat on the table.

"Kneel," Kira ordered.

I knelt, very embarrassed as all the men stared at me, and she filled a bucket with water and handed me a rag and soap.

"Clean his feet and lower legs," she ordered.

I felt indignant at that, but obeyed, only to have her pull me back.

"No," she said.

She removed her robe and knelt gracefully before the man. She picked up one foot in a most gentle way and laid it between her bare thighs, then dipped the cloth in the water and squeezed it over his foot. She applied the soap, next, always very slowly and smoothly, and used her hands to caress his foot as it lay clasped between her thighs. Her fingers began to deftly massage the foot, and she showed me where to push my fingers, how hard to press, and to stroke.

"You must worship the foot," she said sternly, which seemed desperately odd to me.

But soon the foot was between my thighs, and I had to caress and stroke it as the man looked on with a grin.

"Now take it between your breasts," she ordered.

I hesitated, and she reached forward, gently lifting the foot, sliding the sole up my belly and until it rested just beneath my breasts. Then, crouched behind me, she reached beneath my arms and took my breasts in her hands, gently pushing them together around his soapy foot.

This, I should add, was only the beginning, for after doing both feet and lower legs, the man lay back on the table, and I must then straddle him and gently soap up his body with my hands and the rag, and spend long minutes slowly stroking him with first my hands, then my body itself.

With my breasts, groin, legs and belly layered in slippery soap, I knelt on the table straddling him, my thighs together

131

around his hips as I bent forward, pressing my chest against his back and slowly grinding back and forth. Kira stopped me frequently to correct my movements, which must be slow and careful, smooth and lacking any sense of vulgarity.

First I was to use my hips to grind my pelvis up and down, starting from a position where I sat above his thighs, until I was straddling his back. Then I was to bend forward and use my upper body, my breasts, principally, to caress him from shoulders to thighs.

While he was on his belly this was less difficult, but as he rolled over I saw that he had a strong erection. I looked to her questioningly, but her face gave no indication that I should attend to it. Yet neither could I avoid it, as I slid my body forward along his thighs I felt the hard heat of it against my pussy each time I slid over him.

"You may attend him between your breasts," she said.

I had no idea what she meant, at first, but then as she cupped her own breasts I realized she intended that I take his male organ between my breasts as I had his foot. The idea was strange at first, yet the feel of his soapy member between my breasts was not unpleasant. And in truth, by then I was, while still embarrassed, more than a little aroused, as well.

I bent far forward, letting my breasts press heavily against his abdomen, then sliding them back and forth over his erection. He stared at me eagerly, and I smiled, reaching down and squeezing my breasts together around his cock, sliding them from side to side over the soapy layer as he began to roll his hips and groan in pleasure. His cock stroked against my breastbone, and I continued to massage my breasts against it until his come fountained out of the end and he slumped back with a sigh of relief.

Once this happened I had to straighten up and use only my thighs and groin, sliding slowly up and down his body for a time while he relaxed, then dismounting the table and letting him sit up.

"You will learn better," Kira sighed. "Clean yourself."

She pointed towards one of the shower faucets and I padded naked across the tiles and stood beneath it. There was a naked man on either side of me, both shorter than I and both fascinated by the sight of me. I felt my embarrassment rising once again and tried to ignore them as the water poured down over my head and rinsed away both soap and semen.

"You must learn to be less shamed at naked flesh," Kira said from behind me.

"I'm sorry, Mistress," I said.

"Your apologies are without value."

After I had towelled myself somewhat dry she led me from the room and further up the hall. She was once again robed while I remained naked, and I cringed slightly each time we passed someone and they stared at me

We turned down a stone-lined hall and I felt extremely odd padding along naked. The walls were at least forty feet apart and the roof almost that high. We passed a number of people, some male, some female, but all startled and staring.

Then we came to an intersection where the hall met another similar one. We waited there, and she was silent, simply poised and unmoving for long minutes.

"What are we waiting for?" I asked finally.

"You must learn patience. You are a slave. When it is desired that you know something you will be told."

Finally a man arrived, clad in simple black and wheeling a cart. He bowed slightly to Kira, ogled me briefly, then took a six foot high golden pole from the cart and stood it on the floor. It was no wider than my thumb, and I looked down I saw the bottom slip neatly into a small hole in the floor.

He then placed a second pole, this one only a foot high, a few feet from the first and Kira, silent until then, turned to me and motioned me to stand between the two. Puzzled, I obeyed, then spread my legs apart at her command.

133

There were two other small holes in the floor, and the workman produced two inch long plugs which locked into them. Each plug had a narrow gold chain, and attached to the chains were thin gold rings. Startled, I watched as he fitted each of the rings around my big toes, tightening them in some fashion so they would not come off.

I was instructed to raise my hands up and then back behind my head. There they were bound by another thin gold chain which was then pulled down firmly, until my back was sharply arched. I felt fingers at my rectum, and a thin plug was inserted there which seemed to hook up against my tailbone, and attach somehow to my wrists, holding them back behind me.

Kira herself moved forward then, smiling serenely. She clipped two more small gold chains to my nipple rings, then led them up and out, pulling harder and harder until my nipples stretched out, and then the areolas behind them. I winced in growing pain, slowly rising onto the balls of my feet in an attempt to relieve the pressure. At that point she clipped the chains to the pole before me.

She took another small gold chain off the cart, and this time knelt between my legs. Her finger gently caressed my bare slit for a moment, then spread the lips of my sex apart as she clipped the chain to the ring piercing my clitoris. This chain was pulled down, and then back between my thighs. I cried out softly at the pressure exerted, but she judged things in her own manner, then fastened the chain to the smaller pole directly behind me.

"You must learn to be less shamed by your body," she said.

And with that she and the man left me there alone.

I moaned as I looked after them, my nipples already aching and my lower belly feeling slightly queasy from the pull on my sensitive clitoris. Yet I could not move at all. A man walked by, licking his lips hungrily as he passed, then two more in the other direction, staring and whispering.

Two young women approached me, huddled together, eyes wide, faces showing both embarrassment, shock, wonder, and amusement. They were about my age, wearing long skirts and business jackets, long straight hair hanging past their shoulders. They moved so closely together their shoulders were touching as they moved past me, their eyes wide. One pressed a hand over her mouth in an effort to hide embarrassed giggles, then the two hurried down another hall.

I was terribly embarrassed, but there was, of course, not a thing I could do to hide any portion of my body. Each time someone passed they inspected me with varying degrees of amusement, scorn, or excitement, not failing to note the rings stretching out my nipples or clitoris.

My legs ached, and cramps made me groan from time to time, but my toes hurt more, and I was not at all sure how long I could remain so precariously balanced on the balls of my feet. My skin felt hot and moist, for the air, even in the stone corridor, was quite hot and humid. I was soon sweating, and panting softly, my legs trembling.

Hours passed, and the pain in my feet proved too much. I had to lower myself so that my feet were flat on the floor, fighting off tears of pain as my nipples were pulled out that much harder, stretched taut and pulling my areolas up and then the soft, heavy flesh of my breasts, burning with a hot, sharp pain.

The hall became much busier, with groups of people walking back and forth in all directions, all staring at me as they passed. Then fewer and fewer passed, and the halls became quiet and deserted. My stomach grumbled and my throat was parched. My skin was coated in sweat, and I was exhausted and aching all over.

Kira came for me then, and I collapsed to the floor as she finally removed the clips from my nipples and clitoris. I was allowed to return to the shower room and clean myself, then, still entirely nude, was led to a large cafeteria of sorts, where I sat on a wooden bench and ate under Kira's stern gaze.

There were several dozen other people in the room, and all stared at me as I ate, but I was growing less sensitive to such stares by then, and was moreover too hungry and thirsty to give them much heed.

From there I was returned to my room, and quickly fell asleep on the big bed.

Morning came and Kira woke me. We sat on our crossed legs again, and went over our Chinese lessons for several hours. Then she guided me to the cafeteria place once more, for our breakfast. This time the room was crowded with men and women of various ages, and I felt a new embarrassment as I moved among them naked. I was taller than almost all, and I could see eyes turning my way from all across the large room. My chest was tight with anxiety, and I could hardly think, much less taste the food Kira sit before me. I kept my head down, for every time I raised my eyes I saw the people on the other side of the table staring and whispering. None spoke to me, however, nor to Kira.

Afterwards I was taken to the garden, and there, under a hot sun, another woman led me in exercises. They were unlike the kind of things I was familiar with from school. Rather than hopping and jogging here all was slow and smooth movements. Still, it rapidly grew quite tiring in the heat, and my body was soon slick with perspiration, my hair matted against my forehead and neck. I was desperately relieved when Kira came for me at last and led me back inside.

We returned to the shower room, and Kira instructed me to lie on my stomach on one of the padded tables. As before, there were men there, most of them naked, and as before they stared at me, but perhaps I was growing somewhat immune to them, for I felt much less embarrassment.

To my surprise, Kira removed her own robe, and then

136

used a wet rag to moisten my flesh. Soft soap followed, and I felt a deep sense of relaxation as her strong, yet nimble fingers stroked and massaged my back and shoulders. Her hands worked their way down my body, and when I was coated in a layer of soap she climbed atop the table, straddled my body, and sat on my upper thighs.

Her hands continued to slowly stroke up and down my back, and then massaged my buttocks. I could see more of the men staring now, though they were being rather circumspect about it.

Kira's hands slid smoothly up the slippery sides of my body, caressing the sides of my breasts where they pillowed out beneath me. Then her body began slipping forward, and I felt the softness of her buttocks riding up over mine, slowly sliding back and forth before easing higher still. Her small, strong thighs pressed in against my waist as her fingers kneaded the muscles of my shoulders. Her wet, soapy hands began to comb my hair back then, pulling it back behind me and twining it together as she lathered it up in soap. Her hands moved to my temples, fingers caressing lightly, then stroked along the nape of my neck as her groin and buttocks slid slowly up and down.

She did not speak, but I realized she was demonstrating that which I must myself master, and tried to pay attention to the gentle movement of her body and hands, to the feel of her fingers now stroking along my skull, and the slow, soft grinding of her thighs around me.

I felt her breasts pressing heavily against my back then as her hair spilled across my shoulders. She slid slowly downwards, her breasts rubbing along my flesh, sliding easily atop a thick, slippery layer of soap until they rubbed against my buttocks. She halted, then slid upwards again, and I felt her breasts against my wet, soapy scalp.

It felt... very strange, very comforting, and yet, erotic as well. Before very long the presence of the men watching us became less of an embarrassment than a goad to that part of my exhibitionistic nature which had begun to arise since my capture. I watched some of them out of the corners of my eyes, seeing their engrossed they were in the sight of us, how obviously excited and aroused they were becoming.

"Roll over," Kira's voice whispered in my ear.

I was startled out of my reverie, and she rose on her knees to allow me to turn. I felt a fresh sense of embarrassment now as I lay on my back, but Kira showed not a hint of unease as she sat back on my upper legs and began to stroke her hands over my body. I could see the watching men less easily now, but sensed their indrawn breath as Kira's soapy hands moved confidently up over my breasts and began to knead and caress them. Her thumbs and forefingers rolled my already erect nipples between them until they ached, while her pelvis slid up and down over my belly, abdomen and groin.

My arousal deepened, despite a continuing sense of embarrassment and unease at our audience. I felt wicked and sluttish, and was simultaneously appalled and thrilled.

With my legs closed tightly the nearness of her was more of a teasing thing which produced little physical contact with my sex. Yet the sight of her and the awareness of our audience began to set my insides thrumming with heat and desire. I tried to hide this, for she appeared quite casual about her work. Yet as she leaned over and let her slippery breasts ride up across my belly and over my breasts I saw a small flicker of heat within her eyes, and my stomach muscles clenched as further excitement roused within me.

Her nipples were tiny, yet quite long and erect, and I felt them stroke back and forth over my own as her hair slid over my face. She slid back, rising upright and her hands began to move around and around my breasts, circling them, kneading the edges, caressing and stroking as they moved slowly inward. Soon my breasts were throbbing with heat and excitement, the nipples like small pink coals set in the centre. Sharp little flickers of almost painful energy rippled through them both and sent tendrils of fire down into my chest and groin.

I felt my legs slipping further apart, and as her body slid upwards both feet slipped over the sides of the table. My knees followed moments later, and I drew them up and back, placing my feet flat on the table to either side of my hips. This prevented Kira from sliding back below my groin, but she did not appear to care. And then she rose, her face still tranquil, her pelvis turning to the right as she pulled a leg back between mine. Chest and belly pounding with excitement now I drew my left back more and let my right new fall aside.

Kira took my left, extending it straight up, half turning me onto my side as she pulled it in against her chest. I felt her sex sliding in directly against my own, and let out a soft moan of shock and heady excitement. My embarrassment grew worse even as my body was electrified with sexual tension. The sensations as her sex began to slowly, seductively grind against my own were almost unbearable in their intensity.

A small part of myself was wild-eyed with horror and shame, wailing that I could not do such a thing in front of strangers, yet it was lost amid the chorus of pleasure coming from every part of my body and mind. All the inhibitions drilled into my mind since childhood by a lifetime amid English society cried out to stop, yet that dark, wicked side of me rose triumphant, trembling with shocked delight at such daring, such wanton conduct.

The room closed around us, and I raised a hand, squeezing one of Kira's breasts, reaching for her. Yet she would not bend. She ground herself steadily against me, serene as she rode her sex back and forth against my own, still holding my leg upright against her chest.

I could sense as much as see the men around us now. Most had abandoned the pretence of showering, shaving and dressing to stare at Kira's slow and sensual grinding motion. Her chin began to tremble, then rose bit by bit, higher and higher, her back beginning to arch as her hips ground more quickly. The pleasure was a towering wave now, carrying me ever higher, and I twisted my body slightly further to the side, bringing my other leg up around her, grinding myself back against her sex as I brought my hands up to squeeze my breasts.

Her lips parted slightly and I heard the smallest of moans emerge as she arched her back yet more sharply. Her eyes were closed and her fingers clutched more tightly against my leg, grinding it against her small, hard breasts. I realized she was coming, and the knowledge sent my own spiralling pleasure past its peak. I tried to suppress the cry of pleasure as I came, but was only partially successful.

The ecstasy sent me higher and higher, until it seemed that I must explode from the sheer power of the sensations roaring with me. And then as it finally began to subside and some smallest part of my mind awakened, all those eyes staring down upon me acted as a fire beneath my climax, sending it roaring hotter and harder still. My body writhed in the grip of a climax which rose and fell like a bird caught in a high windstorm, my head lolling and jerking bonelessly, my back arching again and again as my groin remained locked tightly against Kira.

Finally it seeped away, bit by bit, leaving me gasping and breathless, chest heaving, mouth slack, completely spent. My legs fell aside, off the edges of the table, and Kira lay forward upon me, her chest heaving almost as strongly as my own.

As I opened my eyes and gazed weakly about me I saw that there were almost two dozen men in the room, circling us at a distance. Most were either nude or in some undress, and I felt a sharp little spike of excitement at the thought of them all taking us right then and there, attacking us like starving wolves, thrusting their cocks into every part of us.

Yet they stayed back, turning their eyes away, pretending once again to be showering or changing or shaving. Kira sat up, her features composed once again, and then slipped off the table. I watched her move over beneath the showers, stepping easily into a space between two young men, ignoring them as she turned on the water and let it pour down about her. Left alone, I found my embarrassment and sense of unease deepening, and rose as well. I could not join her, but moved to the only other cleared space, feeling the eyes and hunger of the men on either side of me as I reached up and turned on the water.

My cheeks began to heat as I let the water rinse the soap from my hair and body, and I marvelled at how I had permitted myself to become so aroused in such a public manner. It was true I had little choice about what was done to me, for I was a slave. Yet none had forced the pleasure upon me. That had come from within, and I did not understand it.

I hurried after Kira as she finished towelling, barely towelling myself in my desperation not to be left alone there. We returned to my room, and I felt a sense of relief as she closed the door behind her.

"Isn't there ah, uhm, a women's shower room?" I asked timidly.

"You must discard your inhibitions," she said. "All inhibitions, all modesty, all sense of shame. You are a slave now. You can have none of these."

I bowed my head in acknowledgement.

"What place is this?" I asked.

"This is the palace of Chow Lei."

"I thought you were all, well, communists."

She raised an eyebrow.

"China never changes. China endures, regardless of what

141

men think or do or say, what governments or dynasties come and go, wars, plagues, disease and floods. Chow Lei calls himself a Communist but he is at heart no different from any provincial governor who has ruled in this place over the last five thousand years. He passes on his taxes and rice and cattle to the government and keeps order among his people. That is all which is asked of him. And so long as he does this he rules here as an emperor would. His word is life or death for men, families, even entire villages."

"Are there other westerners here?"

She shook her head solemnly. "You are the first white skinned person I have seen since I was brought here as a girl. Governor Lei's people will be most proud that their lord has taken a western girl for a slave. He will receive much status. You are already the talk of the palace."

I stared at her in amazement, hardly able to credit her words.

"But... doesn't he worry that, well, someone might find out?"

"And why should he fear? He is as near a God as can be to his people, who are peasant farmers no more sophisticated than their ancestors. Those in the central government care little what transpires here, and when they discover he has taken a white girl for a slave they will only admire his strength and daring. You will never leave this valley unless Chow Lei wills it. Do not think otherwise. Learn to accept and obey."

CHAPTER EIGHT

I was given ample evidence of Kira's words only a few days later. Master Lei gave a banquet for many of the more powerful figures in local industry and bureaucracy, as well as some of his fellow governors. The banquet room was large and beautiful, with three long rows of guests sitting cross-legged behind gleaming, knee-high tables to either side of a broad, red carpeted aisle. The Governor himself knelt behind a table facing them at the far side of the long hall, presiding over things much like a king or emperor.

He and all his guests were dressed in colourful, traditional apparel, nothing at all like the ugly, colourless little Mao suits I had seen so much of on television prior to my capture. I was given a similar robe, bright and glittery in green and blue, but my hair was left down, and I wore nothing beneath the robe.

For the first half hour of the dinner I knelt behind and to the side of the governor, hands on my thighs, head bowed. A few times, in conversation with those around him, he seemed to mention me, and he and others would turn their eyes my way, but I had no idea, of course, of what they were saying.

Once he picked up a not very appetizing piece of seafood off his golden plate and held it out to me with a smile. I instinctively knew I was not to take it with my hands, and leaned my head forward instead, licking it out of his hand. It tasted awful, but I swallowed it quickly and did my best not to show how distasteful I found it.

As dinner was being washed down with wine Lei gestured me to come closer, and then to rise to my feet. I could feel many more eyes in the room turning my way as he raised his voice and spoke aloud for several minutes. A few times his audience laughed, I knew it was at my expense, and fought to keep from blushing at being the centre of such attention.

He appeared to address me then, and I felt a little shock

143

of alarm and anxiety tighten my chest as I thought I recognized one of the words Kira had taught me. I hesitated, and his features darkened as he repeated the word. It was clear he was ordering me to disrobe, and my insides quivered and twisted in turmoil as I undid the front of the robe and then slipped it back over my shoulders.

I had become somewhat used to such attention in the cafeteria, but there all was bustle and chatter. Here the hall was silent, with long rows of eyes turned my way, and I was the only standing person in the room.

Beneath the robe I wore new gold rings in nipples and clitoris, brighter and larger than before. I wore, also, around my wrists, thin golden bracelets which could be clipped together, and a similar pair of anklets. A matching golden collar was tight around my throat, and a small tag hung from it bearing a Chinese character I could not read.

Lei stood, speaking again as he gestured to me, and more laughter spread around the room. He took my hands and raised them up then drew them back behind my head, and there clipped the bracelets to the small ring set in the back of the collar. A sharp tug reminded me to keep my back straight, then he cupped one of my breasts, tugging on the ring. Again there was laughter at his remarks.

Lei slapped me on the buttocks, then directed me to walk, both through word and gesture, and I nervously moved in front of his low table, pacing slowly along its length. Then at further gestures I moved down the long length of the hall, passing before the long table of his guests to the right, walking all the way to the end of the room, then turning and walking back along the other side of the central aisle.

My insides were writhing and my stomach fluttered like a butterfly as I walked, and it was all I could do to keep breathing as I focused all my attention ahead, ignoring the staring eyes on either side. I kept my back, or rather, due to my position, was forced to keep my back arched, which served to accent the firmness of my breasts. My face flushed darkly at displaying myself in such a way.

And yet I felt a rising heat at such exhibitionism. So many people staring at me as I padded up and down nude, so many eyes watching, so many minds thinking. I felt heady with the strange sense of freedom acting on another's orders gave. I could sense the hunger of many I passed, and the envy they felt for Lei's possession of a girl like me.

I returned to the front table and the Governor gestured me around to the rear. The table before him had been cleared back and he took one of my arms, guiding me forward until my lower legs pressed against the edge of the table. I was forced to kneel upon it, then, and at a push forward was bent low until my chin was pressed against the tabletop. This forced my head back, and I grunted as my breasts were crushed beneath me.

Lei held my hips steady, slapping my buttocks slightly as he ordered me to raise my bottom more and spread my legs.

I was breathless with anxiety and shock, realizing he intended to show his guests his mastery, his masculinity, by taking me then and there before them all. There was a murmur among his guests, of approval, I believe, and some small laughter. Then I gasped as he entered me, using a deep, powerful stroke to drive himself deep into my surprisingly moist sex.

His fingers dug into my hips and he thrust in once more, burying himself within me. I groaned softly, watching the long rows of guests turned sideways behind their tables, all staring at me as he began a hard, crude thrusting. The room was silent now except for the growing sound of skin on skin; Lei's belly slapping more forcefully against my upraised buttocks.

His cock was harsh on the soft flesh of my insides, for I was as yet unprepared, but as he continued his powerful strokes my body began to recover from its initial shock, and

145

I felt my inner warmth growing. I felt a sense of the unnatural, as if I were merely in a dream, and the air puffed out of my mouth in small gasps and pants of breath.

Lei continued his strong thrusting, using the full length of his cock, and driving himself straight in. He made no attempt at subtlety, at altering the direction or strength of his strokes. He was using me as a bull would, as an animal, gripping my flanks strongly and pounding himself against my bottom. Of course it was necessary for his reputation to not finish too quickly. And so he restrained his climax, thrusting, thrusting, ever thrusting as my insides were slowly churned into a steaming stew of liquid heat.

'This is a dream. This isn't happening. Oh God. Look at all those faces. Oh it feels so good. Oh it's so shocking, so wicked. What would my friends think!? Oh! Ohh yesss! Oh God forgive me! It feels so gooood! I'm such a whore!'

I began to lose myself in the passion he brought to my body, feeling heat grip me from head to toe. Perspiration stood out on my chest and I could feel the wood growing slippery beneath me as his pounding jerked me to and fro.

He stopped at last, climaxing inside me, and I moaned in denial, being near to the edge of my own orgasm. He stopped at once, of course, for he cared nothing for my pleasure. I felt my insides gape as he withdrew, felt the muscles of my sex clasping at nothing as if they could draw him back inside.

A rough grip on my collar brought me back up so that I was kneeling upright, and then a stronger grip forced my head back further and further, so that my back arched painfully sharply.

He spoke the words which Kira had taught me translated into "Do not move." She had spent considerable time convincing me of the danger of disobeying these words, and that whatever pain I might feel at what Lei did would be as nothing compared to what would happen should I disobey.

But I did not care. I was too aroused, too inflamed by the

146

desires of my body and that wicked, hedonistic side of my mind. I saw him take a flog from a servant, and whimpered as much in anticipation as anxiety.

He was going to flog my breasts!

I knew it was so, and I shuddered, drawing my head back further to accentuate my breasts more. I felt a great wall of shocked desire flooding me, and only a small part of my spinning mind even wondered at it. My breasts were heavy and swollen with lust, my nipples hard and aching.

He spoke the words again, and then brought the flog down.

It was a short instrument, with foot long leather strips bound to a foot long handle. Each strip was, individually, not at all thick or heavy, but when they struck in unison it felt like a swarm of wasps had attacked my chest. I cried out, shocking little sparkles of pain ripping through my soft flesh. One strip nipped at my left nipple and I felt an even deeper sense of heat and pain there.

But I held my position, and as even as the shockwave of pain rippled through my nervous system I felt a bizarre sense of... well, satisfaction, of rightness, of almost gleeful wickedness.

Again the flog whipped down, and once more my cry of pain filled the air, as the flog laced my taut, straining breasts. Again, and again, and yet again the flog came down, and the heat and pain mounted even as I fought to keep from grinding my thighs together at the desperate need gripping my body.

He whipped harder, and I sensed he was less than happy with my obedience. My breasts burned and ached, and tears filled my eyes. I shook there on the table, swaying weakly, yet held myself as ordered, back arched, head back, breasts in vulnerable display as the flog scourged them again and again.

The pain was horrible, and I do not think I could have coped with it had it not been for that strange sense of heat and need, a sense of deepest arousal which felt a wild passion at such cruel abuse. Endorphins were filling my body now, softening the sharpness of pain as I swayed back further. I had been sitting on my heels, and my legs were spread wide now for balance. The flog struck my belly, then lower still, strips slicing into the soft skin of my lower abdomen, inner thighs, and then directly across my shaven sex.

The beating stopped, but I was hardly aware of it at first. I swayed weakly, eyes glazed, body hot, head throbbing, chest and belly and groin aching. I was pulled off the table, my wrists unclipped from the collar, then clipped back behind my back. A Y shaped golden chain was clipped to my nipple rings, then a small Chinese girl was given the 'leash' and led me down the central aisle.

I shuffled along in a dazed state, the sharp pull against my nipples giving me the signals my body required, and was led from the room and up the hallway.

I was led into a very small round room, the walls and roof mirrored. In the centre stood an upright shaft of metal, almost as wide as my wrist, and rounded at the top. The girl positioned me above it, and then turned a wheel set into the wall. The shaft began to rise, and I felt the pressure against my moist, overheated sex. Had I been less dazed perhaps I would have fought to pull away, but instead I felt a wall of delight and groaning aloud I ground my sex against it.

It rose higher and I felt the pressure against my entrance mount. My lips were forced in and back, then began to stretch almost painfully. I moaned still, panting and blinking my eyes, confused but desperate to be penetrated. I looked up to see the calm eyes of the Chinese girl, watching me as she continued to turn the wheel. I felt a sharp ache down there as my pubic lips were forced just that much further back and then the long, cool length of the shaft began to rise inside me.

It ached, yet it felt glorious, and I squirmed and shuffled and moaned and wriggled atop it as I felt it climbing higher and higher into my abdomen.

"Please! Please!" I gasped, not knowing the words I spoke, nor why.

The pain and pleasure both grew, and I was forced onto my toes, back straight, air puffing out of my open lips as I closed my eyes and arched my back.

The girl departed at some point. I don't remember her leaving. I could not think straight.

I could not remember my name. What was my name? When was the last time anyone had used it? Who was I?

It was cold and solid and thick inside me. My belly ached around it. I could feel my cunt throbbing in time with my pounding heartbeat. But the sexual heat continued to grip me. I had to move on the shaft, yet it was already so deep within me. I had to, and so I did, the pain mounting as somehow I lowered myself, inch by slow inch, gasping and whimpering the while, until my feet were flat on the floor and an unimaginable length of cold hard steel was buried between my legs.

Sobbing aloud, I raised myself up, sliding my aching sex up the now slippery pole until I was once again on my toes, then sinking back down once more.

The climax fell upon me like an avalanche and I screamed in release as my body convulsed in the throes of ecstasy. I shuddered and trembled and jerked, several times crying out in pain as my legs forgot to support me and my weight came down more heavily on the impaling shaft. I imagined it sliding deeper and deeper, sliding up through my insides, up my throat, emerging through my gasping mouth, and in my masochistic stupor relaxed my legs. The pain clawed at me and I brought them down once more, swaying and jerking in mindless sensual overload.

And yet that dark need still lay upon me. I clasped my warm, perspiring thighs and legs tightly about the shaft, grinding myself against it, letting my feet come off the floor.

149

The pain grew harsher, but it was a dull, deep pain which only served to thrust me higher into that state of feverish sexual need which had been growing within me. My head lolled as my body shuddered and convulsed, the pain deep inside me rising and falling as my thighs tightened and relaxed in frantic rhythm against the steel shaft.

I was fortunate, I know, from looking back, that the shaft was as wide as it was, and as rounded atop. But in that state of mind in which I then found myself no cares existed beyond my own immediate sexual satisfaction. And as the orgasm finally fled I moaned in soft pain, carefully laying my feet back on the floor to hold my weight. My insides throbbed and ached, and my body was drained and languid, yet I was sated, and wanted nothing more than to lie down and curl up into a ball.

I could not, of course, but must stand there in my weakened state, a bedraggled slave pinned like a butterfly at her master's strange whims.

I felt some small thrum of arousal even at that, but was too weary to give it play. Still, it consoled me through the following several hours as I stood there impaled upon the shaft, and eventually grew to such a degree I once more began to grind myself upon the shaft.

The door opened, however, and the girl returned for me. She wordlessly lowered the shaft, and I was lowered with it, moaning and gasping at the feel of it sliding down out of my body. I would have followed it to my knees had she not casually grasped my loose, tangled hair and yanked me up, then clipped her golden chain leash to my nipple rings and led me forth from the room.

For the first several weeks of my stay there I was summoned to the governor's bedroom almost every evening. There he used me harshly and crudely, apparently out of some need to show his mastery over the hated English. I was usually taken

150

from behind, and often sodomised, but only after performing fellatio - which I came to learn was considered quite disgusting by Asian women, and so not nearly so widespread as was the case in the west.

I was often pinched, slapped and bruised during these sessions, for Governor Lei took no care at all for my comfort. I was also quite strictly disciplined for the slightest of offences, and I came to believe such punishments were intended more for his satisfaction than my instruction.

My bottom, in particular, was strapped almost nightly for some alleged lack of enthusiasm on my part, and I was twice raised by my wrists so that my back could be flogged.

Two weeks into my stay there I attended another of Master Lei's parties. This was quite different than his first affair, being far smaller and less formal, and there was much more drinking, so that Master Lei and his dozen or so guests all grew quite rowdy and drunk. I was stripped naked, at this time, while sitting across Lei's lap, and there he openly fondled my breasts while joking and laughing with his guests.

I was then placed on my knees and performed fellatio on him as his guests watched and laughed in approval, after which I was gifted to any man who wanted me as Master Lei looked on with benevolent approval.

This set up a mad scramble, to be frank, for these men were quite drunken and eager, and I was quickly surrounded and overwhelmed by them all as they struggled with each other for various parts of my anatomy. I was on my knees, and all around me was a wall of naked or semi naked men, pressing in against me, shouting and laughing, pulling me to and fro as they fought over me like dogs. Hands darted out to grasp and roughly squeeze any available part of my body, and my hair was pulled this way and that as they fingered and stroked it. My nipples were pinched and twisted so hard that I cried out as the nipple rings threatened to tear free, and my breasts were bruised and crushed by eager hands even as fingers were thrust into my anus and pussy.

After long seconds of this mauling some sort of position or rank was sorted out, and I was mounted by a large, overweight man, who puffed so heavily I wondered whether he might expire before he completed the act, and if I would be blamed in that eventuality. Another of them quickly knelt before me and I opened my mouth to take his shaft, attempting to perform as I had been taught against his wild, eager thrustings.

The noise they made as they surrounded me, their loud, drunken voices rising and falling in tandem with ribald laughter, was a wall of sound around me, and in combination with the many hands still reaching out from onlookers seeking to stroke my skin, squeeze my breasts, or pull on my hair was quite overwhelming.

And at the centre of it, of course, was the steady, furious hammering of hips against my buttocks, and the savage pumping of a hard penis within my sex, followed by the second penis thrusting into my mouth and as often as not down my throat. I was quickly dazed and confused by these circumstances, and it was not, I think, until three men had completed their use of my body that I began to feel that dark lust begin to move sinuously through the corridors of my mind.

It began to rise steadily, however, as one after another of them gripped my flanks and thrust themselves into me from behind, and the noisy pawing, slapping and grasping continued unabated.

Oh how I was used! So long and so hard and by so many men. I was the centre of male lust, of an animalistic orgy of unrestrained carnality. My throat was soon quite sore, my jaw aching, my breasts throbbing and nipples afire from the repeated pinching. My buttocks were bruised and my insides felt hollow. Yet still it continued, and I felt a masochistic glee at my own abuse, at inspiring such relentless excitement and lust in so many men.

A small climax rocked my body in the midst of such use, yet it served only to heighten my abused senses, and almost immediately on its passing I felt another, stronger building within me.

Occasionally, through the maze of legs and bodies before me, I would see a well-dressed servant, often a young woman, moving about to provide drinks and food, then the picture would disappear as my throat was filled with cock and another male stomach was crushed against my face.

Another climax rippled through my body, then yet another, each stronger than before, yet none took notice as my body was jerked violently to and fro under their eager attentions and their laughter and shouts continued to fill the air.

My anus was pierced then, and a number of men then began to focus their attentions in that area. Yet this was but little diversion to me, for things continued much as they had been. Each man took me, then took me again, and often a third time, as the evening wore on, and I climaxed with such power and repetition that the muscles of my abdomen and chest ached more fiercely from this than from any other cause.

I was barely conscious as the party ended, and was led out of the room and back to my own, where I fell into immediate sleep.

The next morning I was sore everywhere, and could barely move. I lay abed a full hour after waking before I could summon the strength to stumble to the tub across from my bed, start warm water gushing from the faucet, and then sink weakly to the bottom. Kira, having experienced such parties on occasion herself, brought me fruit and rice for my breakfast, feeding me as I sat amid the hot water, and afterwards massaged soft oils into my bruised flesh and excused me from most of the physical activities of the day. We did, however, continue to work on my understanding of Mandarin.

The problem I had with the Chinese language was that it is so unlike English in its application. One must know not merely the word being used, but realize how the tone affects that word. For many, many words in Mandarin have multiple disparate meanings depending on the tone one employs to speak them. This is why westerners have often remarked on the 'sing-song' way of speaking in China.

Kira had developed a practical, if intolerant method for encouraging my learning. She would run me through my words and phrases each day, and pain greeted forgetfulness. One day I might perhaps be forced to kneel with hands outstretched as she quizzed me, and a sharp blow across my open palms with a small leather quirt would greet mispronunciations or lapses. The next day I might be kneeling in all humility, chest against my legs, clasping my knees as I responded, receiving blows across the back when I misspoke. Several times she brought in one of the women I thought of as the 'washer women' to punish me, and I was forced to humiliate myself by placing my body across their laps as they sat so that they could spank me as if I were a small girl.

On this morning, in recognition of my aching flesh, she contented herself with attaching a thin chain to the ring piercing my clitoris, and giving it a sharp tug each time I failed to pronounce a word properly, or remember its use. Needless to say I was quite sore and sensitive there by the time our lesson had been completed. Kira, removing the chain, pushed me back onto my back on the floor and spread my legs, then, giving me a rare smile, bent and began to massage my clitoris with her tongue.

She was quite soft and gentle, yet so oversensitive was my body that even the soft caress of her tongue set it aching and stinging. I did not object, of course, and despite the pain,

154

pleasure and passion began to rise within me. I wondered vaguely if I were some sort of lesbian to welcome such deviant sexual touches, yet it was beyond me to care. What would have horrified me weeks earlier was nothing more now than a chance of physical pleasure.

And so I allowed her to lick me to orgasm, groaning and writhing there on the cold floor, squeezing and caressing her head in my hands as my pelvis rolled up against her. As I came, she licked especially hard, and pain joined pleasure within me in a seamless flood of heat.

We lay together for a time, then I dressed in my blue and silver robe and followed her down the hall into the larger room where Lei's slaves spent their unoccupied time. I had mentally dubbed it The Harem room on first seeing it, for it did seem to resemble my earlier imaginings of some Arab Sheik's playroom. The floor was covered in soft cushions, pillows and mats, and there was a large pool in the centre of the room, surrounded by flowers and plants. Lei had only eight slaves, however, all of them Asian but me.

Five were Chinese girls, all locals, and one was a Vietnamese. And all had long since accepted their fate, in several cases with very little resentment. Their lives, after all, were quite a deal better than the hardship and endless toil they would otherwise have experienced. Not being virgins, none considered they had any chance of marriage now, and so were prisoners in name only. Even if they could have gotten away there was nowhere for them to go, and no likely life awaited them other than prostitution.

I sat gingerly on one of the mats, as Kira pushed several cushions my way before taking her own place. The girls talked with Kira, and I looked on and listened, struggling to pick up whatever I could - which was little. After a time little Jin, one of the other girls, began trying to teach me words by pointing at objects and speaking the words aloud, and big breasted Chyou joined in. I spoke the words in English, as

155

they hoped to learn English in turn, and we passed some time that way.

There was no television, of course, nor even radios for us girls, and so there was little to occupy our time when not required by Master Lei except conversation - and lesbian sex. All the girls had slept together, and found me, my pale skin and blonde hair as much a source of fascination as did others. Jin and Chyou made expressions of sympathy after Kira spoke to them, but giggled as well, and I knew Kira had told them of the many men who had used me the previous night.

They stroked my hair and hugged me, and insisted on opening my robe that they could caress and massage my sore body. Although I was quite sure this was not their real desire I acquiesced, and was soon lying back under Kira's amused eyes as the two, soon joined by An stroked and licked my pale body.

In a sense I felt as I had the previous evening, yet these girls were gentle and kind, and had only my pleasure in their hearts. Jin and Chyou each took one of my breasts, fingers gently kneading and massaging as their mouths and tongues lapped at and suckled my nipples, and An knelt between my legs, doing wonderful things with her tongue even while teasing me by twisting and gently tugging on my ring.

It was not the overwhelming, carnal enthusiasm of the men, but rather a soft, slow, gentle lovemaking which soon had me moaning amid the languor of sexual heat, ignoring my bruises and soreness as desire flowed through my veins.

Lee joined An between my legs, bored, no doubt, and their tongues fought for space as they moved over my sex. Then Kira abandoned her aloofness to strip off her robe and straddle my head, lowering her sex to my mouth.

Long, long minutes passed, for all of us were slow and casual about our sport. The girls continued to chat idly, removing their mouths from various parts of my body to speak to each other, then returning. I, of course, being unable to speak, simply gripped Kira's thighs and did my best to please her.

I was the first to climax, of course. And soon after my body had eased its writhing and thrashing I felt the others begin to work with new energy. They had, it seems, found my responsiveness amusing, and had set about exploring its limits. And so, giggling and laughing, they forced me to climax after climax, holding me down when, aching, sore and drained, I would have pushed them back, continuing to stimulate my body in such a way I had no choice but to roll through churning, aching, exhausting orgasms, one following upon the heels of another until I thought I must surely die.

Even so, even in the midst of my climaxing, I continued to lick dazedly at whomever straddled my head. I was vaguely aware Kira had been replaced by another, and that another girl had followed her, but before long I stopped knowing or caring, licking until my jaw and tongue were too sore, and the girls finally abandoned me to fall into slumber.

CHAPTER NINE

"You feel pain too much."

"I'm sorry, Master," I gasped, struggling to hold myself still.

I lay in bed with Lei, or rather, sat astride him as he sat back against a massive wooden headboard topped by a carved star. He held my nipple between thumb and forefinger and pinched quite hard, twisting and pulling at it as I trembled and winced.

"You must learn to conquer your body's weaknesses. What is pain but heat? Is pleasure not heat, as well?"

"Yes, master," I panted, automatically agreeing.

He snorted disdainfully and released my throbbing nipple, then pushed me aside and stood up. Naked, he walked to a large armour type of chest and withdrew a thin crop, then returned to bed and thrust it at me handle first.

I took it uncertainly and he climbed into bed, then held out his open hand.

"Strike me as hard as you can," he ordered.

I stared at him in disbelief, afraid to, yet knowing I could not disobey.

"Now," he ordered curtly.

I licked my lips uncertainly, then raised the crop and brought it down lightly across his hand.

"I said as hard as you can," he barked.

Fearful, I took a deep breath, then drew the crop back and whipped it down quite hard. It struck the centre of his unmoving hand, yet he did not even wince.

"Harder," he ordered.

He was sitting calmly back as I knelt, showing no concern whatever as I drew the crop back further, rising on my knees. I swung it down quite hard, and again the crop struck with a soft meaty sound, raising a red welt across his unmoving palm.

158

"You can conquer pain if you have the strength of mind," he said. "I have seen you do this, but in a woman's way."

"A woman's way, master?" I asked fearfully.

His hand slipped between my thighs and cupped my sex.

"You turn to this to shield you from the pain. You take the pain and use it to bake the fires of passion inside your loins. This is not a man's way, but women are weak, and so it serves."

He took the crop from me, and stood, then gestured me out of bed. Swallowing nervously, I obeyed, kneeling before him, sitting back on my heels.

"Back," he ordered. "Bend your body back."

I had been his slave for some weeks now, and my body had grown somewhat firmer with exercise, but also looser and more supple. I put my hands behind my head and leaned back until my elbows, and then the top of my head touched the floor behind me. My knees were still firmly on the floor, and my feet in the same position they had as I had sat upon them. Yet my body was firm and straining up and back, quite vulnerable to any discipline Lei chose for it.

Head upside down, I stared at the far wall as I felt the crop slip between my legs and gently stroke back and forth along my pubic lips.

"You are easily aroused," he said.

And I was, for my inhibitions had been torn away, and the enjoyment of sexual pleasure was one of the few delights permitted me.

The crop was thin and rounded, made of some soft, oiled wood which stroked like a feather along my skin. The tip gave my clitoris a tiny slap and I gasped at the sharp sensations which rippled through me. Then it slid up my taut belly, flicked lightly along my already erect nipples, and rolled beneath to follow the contours of my spine.

A fat finger pushed into me, gained moisture, then moved over my clitoris in such a way that I was soon breathless with excitement. It drew back and the tip of the crop slapped gently against my clitoris, then again, in a series of fast, light blows which had sharp-edged flickers of pain rolling through my groin. He paused, sliding the tip of the crop through the ring and then pulling back, tugging lightly but repeatedly at my throbbing clitoris.

I moaned lightly, but felt the pain and pleasure warring within for custody of my body. I could see nothing, and so the sensations felt redoubled as his fingers stroked against at my sex, then began to gently massage my clitoris.

A hand slid lightly up my rounded, arched body, up along my abdomen and over my belly, then downwards to caress my straining breasts and pluck lightly at the nipples. A moment later the crop followed, circling and prodding at my nipples and pulling at the rings. It drew back, and I felt long seconds of anticipation before the tip slapped down against one fat, rigid nipple. It was a light slap, yet the shock flashed through my breast and into my body in an instant, and I moaned anew.

The crop slapped repeatedly at the nipple, lightly but stingingly, then moved to the other as I fought to keep my body positioned properly despite the ache now rising in my spine.

Again he halted, and I waited breathlessly. I could not see him at all, though he knelt beside me, for my head was jammed firmly into the rug and my upside down vision allowed me to view only the room straight ahead.

I yelped as the crop slapped against my clitoris again, then against each nipple in turn. The stings were not enough to fight off the rising haze of sexual need within me, and were instead swallowed by it, sparkling like firecrackers in the dark as heat enveloped my mind and body. My nipples and clitoris were soon sore and throbbing, yet still the heat rose, and each new slap sent a new surge of energy through my veins.

Now he drew back and I sensed, rather than saw the crop rising higher. I cried out as the full length of it slapped across my abdomen, the stinging pain briefly cutting through the sexual mist laying over my mind. Several small slaps with the tip followed, against my clitoris and nipples, then another harsher blow, this against my left breast, bathing it in the fire of pain.

He moved away, and I saw a brief vision of him - upside down, of course - as he moved across the room. He returned with a handful of rope, and knelt beside me, out of my view. I felt him sliding lengths of rope around my right wrist, laying each loop down neatly alongside the next. Then he pulled my wrist back slightly, placing it against my right ankle where it lay on the floor, and then binding the two together.

He moved around me and bound my left wrist to my left ankle, as well, and while my aching back felt a sense of resignation at this indication it was to remain uncomfortably and unnaturally bent that dark side of my sexual mind sent a gush of masochistic excitement through my flushed body. He pressed a hand against my forehead, pushing my head even further back, then gathered my hair together behind me and bound it into a rough braid. He pulled it back behind me and I felt something thrust into my anus, something curved, which hooked against my tailbone and pulled backwards. It took only a moment to realize he had bound my hair to this object, and that my body would most surely remain tightly arched until such time as he decided to release it.

He knelt again and more slaps against my clitoris and nipples had me gasping and moaning. They grew harsher, the crop moving in longer arcs and with more force, and the flashes of pain rattled through my mind and body like raindrops on a tin roof. Yet through it all echoed the rolling thunder of a deep and pervasive sexual passion which easily dwarfed the pain, and even absorbed that pain into its own crackling stormwave of pleasure.

I cried out as another harsh blow struck my chest just below my breasts. Lei was kneeling back now, and bringing the crop down strongly, if slowly, striking me from breasts to thighs.

"Spread your legs," he ordered, as I heaved and moaned and trembled with pain and pleasure.

Half dazed, I obeyed, and the crop lashed at my inner thighs, then struck down with deliberate aim on my vulnerable cleft with force sufficient to send the slender rod sinking deep between my swollen public lips. The pain rose and caught me in a roar of fire, yet the howl of pleasure was greater still.

And then the harsh blows halted, and I felt the tip of the crop rubbing against my aching clitoris. Pleasure and pain screamed through my mind, and then as I began to come the tip snapped down against my clitoris in a fast, sharp spanking motion.

I came with a scream, my voice rising and falling in animalistic passion and ecstasy as my body was racked by convulsions. I have no idea how I held my position, yet somehow I did even as my mind writhed under the power of the explosive orgasmic storm.

As it ended, so ended the spanking of the crop, and Lei rose, moving away once more. He returned to clip wires to both nipple rings, running them up and out at an angle which would force me to maintain my arched position. A similar wire was attached to the ring piercing my clitoris, pulling it out and up in the opposite direction.

Then, with my legs spread, Lei knelt between my thighs and entered me. After the sharpness of the pain, the soft, stretching of my sex and the feel of his slow piercing was luxurious and I sighed and closed my eyes that I might focus more of my attention on the movement of his erection through the soft folds of my pussy.

He was soon deep within me, and his hands moved over

my bowed frame as he thrust in and out with a long, slow stroke. His hips pushed against my thighs with a force which grew with his pleasure, and my body was soon jarred and jerking repeatedly against the biting pull of the wires pinning my nipples and clitoris in place. Still, despite the rippling pains which washed over me, his thrusting penis soon brought me to another climax, and the repeated stinging pains were like flashes in the darkness as I writhed under his touch.

As he finished he stood up, and then left me there on the floor. I heard him talking, but as it was in Mandarin I could not know of what he spoke. Minutes later there was a soft tapping at the door and Lei's barked order opened it to admit Lan, the young Vietnamese slave with the pert round breasts, and Chyou and her large bouncing breasts.

They giggled as they dropped their robes, and Master Lei gathered them into his arms as all three moved past me and into the attached bathroom. I could hear the water being run, and more giggles as the aching in my back continued to slowly gain ground on what remained of the passion my orgasms had left behind. I could relax a small portion of the effort required to remain in my unnatural position, but only by allowing it to be taken up by the pull of my hair against my tailbone. Yet such was the aching in my spine that I slowly allowed myself to do this, ignoring the rising sting in my scalp.

My nipples and clitoris were all straining and stretched out from my body, and each time I eased the tautness of my bow the stinging grew hotter and sharper so that I must again force my chest or loins up and outward.

After a time which seemed like hours the three returned, walking past me as if I did not exist, and the two girls scrambled into Lei's enormous bed beside him. There was more giggling and talk among them, but if it concerned me I could not, of course, tell. Nor could I see them from where I was, or at least, where my head was.

I could tell from the sound of the groans and sighs, however, that either they were pleasuring each other, or Master Lei was using one. I felt dismayed at this, for it dashed my hopes of quick release, and also made me oddly jealous.

It seemed forever before the moans and groans reached their peak and subsided, and then another eternity before the two girls, giggling, slipped off the bed and onto the floor around me, then began to tickle and stroke my body. Chyou licked at my stretched out clitoris while Lan began to tongue my nipples and roll the swollen areolas in her fingers.

I endured this rather than being pleasured by it, for the discomfort and ache had risen too high to be overtaken, and I felt enormous relief as the two finally unclipped the lines from my rings, untied my wrists and ankles, and then tugged the donut shaped hook from my rectum. I let out a long ecstatic groan as I was finally permitted to relax my rigid position. I made my way back to my room, bent like an ancient crone, as the two girls remained behind with Master Lei, and stretched out on my bed for some time before falling asleep.

In the morning my back still ached, and I was surprised, and even, to some degree, proud to see the long thin welts which covered the front of my body from thigh to throat, criss-crossing my belly, abdomen and breasts in many places. The pain was not great, at least as compared to the feel of receiving them, so I had no difficulty in controlling it as I massaged a soft, healing balm against my skin.

Each day held lessons in behaviour and language, as well as various duties related to Master Lei and his guests. But I was not worked beyond my means. I had time for long baths, for walks in the garden, and then after a time, for visits into the town below. These visits were always accompanied, of course, usually by Kira and often by one of the Governor's guards. We would walk among the shops in the marketplace

164

and Kira would explain the products I examined as the shopkeepers and their customers stared at me in frank amazement.

The people considered me a sort of courtesan, rather than a slave. They, after all, had no more freedom than I, and considerably less pleasant surroundings in which to live out their lives. They could not leave their cities, towns, villages and farms, nor contact anyone else outside the province even should they know of such a person. They could work only at what they had been assigned, and their lives hung on the whims of the governor as surely as did my own.

So while they seemed to realize that I was not present of my own free will, the very nature of their society meant this did not serve as any great distinction to their cultural norm. They did, of course, think of me as a woman of sex, but the concept of this is simply not translatable for western minds. They had not been exposed to centuries of puritan Christian teachings on the nature of sex and sexuality, so there was little condemnation in that respect. On the other hand the Asians value virginity in unmarried women to such an extent that a girl known to have been raped had little, if any, prospects for marriage.

There was, moreover, a strange fixation and fascination with western women, and blondes in particular, for their rumoured high level of sexuality. This came from their gleanings of western culture, in particular old American movies, and gave them, and indeed, all Asians, the belief that blonde women were insatiable sexual animals who were in an unending state of heat, constantly longing for their next coupling.

So each time I went down into the town I was the subject of intense attention from townspeople in the area, and would often be followed by giggling groups of children, or hot-eyed young men imagining me out of my robe.

Kira would speak to and for me during these early visits,

for a few daring people would invariably ask questions about me. She would also communicate with those in the markets and shops when we desired some article or service of them. Both of us were, of course, slaves, but the townspeople regarded us as far above them in station, simply due to our association with the Governor, and we could take any object we chose on a whim without causing resentment.

The city outside the palace was bleak, most of the newer buildings built by the government were cheap, ugly and of low quality, and the lives of the people that of what I as a westerner would term extreme poverty. Yet they seemed no less happy for their lack of such basic possessions as electricity and running water. And the country in which they lived was immensely beautiful, with lush green forests rising high along the mountains which rose on all sides. Some of those forests had been cut down to make room for farming, often poppy farming, and on one whole side of the valley the mountainsides were terraced halfway up their lengths.

On hearing of poppy growing I realized the connection between Lei and the drug people of New York, and was amazed anew at how such a thing could lead me from my home and schooling to a life as a sexual slave in a Chinese palace. Surely, I thought, the authorities in Peking did not permit such things. Surely someone would find out and sweep down to arrest the man. And yet he obviously had no such fears.

As I gained more possession of Mandarin I was able to interact more with those around me, with the other slave girls, first, then with others of the servants in the palace. I learned there was a feeling of awe and universal lust directed towards us by most of the male servants, along with some resentment at being unable to sample our services. Among the female servants was a mixture of jealousy at our beauty and ease of life, disapproval of our sexual exploits and some of the same awe the men held.

Because of this, interaction between slaves and servants was limited to idle conversations in areas like the dining hall and occasions when our duties brought us into some slight contact.

The higher servants, however, the Governor's more important bureaucrats and aids, regarded us as spoils of status, rare symbols of the governor's favour, and so we were, to some extent, the subject of political manoeuvring. This was directed at Master Lei, of course, for we had no choice whatever in who was presented with our persons or in what manner or for what time. Because of my novelty I was the most cherished and sought after favour, and knowing this, Lei, outside of occasional parties, rarely loaned me to anyone.

As my language skills continued to grow I became quite knowledgeable about the local power struggles and the politics and personalities of anyone close to the seat of power. I can't say it was not a source of pride to be considered a great sign of favour and status, and despite my English upbringing I too felt a certain swaggering superiority over mere ordinary women as I moved about the palace.

I was, of course, quite demure around those with power, but as to lesser servants, well, they were practically invisible to those with power, while I was a much sought after prize. So it was easy to dismiss their importance. I do not mean to say I treated them badly, though some of the other girls did, but I did feel a certain casual contempt for their unimportance in the scheme of things.

We slave girls were on the arms and laps, or sometimes the beds, of the men of great power every day, after all, giggling with them and sharing food, while the servants were lucky to catch glimpses of one striding down the halls.

And yet still we were slaves, and there were limits beyond which we ventured only at great risk. Chyou and Jin did this one day while laying about the 'harem', bored and sipping idly at wine while playing cards. One of the servant girls, new and young, ventured into the room with a mop and pail, timid and awed at being in the presence of the governor's notorious and beautiful sex toys.

She was quite a pretty thing, however, with wide brown eyes and a lovely, lithe young body beneath her awkward, bulky servant's dress. Chyou, always more arrogant than the others due to her large breasts, and how the men lusted after them, noticed the girl and decided to make sport of her.

As Jin related to us afterwards Chyou called the girl over in an arrogant voice and proceeded to taunt her on her alleged unattractiveness. Then, in her temerity, ordered the girl to undress that they could see what value lay beneath her clothes. The girl, despite her humiliation, had not dared to disobey, and had slowly removed her peasant dress and underthings to stand trembling before the two 'great ladies' in only her skin.

Chyou and then Jin had stripped themselves, the better to compare their bodies, and Chyou had made much of the girl's small breasts as compared to her own, taunting and ridiculing her. Then, amused at the girl's mortified appearance, had forced her to lie back and had begun to fondle and stroke her body. The girl, though rigid with humiliation, had not dared to protest as Chyou and Jin had so intimately explored her, as it turned out virginal body.

Even when Chyou had straddled her head, pinning her arms back with her strong legs, she had not dared to refuse the woman's demand that she perform on her sex, and after much sneering instruction and pulling of hair the girl had managed to bring Chyou to climax with her tongue.

Even this abuse might have been tolerated, had not Chyou (or so Jin claimed), then wrestled the girl onto her knees and as Jin held her, gleefully used the end of the mop to remove the sign of her virginity. As if this were not sufficient they had bound her in position, bottom raised, legs back, and then sought out nearby male servants to perform on her. Seven or eight male servants were brought back and 'ordered' to perform on the sobbing girl (although I have much doubts any had to be asked more than once) before one of Master Lei's senior managers happened by and put a stop to things.

The result of this was that the next morning, in the dining hall before the assembled servants, both girls were flogged, and spent much of the remainder of the day on their knees on a central table, arranged awkwardly for the appreciation of the servants.

The two sobbing girls had been forced to climb atop the table and kneel on all fours facing opposite ends while Gahn Mai, the Governor's senior servant, placed thick wooden shafts at the entrance to Chyou's rectum and Jin's pussy. Each shaft was two feet long, and after each had been slowly driven halfway up into each girl's belly the two were made to back against each other, and the opposite end of each shaft was forced into the second girl.

They were forced back until their buttocks were flat together, the two thick shafts forced deep into their soft, warm bellies. Their ankles were bound together. Their wrists were pulled straight back along their bodies and bound together, and their long braided hair was pulled tightly up and back and also bound together.

Though neither girl was pierced as I was, thin twine was bound tightly around their nipples, pulled straight down with some force, and then through a ring driven into the table there to meet up with the twine bound to the other. Thus any movement by one pulled against the nipples of the other. A small, two-sided clip then snapped closed around first Chyou's clitoris, and then Jin's, binding them even closer together even as they squirmed and bawled in pain.

Worse still, from the sense of violated pride, each girl was then left in place with orders to please any man who might approach them with her mouth. With their hair pulled

169

back so tightly their mouths were unable to close without pain in any case, and the palace servants took great pleasure in watching them take even lowly gardeners and labourers into their mouths and throats.

Lines of men of all ages formed to either side of the table, while female servants lagged back, giggling and snickering at their discomfort. Many of the men took pleasure in jerking them to and fro to hear their cries as their nipples or clitorii were tugged and stretched, and both girls spent a miserable day from which they were quite some time in recovering. Their voices were raw whispers for many days to come, and it was weeks before their jaws and throats stopped protesting the misuse to which they had been subjected.

Of course, this put them a considerable distance ahead of the servant girl, who, as I understand it, was soon afterwards disowned by her family and treated with scorn and derision by the other servants. Although she was an attractive girl Master Lei did not choose to make any use of her himself, instead having her driven to the edge of his lands and discarded there.

I felt this to be quite unfair and even foolish, but of course, did not make protest. I had never reached the level of arrogance some of the other slave girls had towards the lesser servants, but what arrogance I had learned eased considerably after that day. I was always thereafter quite polite to any servant I encountered, and reminded of my own uncertain position and what damage I could do to theirs.

And yet, my learning, my attempts to understand the Chinese languages and people, were for naught. Like all men of limitless power and reach Lei soon had other women arriving to please him, willing or unwilling. And a few months later he bartered me to another Governor even further to the west, and I was placed aboard a large riverboat making the journey through the immensity of the Jinshu mountains. The scenery was breathtaking in its beauty, distracting me from my unhappiness at being taken from the life I had come to know, the friends I had grown fond of.

But I was a slave, and had no say in such decisions. I had no idea why Master Lei had decided to give me to Governor Chow, nor what price he asked in return, nor was I to ever know. In fact, I never met Governor Chow, for after weeks of floating through the rough country of western China I learned that he had no desire to even look upon me. And certainly had neither need nor desire for my services. In fact, the impression I gained from overhearing the words of his assistant was that the very idea of a sexual slave struck him as particularly disgusting.

Nevertheless, as a practical man, and one who recognized the weaknesses of others, he had gone to some difficulty to obtain my person so that he could, in turn, gift me to another powerful man even further to the west. As we were almost on the Burmese border this caused me some confusion, but it emerged the governor whom I was destined to serve was an Indian governor.

I had thought myself entirely resigned to my life as a sexual slave, but it seemed I was mistaken. For when I overheard my ultimate destination I felt a tight clenching of my heart and my pulse began to race with anticipation. India was a free country, with many British and other westerners within its borders. Were I taken there, surely the chances of my making my plight known would be greatly increased. Furthermore the authorities would not tolerate this sort of abuse as they did here.

And so I was in quite good spirits as we continued down the river, and spent much time smiling at the beauty of the lush green mountains which slid past on either side, at the small waves rippling away from the bow of the slow-moving boat, and at the people and animals along the shore.

The sailors, if one could describe them with such a term, found me of immense curiosity, and whenever I was in sight

171

would stare at me with wide eyes, as if I were a strange and exotic beast.

In a way, I suppose I was. How many blonde English solicitors-in-training did a provincial Chinese riverboat man encounter during his life? Arrogant in my position as a valued commodity, not to mention British, I hardly deigned to notice them, yet was aware of their eyes constantly upon me.

One evening, after the sun had set, and the boat had tied up to the shore in a cleared space, I removed my robe and, nude, made my way into the water that I might wash myself. I could not honestly say I was unaware of the eyes upon me, nor claim to feel no measure of excitement and pride at their awe. I bathed casually, pretending an aloofness I did not feel, and hiding the quiver of arousal within my loins.

After all, there I was, alone, a white woman in the deepest mountains and jungles of China, with a dozen sets of hungry male eyes upon my naked flesh. And yet they dared not touch me, for to do so risked worse than death were the governor to discover. And so I was free to tease and taunt them with my beauty and sexuality, free of any fears that they might approach me and force me to satisfy the lusts I raised in them.

I had little to occupy my time with. The boatmen spoke a dialect which made conversation with us all but hopeless, and were a primitive and unsophisticated group in any case. There was one guard present, but he was an older man who glared at me whenever I approached, sullen, no doubt, at being forced to take himself away from the glories of the palace and endure the long and boring boat ride alongside me. The scenery, while beautiful, became monotonous, and I grew bored without my books to read, or any male to satisfy.

During the day it was too hot to do very much but sit still. I had attempted to remove my robe on occasion, but the guard had evidently been directed to ensure this did not happen. This was not for reasons of decency, of course, but so that my pale white flesh would not be darkened and thus the governor's gift somehow diminished. I wore the robe at all times while under the sun, as well as a wide-brimmed silk hat to shade my face.

At night, however, I could do what I wished, and began to strip entirely to do exercises on the shore or the deck of the boat. The eyes of the boatmen would fix upon me as I did so, and their jaws would grow slack as they followed my every movement. I often positioned my body in exaggerated poses simply to amuse myself by teasing them, and drew a measure of excitement from this at the way they shifted and twisted as they sat to hide their erections.

Even as I did this I tried to make excuses for my behaviour, but inside I realized that it was mere exhibitionism, for I had definitely become an exhibitionist during my time in China. Kira and my other sister slaves had been bemused by my response to public nudity and sex, coming as they did from societies where nudity was more common and less associated with sexuality.

Yet even as frequent as my public exposure had become - frequent enough that it no longer embarrassed or humiliated me to be seen in the nude by however many people - I still felt an intense rush of wickedness, of the forbidden, my schoolgirl moral teachings all telling me that no good or decent girl ever showed off her privates in public.

Still, the atmosphere of the palace had been so hedonistic, at least around we slave girls, that there was less arousal because of the casual acceptance of such nudity by all around me. Yet only a few days away from the palace, spent among more common men with more ordinary sensibilities, and I was basking in the forbidden nature of my exposure, revelling in the shock and arousal they so obviously felt at my public display.

One evening, after my exercises and swim had been completed, I positioned myself at the rear of the boat, atop some low crates, and there spread my legs wide, opened my robe fully, and began to pleasure my body. Although I was not within sight of anyone I recognized that one of the boatmen could happen by at any moment, and the wickedness of my behaviour lent excitement to my fingers as they stroked against my sex.

My nipples were erect, the areolas puffed out behind them, my breasts swelling rapidly as my fingers danced along my soft slit, and I began to breathe more quickly as the heat quickly rose within me. I leaned back, looking upwards at the long dark shadow of the mountains behind me, hearing the lapping of water against the boat and feeling its gentle vibrations.

And then the feel of feet moving on the deck.

My fingers rubbed more quickly, even as a slow flush rose to my face. I was behaving wickedly, sluttishly. These were not the sophisticated, corrupt, and jaded men of the palace, but simple peasants. To behave in such a manner around them was unconscionable!

And yet that very fact roused the desire within me, knowing how such nudity, such open display of sexual self-gratification would shock any of these common men. And so as I felt the steps grow closer I arched my back and drew my head back further, panting softly, as I slid two fingers into my body and began to stroke rapidly in and out.

The vibrations ceased, and I could almost feel the shock of whoever had spotted me. I could see a darker shadow against the side of the wheelhouse, and a powerful thrum of excitement washed over my body. I was so wicked! So terrible! So sluttish! What he must think of me!

And as the passion flowed through my body I began to writhe there on the top of the case, greeting my approaching orgasm under the eyes of my secret watcher.

And then his resolve broke, and to my shock the dark shadow was upon me, rough hands grasping my thighs and tearing them apart. Startled but dazed, I looked up into shadow, his back blocking what little light came from the distant fire. A strong hand slapped against my mouth, jamming my head backwards and over the other side of the case, then his cock thrust deeply into my body, easily slicing through the moist folds of my sex as he buried himself within me.

My legs jerked as I sought balance, but I had no real desire to fight him off. Unfortunately, he did not know this, and was rough as he pinned me down and drove himself into my body. A dirty rag was forced into my mouth, and then my slim wrists were pinned back as he redoubled his efforts. His breathing was harsh and ragged as his cock stabbed into me with pounding strokes, and his hips ground furiously against my thighs and buttocks as he used me with frantic desire.

The sudden attack had startled and disturbed the flow of my passion, but now as he forced himself into me and took control of my body I felt the heat rising once more, the power of my sexual need redoubling as I groaned under the brutal heat of his lust.

I writhed helplessly, though with no desire to escape, and he slapped at my face, then clawed at my breasts. I cried out softly, groaning in pain and pleasure, nearly swooning with the severity of pleasure and passion tearing through my body. He rode me wildly through it, and then even as the pleasure slowly began to fade, was gone, darting back into the shadows.

I sprawled back, gasping, pawing at the rag in my mouth to pluck it free, then drawing in deep breaths of warm, humid air. I moaned weakly, letting arms and head fall back once again even as my legs drooped down across the sides of the crate. I felt a deeply sated sense of contentment, as if being brutally fucked by a stranger was the fulfilment of my passions.

175

I pulled my head up, not without difficulty, and twisted my body so that I could prop my back against another crate. I lay still but for my heaving chest, wondering what kind of a woman I had become, what within me responded so powerfully to such raw, animalistic sex, to the savage use of my body.

I recalled my days at university, and the care I had taken to dress myself attractively without risking condemnation. How bizarre that I had now become a creature aroused by publicly exposing herself, by rousing men to such extent they lost control of themselves and attacked me sexually.

What would happen if I ever did find myself back home? How would I control this burning need to expose myself, to degrade myself, to be used so violently by men?

But then I realized this was not a consideration I really needed to devote my thoughts to, for my freedom, even if I did wind up in India, was unlikely.

I sat up and closed my robe, giving a little shudder at the warmth and sensitivity of my breasts, then slid off the crate and went to my mat to find my sleep.

CHAPTER TEN

My first introduction to India was not pleasant. The boat stopped at a small, dirty town and I and my guard disembarked. I was, of course, excited and curious about this new land and its people, but that excitement was tempered by anxiety about my own future. That anxiety was little aided by the sight of the townspeople, who seemed quite stricken by poverty, and moved about with eyes cast down and faces filled with wariness and fear whenever they chanced to be near a figure of authority.

The car waiting for us was ancient and dirty, one of the windows cracked, the springs in the seats broken, the fabric much stained and torn. We set out through the town, and then onto a dirt track which would have been quite flattered to be termed a road. The track was filled with holes so that the car frequently lurched from side to side, and bounced up and down. Several times it drove off the road into fields adjoining it as the driver spent long periods of time with his eyes glued to the rear view mirror staring at me, rather than upon the track itself.

The man was as dirty as the car, wearing a ragged looking white robe which resembled little so much as a very cheap, plain nightgown. If either it or its wearer had recent acquaintance with either soap or water I would have been much surprised.

The drive took almost two hours, most of it spent with my hand tightly grasping the handle of the door to prevent my head from bouncing upwards against the roof. The heat was appalling, and I was panting and sweating terribly within the first ten minutes. I longed to open my robe somewhat but feared the driver would lose all control were I to do so.

The final quarter of our journey was spent on a paved road, but again, such description greatly overstates the case. The pavement was much cracked and patched (though not patched sufficiently) and there were uncountable potholes scattered along its length. The car shook and rattled violently as the driver increased speed, and as his eyes continued to monitor my person as opposed to the road ahead I wondered at our chances of reaching our destination intact. For we now passed similar cars and trucks racing past in the opposite direction, and I had little confidence the rusting, creaking automobile would survive a collision of any force.

At long last we reached the city of Rankghar, as dismal an assault on the eyes and nose as anything I had yet encountered. The streets were filled with beggars, many of them terribly scarred, blinded, or with missing limbs. Several of them raced alongside the car, shouting and gesticulating, holding forth their hands for alms as the driver cursed at them and swung the wheel violently back and forth in an attempt to hit them.

The smell of human and animal waste rotting under a blinding sun clogged my nostrils, and made my eyes water as we dodged in and out of narrow streets behind trucks, tractors, ox drawn carts, and assorted mobs of people with livestock.

Finally, we arrived at our destination, a singularly unimpressive pair of wooden gates held together by a rusting chain. A ragged looking man with a rifle slung over a shoulder slouched towards the driver's door, then leaned in to speak with our driver. The conversation lasted far too long, given the heat, and occasioned much snickering and ogling of my person.

Finally, the man slouched back to the gates, unwrapped the chain from one of the gates (which leaned weakly outward) and dragged them open. The driver raced the engine and the car lurched forward. We found ourselves in a paved back court beneath a tall, squat, ugly looking building. A variety of cars and trucks were parked about, most of them in no better condition than ours. Off to one side was a large gathering of garbage cans, the trash overflowing onto the ground and the smell assaulting my nostrils.

Another ragged guard approached the car, and more snickering occurred, while the Chinese guard who had accompanied me exited the car and motioned me to follow. He spoke to the second guard in a language with which I was unfamiliar, and the pair then led me through an open door and into the bowels of the building.

The hall inside was narrow, with floors, wall, and roof of chipped, cracked concrete, and bare light bulbs dangling overhead. We met up with another guard, this one wearing a cap which appeared to signal he was an officer of some sort. He examined papers the Chinese guard presented, and then signed them. From there he roughly took me by the arm and led me away.

We did not, as I had expected, go upwards, but rather, took a dark stone stairwell down into the bowels of the building. We made three turnings, going ever deeper, before emerging in a dark, damp, and yet refreshingly cool stone corridor which, other than its temperature, had little else to recommend it. In all other respects it was similar to the one above.

We turned a corner to another similar corridor, and I saw with some trepidation that the walls on either side were lined with low, narrow, strongly built doors, each of which had a barred window and a heavy bolt on the outside. The guard led me to one such and opened it, and I my heart sank as I saw that it was indeed a cell of some sort.

There was a bare bulb in the ceiling, of low power. It lit a stone room no more than six feet square, empty save for a hole in one corner, and a thin and filthy mat in the other. The guard pushed me inside, and followed, then thrust me abruptly against the wall. He leered at me as his hands tore open my robe, and his eyes widened with lust as he beheld my nudity. I could almost smell the heat and lust he exuded as his hands reached out and almost reverently cupped my breasts, then began to squeeze them with a hot urgency which seemed to transmit itself to me through my breasts.

His fingers were hard and hot, and my breasts ached as they dug deep into the soft flesh, kneading and pinching it. Yet it was a hot ache, an ache which seemed to feed on his own lust, on his obvious excitement for me. He was a crude, thuggish man, dirty, with foul-smelling breath, yet I was at his mercy, and as his hands raced over my body I felt a fiery ache beginning to rise in my loins.

He spoke rapidly in Hindi, which I could not, of course, understand, and his eyes darted back and forth between the doorway and my body. Due to the heat I had braided my long hair into a single tail. This he took hold of, using it to roughly yank my head back, and then jammed his warm and dirty mouth against my own as he continued to maul my breast.

He thrust me back with a further leer, feral eyes still watching the door warily. He said something else, then turned and casually stripped off my robe completely, followed by my slippers. He smirked as he looked upon my nudity fully, then pushed me back against the hard stone wall. I now noticed the heavy iron clamps, ancient with rust, bolted to the wall. One, larger than the others, was almost at the proper height for my throat - almost. I was forced onto my toes as he swung the clamp closed, a thick, curved iron collar which pulled in tightly against my neck just beneath my jaw, and was bolted into place there.

My arms were raised up and out and similar heavy shackles snapped around them, bolting them directly against the wall, as well. There were lower shackles, but my captor hesitated, then went to the door. He gazed up and down the hallway, then returned quickly, undoing his dirty trousers.

I felt my stomach fluttering with a mixture of anticipation and disgust. He truly was a filthy beast, yet he was clearly about to use me. Bound with heavy, cold iron to the hard stone wall I felt very much the helpless prisoner as he pushed his groin in against me. He spoke again, softly, muttering, jamming his hardness against my soft sex. He forced my legs further apart, then forced himself into me. This left me half hanging from the heavy metal shackles, which pushed in harshly against my soft wrists.

He used me roughly, grunting with pleasure and obvious relish, thrusting furiously up into my body as his dirty fingers dug into the soft flesh of my buttocks. He panted and gasped as he drove his loins against me, his eyes nearly closed as he threw his hips forward. It took under a minute for him to give a shudder and release his seed.

He drew back with a groan, stood still a moment, then quickly did up his trousers and bolted my ankles against the wall. Then he was gone, leaving me in place in the dark, hot, fetid cell.

"Welcome to India," I whispered to myself.

My body was already overheated from both the air and the quick, ruthless sex, and I stared about me feeling as though I were, for the first time since my initial capture, in the life of a sexual slave. For this was the sort of thing I had expected on hearing I was to be taken to China, the kind of thing I had imagined was the fate of any sex slave. Yet things had been so very different at Governor Lei's palace that my belief in the treatment of slaves had been challenged. Now I was brought back to earth. As in China, I was in a rural back province where the governor enjoyed great autonomy and, I guessed, little fears of close supervision from the central government.

Unlike Governor Lei, however, and going strictly on what I had observed to date in his subjects, servants and cities, he seemed to exhibit rather more of the type of behaviour one would expect from a third world dictator. Nor did there appear to be the type of wealth that Governor Lei had access to.

181

While it was true I had only seen the rear of the building under which I was held, and its lower levels, it bespoke a considerably poorer man than Governor Lei, and the city around it seemed to echo that theme.

I stood unmoving, locked against the harsh stone, hoping my stay was to be short but with growing fear that that was not to be so.

After a time cramps began to move through my legs and thighs, and my back became stiff and sore. My lower jaw soon ached from the pressure of the heavy collar bolted around my throat, but I had not the strength to keep myself on my toes for long.

With nothing to exercise my eyes upon my ears began to take in the sounds of this place, and they were far from encouraging. Not far away I could hear a moaning which bespoke pain and hopelessness, and then further, a distant cry which came again and again, a man in some considerable pain. The cries grew louder and more frenzied, then stopped abruptly.

The sudden scuff of feet on the stone outside caught my attention, and a moment later the bolt was thrown back with a loud metallic protest. The light snapped on, and I narrowed my eyes, blinking and squinting as two men stepped in, unshackled me, and dragged me out of the cell.

I was led back up the hall, then up the stairs once more. Neither of the men talked to me, and both clung tightly to one arm, as if I would break free and somehow escape. We climbed several flights of stairs, more than I could recall descending, then emerged into a narrow corridor which led, only a short distance away, to still more stairs.

I was in good shape due to my constant exercises, but was still panting in the heat and humidity as we reached the top. A guard there opened a steel door and I was taken through to a far more luxuriously appointed hall. The roof was still low, and the walls of dull, institutional concrete, but the floors were covered in thick, brightly woven rugs, and tapestries covered most of the walls. The doors were of polished wood, with enormous, old-fashioned keyholes beneath the handles, little windows atop the frames.

Inside the room I was taken was an unfortunate collection of what looked suspiciously like purpose made, heavy wooden frames and objects designed to cause people pain, or at least, to hold them in restraint while pain was given them.

In the centre of the room was a three dimensional square frame made up of two by fours with an overhead lattice. Hooks and rings ran along all the inside edges of the frame, and a small chain was attached to a hook in the direct centre of the overhead lattice.

To the left was a narrow frame of polished wood. A triangular piece of wood a foot in length sat atop a narrow metal post. A wooden penis carved with ridges sat in the centre of this wood, thrusting upwards. Shackles were bolted to a pair of metal posts below. Beyond that was a wooden beam laid on its edge, shackles attached to the metal legs supporting it.

To the right stood a flat upright frame with two small holes about where a girl's breasts might be, and what resembled a large, thick, carved wooden penis sticking upwards at a very sharp, almost vertical angle. There was a second such object at the top of the frame, angled out and then down, on a hinged arm. A pair of pegs thrust out horizontally on either side just a little below the lower 'penis', spaced widely apart, with shackles attached to the sides of the frame a little below these.

There were hooks running all along the walls, and an amazing assortment of flogs, crops, switches, whips and paddles hung from these. Below this was a shelf filled with an untidy assortment of leather and chain restraints.

And standing in the middle of all this was a tall, very

thin, greasy looking man with a ferret face, slicked back hair and an eager expression. He spoke to the guards, who released my arms and then stepped back. At another word from him they left, closing the heavy door behind.

I did not know who this man was, but of course, did my best to appear pleasant, smiling in my most obedient and helpful way.

He spoke softly, but coolly as he stepped towards me. I could not understand a word, however, nor did he seem to care. He examined me with a smirk then slapped my face. I staggered back a half step, then straightened myself. He said something, but of course, I could not understand. Again he slapped my face. This time I held my position, and he glared.

He moved away from me, to a small table set against one wall, and took from it a pair of leather gloves, which he donned. He returned to me, again speaking low and coolly, then took my braided hair and quite roughly yanked me around to the frame on the right side of the room.

He pushed me, face first, against it, so that my breasts pushed against the small holes, and began to slowly push through. He slapped at my buttocks, shouting at me and gripping the wooden cock. I realized he was ordering me to mount the thing, yet I was at a loss at how to do so.

Then he showed me two places at either side of the frame where one could step. I did so, awkwardly lifting myself up a foot or so, gripping the top of the frame for support as he held my hips and manoeuvred me against the penis.

I felt it nudging my soft lips, and swallowed nervously as I began to settle downwards. I bent my legs, feeling the pressure of the wooden penis as it was forced between my labia and penetrated my body. I felt the hard, cool wood sliding forward, pushing aside the soft walls of my sex, forcing my tube open as I slid lower. With the thing halfway up inside me I was able to step on the floor once again, and bring my legs together, then settle slowly downwards.

His hand pushed against my back, pressing my body harder against the upright wood, and I felt my breasts pushing against those two holes once again. Neither of the holes was much wider than a teacup, but my breasts were soft and malleable. Then he moved behind the frame and I felt his fingers on the other side, pinching at my flesh, grasping my nipples tightly and tugging my breasts through the holes.

He worked his fingers, pulling and squeezing, pinching and twisting until my chest was flat against the frame and my breasts had been entirely worked through the holes, swelling out on the other side. Something just on the other side of the frame then closed in around them and I cried out at the pressure which pinched in on all sides. (My breasts were squeezed into a hole no wider than a silver dollar, bloating out painfully beyond that like overfilled balloons).

I felt a slap at one breast, and cried out. Another slap struck my other breast, and both began to sting and throb. I could not see through the flat frame, and imagined all manner of terrible tortures being done to my sensitive breasts. Yet I could do nothing to defend them, nor even pull away.

He came around the frame once again and drew my arms together behind my back, then placed a collar around my throat, and attached a small chain to my wrist restraints so my hands were locked up high beneath my neck.

He returned to the other side of the frame, and I stood anxiously, my breasts throbbing. I gasped as I felt a touch, yet it was soft. I felt my swollen nipples pinched and rolled between his fingers, plucked and twisted lightly. I felt the rings pulled outward so that my nipples strained, then felt them undone and removed. A moment later something soft struck my left breast with a light 'Crack' of noise. It stung, yet the sensation was not heavy enough to be termed pain. Whatever had struck seemed no more than an inch or so wide, probably leather and, almost certainly capable of causing much more pain.

It struck again, again directly against my nipple, then again, and again. It switched to my other breast, my other nipple, and began to alternate. Both nipples were quivering and swollen, hot and buzzing with pain and hot, dark, sexual electricity. He halted, and I felt his mouth closing around one of them, taking it and the areola, as well as the centre of my taut, swollen breast into his mouth. I felt the heat and moisture of his mouth around my breast, his tongue lapping at my quivering nipple. Then his teeth drawing in, pinching lightly but repeatedly so that my flesh ached.

His mouth drew back and the hard, stinging blows resumed as I wriggled and writhed on the other side of the frame. The wooden cock was a thick, immoveable thing within my abdomen, and every movement of my body jerked my soft pussy sleeve around it, causing me to gasp and groan as my sex was stretched and strained. I had eased down from my toes and found that I now had almost the entire length of it within me. Yet as I neared bottom I found that the space between it and the frame from which it protruded narrowed, as well, until just above the base only a thin sliver of space remained.

And the very top of my sex was caught in it, pinched against a round little lump which by design or chance stuck out from the frame in just the right place to jam against my soft clitoris. I raised myself up as the pressure against my clitoris sent a throbbing pain through my body, moaning anew as my toes and the balls of my feet protested.

He continued slapping my nipples, and both were now on fire. My breasts were throbbing with heat, as well, being squeezed and constricted at the chest, and my nipples were ultra sensitive little coals sitting at their centre.

My body was jerking against the frame, my breasts tugging against the tight, remorseless grip of the frame, unable to pull free. I was puffing and panting, trying to fight through the pain to the sexual heat I had held only minutes earlier.

He stopped, and my breasts throbbed on the other side of the frame. A moment later he appeared around the other side once more. He examined me, then reached between my legs, feeling the base of the wooden penis where it impaled me.

He was carrying a short crop, much like those I had seen before, save it had a soft, wide, tip. He used the crop on my buttocks now, the narrow flexible body of it striking across my bottom harshly, causing me to jerk against the frame and cry out. He smiled at this, then pressed his body against me. I felt his trousers drop and his manhood spring upwards, its warmth sliding along my inner thigh.

He forced my legs apart, which brought me down harder on the wooden penis and pulled at my breasts. Then he forced himself against my anus, jamming the hard, knobby head of his penis forward until he was able to force my sphincter muscle apart and enter me. He thrust himself in and up with hard, short little jabbing strokes that sent his hard penis climbing higher and higher into my body, and soon his hips were pressing flat against my buttocks as he gripped either side of the frame and ground his body against me.

The frame was not a great deal wider than my body, and he slid his hands around it, able to cup my taut breasts easily, pinching my swollen nipples as he rolled his hips slowly, twisting his cock about within my anus. He whispered into my ear once again, soft words which were not, I was sure, flattering, then began to pump his hips in and out.

I was almost fully impaled upon the wooden penis now, and my clitoris ached as it was caught against that hard little bump. Yet worse was to come.

He reached above to the arm which hung from the top of the frame, swinging it down so that the long, thick wooden penis it held was against my mouth, then gripped my braided hair and forced my head back. He pulled the arm down further, until the wood was jammed against my lips. A moment later I tasted the hard wood as it filled my mouth. And then he pulled lower still, so that it entered my mouth.

My throat ached as the wooden plug was forced into it, inch after inch sliding through my lips, over my tongue, and thence downwards. Its length was prodigious, and it pushed past my throat and into my very chest before my lips were crushed against the base of the arm holding it. At that point he used two straps, one to either side of the penis, and attached to the arm, to clip tightly to the sides of my collar and thus lock me in place.

He then focused his attention on sodomising me, working his hips with more strength, his cock sliding in longer, more forceful strokes until his hips were pounding against my backside, crushing my pelvis against the frame. He reached around the frame once more, pinching and twisting my nipples, slapping at my sore, swollen breasts, then spreading his fingers wide to encompass them and squeezing them harshly as he pounded his erection up into my rectum.

I had long since mastered the ability to breathe even while my throat was filled. However, the hardness of the wooden penis was far different from the softness of a man's cock, which, however rigid, was far and away less bruising and uncomfortable. My throat began to ache terribly, and the variety of pains assaulting my body began to give me a slightly disembodied sensation so that I had the sudden dazed thought that the wooden penis was, in fact, all one piece, that I had been impaled literally, the hard wood thrusting straight up through my body and emerging from between my lips.

Oddly, this not only did not frighten me but a crackling sexual heat seemed to spread out through my body. Pinpricks of shock fluttered over my skin and my chest tightened to the point where breathing was even more difficult. I stared up at the wood which protruded from between my lips, imagining it to be the same wood which was jammed high into my belly, imagined myself spitted, skewered by its long length in the ultimate demonstration of cruelty.

My pelvis was jerking and grinding against the frame, against the hard penis inside, and against that awful bump which was rolling and pinching my clitoris, and my breasts continued to throb painfully. I moaned softly, getting cross-eyed as I stared at the wood above me, feeling the hard wood filling my throat and sliding down into my very chest.

Impaled. I was impaled. My mind swirled and tumbled, and I felt a sense of shocked delight at being so savagely wounded yet feeling so little pain. Impaled, I thought, impaled even as he sodomises me, even as his cock pounds into my body and his hands maul my breasts. A cruel man with no mercy to treat me so.

A climax welled up within me, a climax I thought surely would be my last in this life, and I imagined now that I could feel the thick round wooden post in my stomach, sliding up through my body and out of my mouth, imagined I were to be used so casually and then cast aside. I shuddered as I came, my pussy clenching repeatedly around the hard wood, my rectum squeezing down on his manhood as it thrust upwards again and again.

Sparkling lights filled the world above me, and I felt my vision swim, then fade.

I woke slowly, groaning as I stirred. I found that I lay upon the floor, and my captor, my tormentor, my new master, stood above me glancing down with an arrogant look of contempt.

I was rolled onto my belly, my sore breasts flattening beneath me, and my arms were pulled together behind my back. I was dazed, but still moaned weakly as I felt something heavy circling them just above the elbows and then drawing them forcefully back until the elbows were jammed together and my shoulders screamed.

He gripped my braided hair, dragging me along the floor

to a small cage in a corner. The cage was no more than three feet in height and length, and perhaps half that wide. It was made of heavy iron bars going both vertically and horizontally and looked strong enough to hold a lion. He opened the side of this cage and used a firm grip on my hair to force me onto my knees and then inside.

He reached behind the cage and drew out a long thick metal bar, then thrust it lengthwise through the cage a foot or so below the top. A moment later my tightly bound arms were lifted up and over this bar, then folded down across it and bound in place. The side of the cage was locked into position, and I was left like that, with my bottom held high, my face pressed against the bottom of the cage, and my arms drawn back together and folded painfully up over the bar.

I stared out through the bars, still dazed, feeling only a little aroused now at being caged, at being treated like an animal. The discomfort in my arms and shoulders was intense, and growing worse with every minute of immobility.

Soon the pain was intense and I was sobbing against the bottom of the cage, tears spilling onto the rough wooden floor. Every movement brought sharp, jagged agony to my arms and shoulders. It was the kind of pain that would drive a person mad within a short time, yet I could do nothing but endure. After an eternity my arms and shoulders became so numbed that the haze of pain dimmed and I was at last able to slow my breathing.

Yet long hours passed and I whimpered and moaned in my misery, wanting nothing but to be released from the unending pain.

I could not easily judge the passing of time in that place. But it did pass, and I became aware of movement in the room, my tormenter returned to view my agony. He opened my cage, unsnapped my arms and drew out the bar, and agony made me scream as my body finally moved. My shoulders shrieked as he roughly yanked me from the cage, and I babbled and sobbed and cried out again and again as he ignored my discomfort, and, heedless of my stiff, aching flesh, dragged me away from the cage to further his amusement.

He lifted me enough to then drop me belly-down across the padded bar. My legs were spread wide and bound tightly with rough rope that pinned them to the legs of the bar at ankle, knee and thigh. He moved behind me and passed a rope below my body, then drew it upwards. There were two loops in the rope, and as he raised them so that my dangling breasts passed through them. He pulled on the ends, tightening the harsh rope, squeezing my breasts out as he had done earlier, forcing them into fat, hard balls of flesh before he tied the rope off behind my back.

Thinner cords were tied to my nipple rings, pulled down and slid through a ring set into the floor there, then tugged sharply so that my nipples stretched, my areolas strained outwards and my breasts began to distend. Only then were the cords tied off. My head was raised up and my hair, still braided, was bound in cord and tied to a hook overhead, holding my face level.

He then fumbled free his erection and thrust it into my open mouth. I was too dazed to perform with any degree of expertise, and, indeed, had no time to even consider that I must before he had forced himself deep into my throat. From then there was no opportunity to practice the art in which I had been trained, for he used my mouth and throat roughly and crudely, his testicles swinging below as his hips worked, his skinny abdomen crushing my nose each time he drove his cock into me.

My head began to throb as he continued to thrust in and out and my vision began to fog. His abdomen continued to hammer against my face with painful and dizzying force, and I could do nothing but hope loss of consciousness would release me from my misery and pain.

Then he drew back, and his cock slipped out of my throat

with an almost audible pop as he moved behind me. A moment later he was thrusting just as savagely into my pussy, his hands slapping at my buttocks, his hips hammering against my thighs as he drove his erection into my belly with deep, powerful strokes. He halted, pulling free, but I sensed this only belatedly, my mind dizzy and confused.

The whipcrack of noise arrived with new pain, and I realized, though I could not see behind me, that he was whipping my bottom. The pain was sharp but I was too grateful for the sweet air I was now gulping through my aching throat to pay it the attention I otherwise might have.

Soon my entire backside was afire, and this penetrated my thinking enough to make me moan and whimper, yet I could only bear it.

He halted his attack, and I felt him thrusting into me once again, using his erection like a weapon to stab savagely into my body. When he finished the light disappeared, and after a time I realized I was alone. My jaw was slack, my scalp aching. The pain surrounded me and tears trickled slowly down my cheeks.

My mind fogged as it had before, and once more the fog was cleared by the sharpness of noise and movement, by rough, uncaring hands untying the cord from my hair and releasing my nipples. I was lifted upright, though my legs were still bound straight and wide, and had a moment to observe my swollen breasts, almost purple with pain, before the rope was released.

The agony was indescribable. As the ropes pulled free, as the cruel pressure binding them released, they caught fire with returning blood and I screamed raggedly through my aching throat. My captor showed no sympathy whatever, slapping and fondling my breasts, snickering at my screaming, laughing as I thrashed madly in place.

He dragged me back to the cage and heaved me into it, but this time did not bind my arms up, but contented himself with merely closing the cage door and walking away. I curled up on my side as best I could, knees drawn up against my chest, trying to shake off the memory of the stinging in my scalp which had left me with a throbbing headache. My bottom ached terribly, but that was almost reassuring in its consistency. I knew from past experience it would soon ease.

My breasts, however, continued to throb. They were quite hot and red and every movement made me wince and curse. Yet that pain too slowly eased, leaving only the continued discomfort in my shoulders. After a time, exhaustion brought an uneasy sleep. I wakened to see a bowl of water in my cage, and slurped it down eagerly, then lay down my head once more.

My shoulders ached less now, probably because they had simply gone numb, and I felt a little better. I looked out through the bars of my cage and wondered at what the immediate future held in store. This place was so far outside what I had thus far experienced I had no way to accurately predict, though I strongly suspected further punishments were my fate. I had never before been punished merely for the sadistic satisfaction of my master. Always before it had been to teach or punish me. This left me with the worrying thought that every day might bring fresh pain and misery so long as I was in this dreadful place.

Yet there was no appeal, and certainly no escape, not bound and caged as I was.

Caged. What manner of man would put a girl in a cage anyway? What kind of satisfaction did he gain from seeing me locked up in this way? I found myself reliving my times in China and wishing I could return there. I wondered what the girls were doing now.

I managed to sit up, though my head was pressed against the bars, and looked out into the room once more, staring at the various frames and wondering to which I would be guided when my new master came for me once again. There were any number which he had not used, some of which had purposes I could only guess. Why couldn't this man simply enjoy my body as others had? What need had he to give me pain and discomfort?

That was, I realized, a pointless question. He gained pleasure from my pain. This meant I would be given more pain, until, perhaps, I reached that point where my body, or perhaps, my mind, could no longer endure it.

Was I to be tortured to death or madness by this nasty little man? I recalled my feelings of impalement from the previous session, and felt stirring in my loins once again at the thought. I pictured myself impaled in that manner, displayed to all, the perfect picture of a poor, naked girl brutalized and mistreated. How sad, and yet erotic I would seem to be such a helpless victim of cruelty and evil.

My stomach grumbled and I felt a small wave of butterflies take flight within. I had not eaten since arriving in this city, and barely drunk, for that matter. Surely my captor did not intend me to die in such a mundane way. Surely my death would be accomplished through some grand and terrible punishment which would shock any who heard of it, some sinister, terribly perverse torture which would make men's cocks throb and women's nipples tighten within the cups of their bras.

The door opened and he entered, and my heart began to beat more strongly. I felt my nipples quiver lightly, still swollen from his earlier attentions. My breasts were still pinkish, the skin sensitive to even the breath of air.

He approached the cage, smirking, then opened the door and reached in, taking my hair, still in its braid, causing me to curse myself mentally for ever tying it back into such a convenient hand hold.

He spoke to me, whispering, cooing into my ear, his voice an eager, excited sniggering thing as he half dragged me towards the simple frame to the left.

This frame consisted of a thick, heavy post which rose from the floor. A horizontal steel bar perhaps two feet long was attached to one side of the post near the top. A pair of shackles were bound to each end. Another steel bar, this one vertical, and perhaps a foot long, rose straight upwards from the centre of the post, and a length of wood rested upon it. This wood was no more than a foot in length, polished, and set on its edge so that the top surface was no more than an inch wide.

I was dragged to this, and through curses and brute force was made to straddle the narrow length of wood at its top. I was just able to do this while on my toes, though the thin wood pressed up against my sex so that it forced apart my soft labia and was driven up between. A moment later loose shackles were chained to my ankles to ensure I did not dismount. There were two tall, narrow posts in front of and to the rear of me, and after my rings were replaced, my tormentor bound narrow cords to all three, attaching them to the post before me.

Above me, unseen until then, was a hook, and dangling from that hook was a long length of thick chain. He drew the chain downwards directly above my head, then, to my surprise, wrapped it around my neck, and clipped it into place. He smirked at me a moment, and then left me alone once more.

This seemed entirely too simple to me, and I looked about nervously for the source of the pain I was surely expected to receive. It took surprisingly little time for understanding to dawn, as my toes grew weaker and I was forced to drop more and more weight onto the thin edged wood I was straddling. As I did so the chain about my neck pulled in more tightly. It did not make breathing difficult, but it was apparent that any significant movement on my part, such as falling off one side or another, would cause me to choke.

The pressure of the wood against my sex was painful and

bruising, and I shifted my weight frequently in an effort to ease the pressure and pain. This only caused my entire groin to soon throb with soreness, and as I attempted to lean backwards my tailbone was soon aching as well. The wood jammed upwards towards my clitoris, as well, but though that ached slightly, it did not produce any real discomfort except in the sense that my body was beginning to respond to that darkness within my mind.

I do not know what part of me thought eroticism might be attached to my position. As I have earlier explained, I had found within myself a degree of submissiveness and masochism, a hungering for abuse and outrageous treatment. This punishment, so obviously focused on abusing my sex itself, seemed to me to be a particularly shameful thing to do to a girl, and that inspired the darkness in my soul and the feverish deviance which was now a part of me.

I eased forward slightly to ease the pull on my clitoris and nipples, as I was unable to take very much weight off my pussy I could feel it sliding heavily along the cool wood, could feel the narrow, rounded edge sawing along my bruised, aching flesh between my pubic lips. The pain sent a shudder through my body, for it held the seeds of unnatural pleasure with it. I found myself easing up on the muscles of my thighs and legs, almost unconsciously allowing more weight to fall on my sex, doing this with a soft, repeated flexing of muscles so that the wood seemed to be jabbing heavily against my groin.

I slid slowly forward again, gasping as my throbbing pussy slid along the wood. I eased back, and again the wood sawed along my sex. But I was growing rapidly more aroused now. And as I slid further back I watched the cords tighten against my rings, and felt a growing sting from my clitoris and nipples.

I relaxed my legs entirely, and all my weight came down upon that narrow edge of wood. I shuddered and closed my thighs tightly around it, arching my back slightly, working my lower hips in an attempt to slide. I could not, and pressed my toes against the floor once again, relieving some of the pressure. That relief felt heavenly, and as I slid my groin forward a gush of hot, liquid heat flooded my lower belly.

I slid forward several inches and held my position, shuddering, letting all my weight come down upon my sex, then pressed my feet down once more and slid myself backwards. It hurt, but it hurt so wonderfully I almost climaxed.

I slid back until my clitoris was straining, until my nipples ached, and then arched my back, leaning back further so that the pull on my nipples would grow even more strongly. I was being tortured, a poor, helpless, beautiful naked girl being outrageously brutalized by an evil and disgusting heathen.

I leaned forward, slightly dizzy, and felt another wave of delicious relief as the sting on my nipples eased. I let all my weight down once more, gasping and shuddering as I lifted my feet off the floor, holding them locked together at the base of the post. I let my weight ease forward and then back before finally taking some of my weight on my feet once more. Heaven! The relief was intoxicating, and I slid slowly forward, letting the wood saw along my sex. The wood was slick now, moist with the juices of my throbbing sex. Orgasm approached, hot, heavy and powerful, and I slid further forward, letting more weight fall against the wood.

Then it hit, and I shuddered, my body convulsing. I raised my feet and rode the wood, my hips and weight rocking me back and forth, my body swaying and trembling as the power of the climax swept powerfully through mind and body; the throbbing in my head from pleasure and pain. Yet I had to go on, had to continue grinding myself down upon the harsh wood for as long as the orgasm continued. Any movement back would rob me of that glorious storm of ecstasy, and I could not bear the thought.

My lower body continued to buck and hump, my head jerking back and forth, my body rocking in place. Then the climax faded, and with an explosive gasp I slid backwards, loosening the chain and drawing deep breaths.

I was sick, a sick girl. I deserved to be tortured.

Yet even as I breathlessly acknowledged this, the warm, delicious tingle of orgasm was still just barely detectable in the back of my mind, and the memory of what it had been made me willing to do anything to get it back.

I was not to be given that opportunity, for the door opened and my master walked in. He gazed me with another smirk, fondling my breasts and whispering what I imagined were threats into my ear. He bent, sliding his hand along my trembling thigh, and unfastened the chain binding my shackles. He then lifted my right leg up and back, fitting the ankle to the side of the horizontal bar behind and below my 'seat'. A moment later he lifted my left ankle, and did the same, forcing all my weight down upon my sex.

I moaned in growing discomfort, for even with the sense of sexual need still gripping me this made my pussy ache more powerfully.

I clenched my teeth and choked back a cry as the hard edge of the wood was forced up even harder between my swollen pubic lip.

He smiled, running his hand along my sex where it was split by the wood, then removed the chain from around my neck, moved behind me and seized my still braided hair. He pulled back slowly and smugly, forcing my head backwards inch by inch. As my back arched the flesh tightened across my hot, sensitive breasts, pulling much harder against the cords bound to my nipples. Soon I was looking almost straight to the roof, and then my hair was bound behind me to the rear post.

He left me again then, to try and make some accommodation with my steadily rising pain. The stinging of my nipples soon began to fade into the background as the soft, warm flesh of my groin pressed against that narrow length of wood with unrelenting pressure. I could not now do anything to ease my weight and bring myself even temporary relief. The ache grew sharper, the pain hotter, until that part of my body was afire with a terrible agony.

It was such a terrible thing to do to a woman, to attack that place which was designed to give her pleasure, to bring such crude force to bear upon that place where she was so sensitive and defenceless. And this again raised my ardour. A strange kind of fever began to run through my blood as endorphins flooded through me to fight the pain. I felt almost a sense of euphoria, a light-headedness.

He entered the room once more, accompanied by three other men. The newcomers stared at me in delight as the man who had placed me in that cruel position spoke. Pride and smugness filled his voice as he waved his hand at me, pointing towards my red breasts and outstretched nipples, then plucked the cord attached to my clitoris.

I moaned as they stared at me, shifting my weight as much as I could on the hard edged wood, rocking back and forth as the pain and pleasure warred within me. Their eyes surrounded me, staring, excited, aroused by my pain, by my nudity, by the wickedness of what was being done to me.

They touched me, my breasts, my buttocks, my hair, and fingered the rings of my clitoris and nipples. They spoke questioningly towards him, and he replied knowingly. He ran a hand along my chest, stroking my arched body, sliding his fingers between my legs to press against my burning labia where they were jammed harshly into the wood.

My body was trembling violently by then, the pain having twisted into a throbbing, aching pleasure as lust swept through my body. I felt as though I was being cleaved in half, as though the edge of the wood had shrunk to razor sharpness and was slicing slowly but surely up between my legs. Yet a kind of rapture gripped me, and every inch of my skin tingled with life and desire. Another climax roared down upon me, and I screamed, my body jerking spastically. I felt a sense of overwhelming pressure in my head, and the light began to fade out around me.

CHAPTER ELEVEN

I coughed, my throat aching, and spat out water. A moment later I opened my eyes and licked at my lips, some part of me recognizing the extreme thirst which had been gripping me since I had landed in this country. I looked up from where I lay on the floor in time to see another pail of water thrown upon me and opened my mouth to capture what I could. Water sprayed over my still pink and sore breasts, and ran down between my legs to where my groin ached hotly.

He took one of my ankles and dragged me aside, and I saw that a small, narrow portion of the floor had been raised up. Beneath was a well-padded space something less than six feet in length and quite narrow. It was to this I was dragged, and dropped into, my arms still bound tightly together behind me, elbows locked as one. The sides of this little coffin pressed in tightly against my shoulders, and my feet were firm against the bottom as he knelt above me.

In short order strong straps bound me in place at ankle, calf, knee, thigh, hip, waist, chest, throat and head. Two blocks of padded wood were pressed in to either side of my head, jamming in against my ears, then the turn of a crank produced a pressure against the top of my head as the little box grew smaller still.

He stepped back and lowered the lid, which was padded thickly along its lower part, and less so at its top. The lower part pushed down firmly against my legs and belly, while the top only brushed my lips. I could not move in any slightest way, nor hear, nor see in the darkness. I was alone, as in a coffin, alone with my pain and bruises, with my misery and fear.

I was not claustrophobic when I entered that tight, suffocating box, but I certainly was when I was dragged free of it. Hour after hour of complete immobility with only my own screams of frantic despair for company. Hour after hour of desperately wanting to move even a little, to bend my aching back or legs or scratch my thigh or above all to relieve some of the intense, agonizing pressure on my tightly bound arms and locked shoulders, pressure which threatened to break my mind, to tip me into ravening insanity.

Every few hours water spilled from a crack or hole which was located above my mouth, and I would snap at it like a starving beast, licking and sucking at whatever moisture I could reach. The rest of the time I bathed in the sweat of pain and misery and heat, trying to draw shuddering breaths through that same small hole and expand my chest against the relentless pressure pushing down against my breasts.

I was probably in that horrible pit, that coffin, for no more than a day. I do not believe my master's patience would have permitted him to spend any longer upon a torture he could not witness. When I was dragged free I was barely human, ready to do anything, including throwing myself off a cliff, to ensure I was never again returned to it.

His fingers dug at the straps around my arms, and then, my mind still swimming in dazed pain felt a new gush of agony as my shoulders, so long forced back, were finally released. I screamed through my dry, ragged throat, sobbing and wailing at the return of sensation, at long frozen muscles at last set free.

Perhaps he was feeling more kindly towards me now, for after sodomizing me, he merely strapped my ankles against the backs of my thighs, shackled my wrists behind me and had me kneel upon the floor in the corner where he settled my still badly bruised and aching sex down upon a thick, ridged metal penis bolted to the floor. It ached as it forced the lips of my sex apart, but compared to the pain I had already endured it was as nothing.

I was expecting something much worse, and waited anxiously for him to do it. Even when he left I did not believe he would leave me long in such calm circumstances. Yet after long minutes had passed, minutes which had, I think, become hours, I accepted it with gladness. Despite the thickness of the metal impaling my aching sex I was no longer in extreme discomfort. My arms were gloriously free, even if my wrists were bound together behind me. Every movement made my shoulders ache and groan in the joy of release. I felt an almost sensual delight in simply shrugging my shoulders and shifting my torso. Such freedom was intoxicating.

I thus had time and the ability to think upon my situation in this new place, and to recognize that I had a need to do something, however desperate, to free myself before my twisted master damaged me permanently, or worse. I did not know what that something would be, but I resolved to be alert for any opportunities in future.

It was only a few hours before my master returned, and he immediately removed me from my comfortable position and set about preparing me for one which would be considerably more awkward.

He placed me on the floor on my belly, then quickly attached ropes to the shackles about my wrists and ankles. Moments later those ropes were joined together and I was being lifted upwards, still in a horizontal position, wrists and ankles pulling together above me so that my torso was bowed and my back ached.

As before, the little man watched me with excitement, standing back as I hung in place, turning slowly in the centre of the frame, all my weight focused on a single rope bound to the hook above. After some minutes the weight of my torso had bowed my body further, and I was lowered so that my belly touched the floor. This was not to be a reduction in my discomfort however. With the slackening of the ropes binding me new ones were added, and the old ones removed. Now both wrists were placed directly against the sides of both ankles, and all four were bound tightly together. That done, I was again raised high as my master watched with excited eyes.

He moved about me, viewing me from different angles, then darted to the corner and there drew a long length of cord. He returned, roughly gripping my long braid, then bound the cord into it and tied the other end to the ropes looped about my ankles and wrists. This had the effect of forcing me to hold my head horizontally, or accepting the pain as the cord yanked on my hair.

Not done, he dashed behind me, tying ropes to both legs just above the knee, and running those ropes to opposite sides of the frame, so that my thighs, still aching and burning from previous torments, were spread wide once again.

As before, he circled me, smiling in self-congratulation, observing me from all angles. He then stood before me, his groin at the same level as my face, and drew out his erection. Due to the taut pull of the cord on my hair my mouth was forced wide, and into it he plunged his erection, unhesitantly thrusting it deep into my swollen, bruised throat.

He then grasped my head between both hands and began to use my mouth and throat with long, frenzied strokes, his erection pumping wildly inside me, his belly slapping painfully against my face, crushing my nose with each thrust. He lasted only seconds in this manner before I felt his cock softening. He withdrew at once, beaming at me and then turning away.

He left the room, and my body, already in discomfort and pain, began to throb and go numb, to burn and ache. What felt like hours passed as my mind slowly developed that same numbness, a sense of dazed incomprehension. It was some time before he returned for me, but I remember nothing of it. I wakened to some sanity in the cage, once more, still without food or water, and spent the night clutching my empty stomach and trying to sleep.

Morning came, or what I assumed to be morning, and the return of my tormentor. This time I was stood straight and my arms chained overhead. He threw several buckets of water on me, then soaped me from head to toe before rinsing me off with more water. He wrung my hair dry, then produced a brush to work out the worst of its tangles before leaving me alone. It was perhaps an hour or two later when he returned, bound my wrists behind me, and led me out of the room. We went down the stairs and along a somewhat more comfortably furnished hall. Yet there was to be no improvement in my fortunes.

The room we entered was large, but bare and windowless. The walls had been painted with scenes of women in torment, but were obviously ancient, the paint faded and in some cases flaked and peeling. An empty, roped-off area covered its centre, and two score men circled its edges, most in small groups, chatting and sipping from cups and glasses.

I was led forward naked into the midst of their hungry, staring eyes, and leering faces and felt a growing sense of anxiety - mixed with the arousal I had come to expect now as my exhibitionistic side came into its glory. I was taken into the centre of the roped off area. There my wrists were lifted high above me and chained to opposite ends of a metre long steel pole. My legs were spread apart similarly chained, then the chain holding the pole above me was raised upward.

Moments after my feet left the floor I was jerked to a halt, for the lower pole was, it seemed, chained in place. Yet the pressure of the chain above my head was unrelenting as it sought to raise me higher. I felt the pressure of the shackles digging into wrists and ankles, my flesh burning and aching. My arms and shoulders strained, and the pressure ran along my spine so that it seemed to pop and creak.

There was no gag to silence my gasps, which became cries and then sobs as the pain mounted. I attempted to restrain myself, even as the sweat stood out on my naked flesh and the pain tore through every part of my body.

The little man who was my master was speaking to the

men viewing my torment, and I could see the pride in his movements and hear the satisfaction in his voice. The pressure mounted higher still, and my entire body screamed in agony - causing me to do the same. My voice echoed about the vast, empty room, yet none of the men appeared disturbed. Quite the contrary, each of my shrieks and cries seemed to raise their excitement, and I perceived that they, like my master, were deeply aroused by my agony.

My four limbs strained in different directions, and I felt more popping in my shoulders and knees. I thought that I was about to die, that the peak of the spectacle would be my flesh torn asunder so that the leering jackals surrounding me could achieve the satisfaction of seeing my beauty destroyed. Yet my torment was not to be so quickly complete.

Just as the agony became such that my vision grew hazy and I began to feel faint it eased off, bit by bit, relaxing its pull on my body until I merely hung limp from the upper pole. I was able to breathe somewhat easier now, and a feeling of deep relief spread through my body.

My new master began to beat me then, with a short flog against my back. It stung, of course, yet it was as nothing compared to the feeling of being pulled apart, and as I saw the excitement in the eyes of the men watching I felt a small quiver of arousal between my legs. To be whipped so, in front of so many people, hanging from my wrists, struck to the soul of my dark, masochistic desires, and even as the flog lashed my soft flesh and I cried out in pain the throbbing between my legs grew more powerful.

He dropped the flog, and I turned my head briefly, eyes widening, chest tightening to see him carrying a heavier cat-'o-nine-tails. It lashed my lower back, and my cries rose higher. The cat stung much more, like claws across the skin, and my body jerked and swung to the pain.

Yet still my sex hungered, excited by such torment, and even through the pain I could sense the moistening of my pussy, the desire to feel the touch of a hand, or a man's penis, or even, and I gasped at the thought, the cat itself.

The blows halted, and I hung weakly, quivering, my body twitching. My long hair was tangled about my face, and I shook my head slightly to clear some of the golden tresses from my eyes, then shuddered as I saw him approach me carrying a long, thick whip. It was a bullwhip, and never before had I tasted its kiss. It dangled from his hand and slid along the floor behind him like a dangerous snake as he moved out of my sight and behind me.

I tried to brace myself, feeling a wonder and fear that he would use such a thing on my soft flesh. The whip made a sound like none I had heard before as it was cast through the air, and the force of the blow as it cut across my back was a hammerblow compared to the needles I had already been given. It sent the breath exploding from my lungs in an animal howl of agony, and left my flesh feeling ripped, torn and burning from my right shoulder to my left waist.

It struck again, and again I could not repress the scream of tortured pain which flew from my ragged throat as it snapped about my waist, leaving a red welt like a belt. Again it struck, and again, slashing into my upper back, then my lower. My insides twisted and roiled, as the pain built up around me. But then it could climb no higher, it seemed, and began to form a screen of heat around my mind and body which diffused and softened the sharpness of the additional blows.

My body continued to jerk to the lashes, and I felt a sense of amazement that I was to be the victim of such cruelty, yet also an excitement, for that dark hunger was coiled deep within me, slowly spreading out as it gloried in the heat and lust of the men surrounding me, as it revelled in their despite, in their desire to see me punished and tortured. My pussy throbbed more than ever before, and the pleasure continued to grow, soaking up much of the pain even as my master changed the direction of his blows.

He turned slightly, shifted his arm and snapped it out sideways, and the long whip flew, striking my back with a sideways motion which curled the first foot around my ribcage and sank the tip into my right breast.

I was shocked, stunned, and as the pain flashed through me I screamed in agony. My body thrashed and twisted in frantic desperation as the watching men leered in delight. Again the whip slashed around my chest, and again sent my already wounded breast bouncing upwards from the force of the blow. The whip landed again, this time lower, curling around my hip and downwards. The tip sank into my inner thigh, but even as I screamed I knew it had missed its target.

Oh no! Oh no!

Yet that dark, terrible side of me exulted.

Yessss! Yesss!

To be whipped there! Not by the soft, light strips of a flog, but by a real whip, the whip of pirate fantasies, the whip of slavemasters in the deep south of the United States! The hiss and crack as it struck was a vivid aural shock which drew me into the realms of cruellest fantasy, but even there I had not imagined anyone would be so terrible as to let the hard, wicked lash of such a whip even approach the delicate centre of my mons.

I tried instinctively to twist my body in some way so as to block the following blow, to close my legs to protect myself. Yet I could not, and some part of me did not wish to anyway. I felt the lust and desire of my sex, felt the soft lips swelling, opening slightly, pouting with desire, and then the whip curled around my hip once more, slicing downwards across my abdomen, the tip making a soft, wet crack! as it bit into the soft flesh of my sex. My hips were thrown back and up, and the air left my lungs. A crescendo of agony and ecstasy screamed within me, roaring together in a maelstrom of sensory overload. The impact of the harsh leather gave me a horrible, shocking gush of savage exultation.

A few of the watchers applauded, but I could hardly hear them through the roaring of blood in my ears and the shriek which erupted from my mouth. I swung, gasping and gurgling, from my wrists, legs twitching and jerking as I instinctively tried to close them. Yet I could not, and a mixture of horror and carnal delight gripped me as I waited the next blow.

Again! Again! the darkness cried.

No! No! my mind wailed.

The whip landed again, no more than an inch lower. I felt it slice into the soft flesh just above my buttocks, hissing along my fragile flesh as it curled over my hip, then sink into the quivering skin of my abdomen before the tip struck just below my clitoris with a powerful blow of agony.

I screamed again, hips exploding backwards, body swinging wildly as my legs jerked and twisted. The pain was horrific, yet the rush, the rush was... indescribable. I felt as though my sex were a volcano ready to explode, as if the heat inside it would gush out onto the floor, as if the sexual pressure inside my head would tear me apart.

Again the whip hissed through the air, curling around my shaking body and snapping at my groin. Now it curled around my left hip, now my right, but always the tip was directed at my burning, swollen sex, and the pain and pleasure both became unbearable, tearing at my strength and sanity.

The tip of the whip slashed in between my legs now, as my tormenter became more cunning, slicing in and upwards directly along the line of my bare sex.

And I came. I came like a maddened, frenzied animal, my body thrashing wildly, head jerking violently and bonelessly about as the storm of sensation lashed my fragile mind. Muscles spasmed and nerve endings snapped and crackled as the climax rose higher and higher still, fuelled by still more blows from my master's terrible whip.

He shifted his aim once more, letting the whip strike against my back, and the stunning heights of pleasure began to sink. Then he sent the terrible thing curling around my ribs once more, causing my breasts to dance and shake, to recoil against the violence inflicted upon them, and the climax seemed to spiral upwards once more, spreading out, seizing me in its grip and shaking me like a rag doll. I could not think, could not breath, and soon even screams were beyond me as blackness began to fill my vision and the pain and pleasure faded away with the light.

I lay on my back in my cage, semi-conscious, throat sore and swollen, body on fire with pain, swimming in sweat, hair a tangled mass, much of it matted against my perspiring face.

At some point water, a pail of it, was thrown upon me, and I half woke from my haze, sputtering weakly. Bowls of water and some foul smelling food were placed beside me, and the shadowy figure who brought them withdrew, slamming the door behind him. My trembling hands fumbled for the bowls, almost spilling the priceless water. I quickly gulped down the entire bowl, despite the pain to my aching throat, then somehow managed to force down some of the soft rice-like food.

Four more times came the pail, water splashing over my naked body and running out of the cage and onto the stone floor, and thence into a drain in the corner. After the pail would come the small bowls of food and water. I do not know if this was once each day, or twice, or three times, though I believe it was twice.

Finally, he pulled me out once more, then forced me to my feet. He reached above him to where a pair of shackles hung from a chain, lifting my left wrist up to place it in position. I did not think to resist. Resistance had been beaten out of me, yet some instinct for self-preservation caused me to shoot up my other hand and to grab at the shackle. Without

210

my mind forming any thought or plan, in nothing but ragged determination I slapped the shackle around his wrist and then fell back as he cursed and yanked at it.

His other hand was free, yet one was caught immovably in the shackle, and he could not release it. I saw his eyes shoot across to the table a few feet away, and the key sitting on its edge, yet try as he might he could not reach it. He turned on me with fiery eyes, cursing me in his own language, no doubt threatening immense pain and torment did I not release him at once.

I simply sat back on my heels, panting for breath, fighting against the weakness and pain, watching him dully. The door was heavy and closed, and no one came in answer to his shouts. Slowly, some semblance of intelligence returned to my mind and I realized my inevitable pain would now only be increased for such temerity. Yet I regarded my tormentor with loathing and hate, and contempt, for he was no true master, a weak man in mind and body.

I stood up, and he rained more threats upon me, yet a nebulous plan formed in my mind. I moved to the desk and took the key, then went to him. He put his hand out impatiently, yet instead I raised the key high to the shackles. His free hand rose at once, as if to snatch the key from my hand, and as he did so I dropped the key and seized his wrist in both hands. I was strong, from my exercises in China, and he was weak and spindly. Before he understood my intent I had his other wrist into the second shackle and the iron closed tightly about it.

More shouts and snarls of rage followed, yet I did not care. I moved to the wall, to the crank I had seen him use, and turned it, not without effort, so that his feet rose off the floor and he dangled from his wrists. There was much satisfaction in seeing him so, and I sat back down against the wall to rest.

Perhaps an hour passed, or two, before I rose once more.

He was hanging limply by then, for hanging from ones wrists was exhausting. I removed his clothing, and then began to beat him. I was still somewhat dazed, but enjoyed myself even so, raining blows with the whips which had caused me the most pain, focusing as much attention on his groin as he had mine, but neglecting no part of his spindly body. I whipped him until my arms were too tired to raise, then sank exhaustedly to the floor once again to rest. By this time he was trembling and sobbing and begging, and I felt even more disgust for him.

It was time to leave, if I would, and though I was not thinking very clearly at this time, I had little doubt about what my master would do to me when someone eventually came along to free him. I squeezed through the door, closing it behind me, and made my way slowly and tentatively up the hall. In the next room I found a water tap, and drank deeply, until it seemed my belly sloshed with liquid, then ducked my head beneath it, soaking myself.

I don't know how I managed to continue to move. I was an automaton, unthinking, operating solely on instinct. I made my way through the quiet corridors, past sleeping or drunken guards, and out an unguarded door and thence to the street.

Naked, I staggered through the street until a kind hearted person - I know not who - seeing my dazed and unclothed state, and concerned about my welfare, took me a little ways up one street and down another and then guided me towards the American embassy. Those worthies, seeing a white woman turned up at their door, perhaps assumed I was one of theirs and took me in. However, I was not to remain for long.

I do not know if news of my true identity arrived, or if news of a search by my master caused them to react. Most likely, they wished to avoid any unfavourable publicity, anything which would cause them difficulties with the local government.

212

I was taken out of the place only two days later, and placed in a small car with tinted windows. We drove to the airport, and I was placed aboard a small private jet.

I was the only passenger, which I thought a bit of a shame. The aircraft reminded me of the one which had taken me to China a year or so previously, and thinking of the events of that trip aroused me quite a bit. Had there even been a single steward or stewardess I most likely would have attempted to draw them into sex, but there wasn't, and the door to the cabin remained locked.

I expected a long ride, and was more than a little bored and irritated at being locked alone without any form of entertainment. Partly to amuse myself, and partly excited at the wickedness of doing such a thing, I drew my legs up across the arms of my seat and began to masturbate. Then, my excitement rising, I dared to strip completely and, naked, pranced about the long cabin, going so far as to flatten my breasts against the door to the pilots' cabin.

Then I returned to the centre of the main cabin, lay on my back in the middle of the floor, spread my legs, and masturbated again, doing so as lewdly as possible, groaning in pleasure, rolling my hips wantonly, and thoroughly enjoying being a slut amid ordinary, respectable society.

I had just finished, and was lying still, sighing happily, when I felt the slight jerk which signalled we were landing. I stood up in surprise, going to one of the windows and staring in surprise at the small, dusty land around us, then turned and quickly got dressed. I thought perhaps we had landed for refuelling, and hoped to be permitted to go out and wander about. I thought that since we had been flying west towards England, we must be somewhere in the middle-east by then.

I wondered if I would be able to see the pyramids.

The aircraft came to a halt, and I peered around dubiously. The runway seemed to have been paved in the middle of a desert, with not a single building nearby. I looked towards the pilots' door, but there was no movement there. Then I heard movement behind me, and turned to see one of the aircraft's exit doors opening. I stood up curiously and walked forward, unsurprised to see an Arab man in a drab brown uniform pushing the door aside.

He looked at me, then motioned impatiently for me to come forward. I obeyed, and he took my arm and led me through the door and down the few steps required to reach the runway. At that he released me, turned back up, and closed the aircraft's door once more, shutting it into place. I stared at him in surprise.

"Here. What are you doing?" I demanded.

He ignored my question, presuming he understood it, and took my arm again, leading me away from the aircraft.

"Where are we going?" I demanded.

He led me further away and behind us the engines roared as the aircraft began to turn around and head back up the runway.

"What's going on?" I asked uncertainly.

The aircraft picked up speed and then took off. The man released my arm, looked me up and down, then moved to a small jeep I had not noticed previously, got in, and drove away. I stared after him stupidly, then looked around me at the runway, and mounds of sand in all directions. I still could see no sign of any type of building. Above me, the sun beat down, and then the wind began to blow softly, sending sand across the runway and swirling around my feet and into my hair.

"What have I done?" I said aloud, turning slowly in place and looking about me.

I was fairly sure they would not simply have sought to fly me here to die. They could have had me killed by simply giving me back to the Indians, after all. But where was I and what did they intend? I walked off the runway, which was helping to bake me in the heat, and quickly found the sand at the edge rather difficult to walk in.

I was still wondering what was going on when I saw movement in one direction, and followed it with my eyes. It was, I determined, approaching. After a bit I realized it was a horse, a man on a horse, and thought of how odd that was. The horse grew bigger and bigger, until I could make out that he was quite large, black, and bore a man in a black robe on his back. He had one of those Arab type headdresses, but he seemed stern of face, and handsome as well. The horse drew up not far from me and the man looked at me silently from under his headdress.

"Uhm, hello?" I ventured.

He stepped down from his horse and crossed to me, then, without a word, backhanded me so that I cried out and staggered backwards. He gripped the front of my blouse and tore it open, then twisted me around and yanked the tattered remains off my back. A moment later my bra was off, and then I was thrown forward onto my face in the sand. I sputtered and cried out as he loomed over me, but he did not strike me. Instead he gripped my skirt and yanked it off, along with my panties, then even removed my shoes and socks before throwing me onto my back.

Still silent, he spread my legs, and I gasped and whimpered, not daring to resist as he opened the bottom part of his robe and drew out a long, thick erection.

I had been used, ravished and abused by many men to that point in my life, but never before had I seen such a monstrous erection. He looked fully a foot long, and immensely thick, and so despite my experience I gaped at it until his hand slapped against my face and threw my head back into the sand once more.

He thrust himself against me, and fortunately my pussy still held the moistness of my earlier self abuse, for he had little time nor patience for my body to accommodate itself to him. I cried out nonetheless as he crudely forced the soft

215

lips of my sex wide and punched his long, thick member deep into my belly.

He seized my thighs roughly, spreading them wider, yanking on my body as he thrust himself forward, still soundless as he drove himself forward again and again, forcing inch after inch of his enormously thick organ into my quivering body. I sobbed weakly, but knew enough not to resist. His erection was like a club, like a spear thrusting deep into my body, reaching so high that the soft, spongy nose mashed against what felt like my actual cervix, then began to beat upon it as his hips thrust in angry, savage passion.

He used me violently, silently, his dark eyes boring into mine as his hips worked with deliberate force. His hands forcing my thighs back and apart, holding them in place with a grip of iron as he drove himself into me.

And then, just like that, he was done. I had no warning of it, no realization that he had achieved his climax. He rose, gripping me roughly by one slim ankle and dragging me along with him through the sand to the side of his horse. He dropped my ankle then and opened a saddle bag, from which he took a long length of rope. He quickly unwound it, pinned my wrists together and then bound them tightly in place.

Still not speaking, he turned and mounted his horse, wound the other end of the rope about the horn of his saddle, and signalled the horse to start forward. Staring, mouth agape, I watched as the horse moved off, then abruptly realized my position and moaned as the rope reached its limit and I had to hurry forward, breaking into a trot.

Already I was sweating, exhausted, shocked by the sudden unexpected violence, and having difficulty with my heavy breathing in such a hot, sandy atmosphere. Yet he ignored me, the horse setting a deliberate pace which I had no choice but to match. It was too slow for a run, or even a trot, but too fast for me to walk. So I was forced to alternate, now trotting, now jogging, now trotting again, getting more and more out of breath as we left the runway behind and moved down a very narrow path between enormous sand dunes.

Nothing lay behind them but more sand, and I moaned helplessly as the horse continued blithely forward, the man never turning as I tried with more desperation to keep up.

My bare feet sank deep into the hot white sand, and I was soon lagging badly, the force of the rope often yanking me forward so that I stumbled. Twice I fell, and was dragged through the sand a short distance before managing to get to my feet. Finally I fell and could not stand, and was dragged through the sand by the wrists, coughing weakly and moaning in exhaustion and overheat.

I managed to roll onto my back after a minute, which eased the pain to my breasts, yet I had no way of climbing to my feet, and no strength left either. I stared up at the sun, panting for breath and coughing in the sand raised behind his horse as I was dragged along.

Finally the horse stopped, and I lay still, moaning, chest heaving, sweat pouring off me. His shadow loomed, and he gripped my wrist, pulling me up, then over his shoulder. He carried me like a bag of potatoes back to his horse, then as if I weighed nothing, turned and flung me up across the horse before climbing up behind me. I lay face down, moaning, as the horse started forward again, bouncing lightly as he kicked the horse into a faster stride.

The sand hardened, and then became dirt, and scrubby little bushes began to appear. Then we were in among a group of trees which surrounded a small pond of clear water. He unceremoniously lifted my head up and flung my body back off the side of the horse so that I fell into the water. I sat up, sputtering and coughing, but made no effort to stand. I was relieved, and scooped water up in my palms to slurp thirstily.

He ignored me at first, seeing to his horse, unfastening its saddle and gear, then leading it up a bit to drink from the pond. As it was doing this he set up a small camp, and gathered twigs and small sticks for a fire. Only when that was completed did he yank on the rope still bound to my wrists and pull me out of the water. He led me, dripping, to one of the trees, and threw the rope over a low branch, then pulled it down behind me. The branch was only a foot or so above my head, and my hands and arms were pulled up over my head. As he continued pulling the rope tightened around my wrists, and began to cut into the soft skin. Then the skin of my arms scraped over the branch as they were forced down, and I was lifted off my toes.

He pulled on the rope until my arms were bent back over the branch, the crooks of my elbows jammed painfully against the hard wood, and my hands down behind my neck. Then he led the rope between my thighs and pulled it up hard so that it wedged in between my labia, curled it over my right hip, around my waist, and back over my left hip to tie together at my abdomen.

I was then left in place as he continued to attend to setting up a camp.

CHAPTER TWELVE

I have to say that at the time I had a young girl's view of Arabs and the middle east. Which is to say that I did not think it strange that a man in a flowing robe, riding a horse, would have taken captive a European girl he happened upon. Nor did I wonder at the absence of cities, or even towns. In fact, my only surprise at my treatment to that point was that the man had ridden a horse rather than a camel.

I thought, as I hung there, that I was destined for his harem, or something similar, perhaps to be masked and hooded and hidden in some type of enormous tent with his other harem girls.

And the idea of being a slave to Arabs, to be a prisoner in a harem, was, to be honest, not an unpleasant one to a person of my curiously masochistic sexual desires. As I watched him strip naked and step into the water, I could not help but admire his powerful masculine body, his firm jaw and dark, flashing eyes. I felt a little shudder of excitement pass through me at the idea of being the sexual plaything of such a man.

His treatment of me to that point had hardly been gentle, yet he had displayed a strength and will which I found quite impressive. In all respects he seemed a far and away more exciting master than the one I had so recently been imprisoned with.

You might be amazed that a girl would even consider such things, would possibly find any aspect of such a situation intriguing and exciting. But as I have already demonstrated, I was no longer an ordinary girl with an ordinary sense of the proprieties. Being slapped and taken, being treated strongly, being bound in discomfort, all these were rather normal aspects of my life now. And so while I was in quite some discomfort due to my position, I was not sobbing in misery and fear as would a girl fresh off the streets of London or New York.

In fact, even the position I was in was not beyond my ability to find comfort. For while my arms ached quite badly at the elbows, where they were holding up a good portion of my weight, the rope attached to my wrists was also pushing in quite hard between my legs. And the pressure was beginning to inspire the same sort of throbbing, aching pleasure as had the narrow piece of wood I had been forced to straddle in India. There was less pain to go with it, however, because the rope was soft where the wood had been unyielding, and because most of my weight was on my arms.

I was in pain, but pain and I had long acquaintance, and the near nymphomania which now seemed a part and parcel of my personality required quite a bit more discouragement than it was now being offered. Especially as my mind raced with the possibilities and fantasies of a life in the harem of the handsome, strong-willed man who had captured me.

I watched the sun glisten off his wet body, watched as he soaped himself up, watched his hands sliding over his muscular chest and arms, then down his trim stomach. He stepped into shallower water, and I panted and licked my lips as he cleaned himself. I found myself wishing I could be there with him to help him bathe, to use my own hands to soap up his groin, and the soft, but lovely long penis dangling there.

I remembered again how thick and long he had been as he had driven himself into my body, and felt my groin thrumming with desire to be taken by him again.

He finished his bathing and rinsed himself, then strode from the water, back straight, head high. A little ripple of sexual admiration passed along my spine, and I moaned lightly in hopes of drawing his eye. He ignored me, however. Instead, naked, he set food into a pot and placed it in the fire he had built. That done he stood up and pulled on his robe, belting it at the waist, then pulled on the headdress which covered his head and neck.

He continued to ignore me, and his strength of will, of character, served to impress me further, and to give my loins even more desire.

Suddenly he rose and turned towards me. I felt my heart pounding and blood racing, wondering if he would take me once again, or perhaps torture me as my previous master had. He walked up beside me, his height allowing him to look down on me even while I was suspended many inches from the ground. He did not look aroused, but rather calm and considerate. He regarded my body for a moment, then reached out and cupped one breast.

He spoke, but the words had no meaning to me. However, as he fingered my stiff, swollen nipple I was sure he was commenting on my evident arousal.

He took a long, frightening looking knife from his belt but I had only a moment's anxiety before he sliced the rope free and I fell at his feet. He took my arm in a powerful grip and half dragged me towards the fire, then set me down. He sat next to me, completing his cooking, not looking at me until he removed the pot from the fire. He produced a wooden spoon and began to eat a kind of thick stew. After several spoonfuls he turned toward me, holding the spoon laden with stew before my mouth.

I licked my lips, then opened my mouth and took the stew off his spoon. He nodded slightly and fed himself once more as I swallowed. I had no idea what it was, and tried not to imagine. It was quite tasty, however, and when he held the spoon out for me once again I quickly opened my mouth and took it.

In this way he fed the both of us, though he, of course, took the lion's share (like a lion would, I thought, with indecent admiration). The sun was setting by now, and I could not help but think of what a romantic setting I was in, there in the small oasis next to a strong, ruggedly handsome Arab. Perhaps he was a prince, I thought, taking water from a steel cup he held to my lips.

I was set to wash the pot and cup after dinner, and then, with nothing to note any change in his thoughts towards me, he took my arms, set me firmly down upon hands and knees, and positioned himself behind me.

A sudden gush of excitement flowed through my belly and my chest tightened with anxiety as I felt his hands on my hips. A moment later his cock rubbed back and forth against my bare slit, and then pushed into me. I was wet in an instant, and raised my bottom like a bitch in heat, shifting my knees apart in the soft grassy dirt as he slowly forced his immensely thick organ into my welcoming body.

I could not help groaning lightly as he filled me to overflowing, as the soft, elastic walls of my sex were forced taut around his hard, ridged erection. Already I was breathing faster, my heart pounding harder, and each new thrust brought him deeper and deeper, to the point of cramps and aching. Yet it was a delicious ache, and as he seized my flanks and began to use me in earnest I savoured every stroke, revelled in the hard, firm pounding of his hips against my bottom, and gloried in the rising moon as it bathed our bodies in pale white light.

I came in no more than two minutes, came powerfully, and made little effort to disguise my pleasure. I wanted him to know how much I lusted for his touch, how enthralled I was by his hard use, how much I welcomed being his slave.

He continued to thrust into me, strongly, firmly, but unhurried, his thick organ pumping back and forth, in and out of my straining opening, jamming deep within me on each stroke and rocking my body forward in the sand. The sexual heat never left me, and even as the first orgasm faded my body continued to thrum with sexual tension and need.

I loved it. I loved it. I loved it. I felt truly in my element, being used by such a powerful man, forced to his bidding, to please his sexual desires. His hands did not roam my body, but remained firmly on my hips, thrusting steadily, hard powerful strokes jerking my body in a delicious rhythm.

I came again, more powerfully, my head thrashing from side to side, the air puffing out of my slack mouth as every fibre in my body flared with white-hot pleasure. I was being ridden by a real man, ridden like I deserved to be ridden, used as I was meant to be used, and I gloried in it. I came a third time, grunting weakly, unable to think or talk, hardly able to breathe at the clamour of sensory joy within me.

And still he rode me, rode me as my arms sagged, as I sank to my elbows, breasts dangling against the ground. Yet I was immediately brought up short. A harsh hand gripped my loose, tangled hair, yanking my head up and back so that I cried out in pain, forcing me back onto my hands, and then resuming its place on my hip.

Yet again, I did not resent this. Rather, it aroused me once again, as a display of his strength of will and character, of his mastery over me. He would not let me slack in the slightest thing, this master. I was his and would know it. He continued to drive himself into me, his powerful hips slapping against my buttocks again and again, and my heat rose once more.

But then he gave a final flurry of fast, shallow strokes as his orgasm arrived. He was silent, yet his fingers dug in harder against my flanks, and he forced himself even harder against me before stopping, his cock fully enveloped by my sex. He knelt there for long seconds as I felt his erection softening, then he slipped back and out. He slapped my buttocks lightly, then stood and moved away.

I was hog-tied that night, wrists and ankles bound together behind my back. Yet he was not needlessly cruel. The rope was not as tight as it could have been, as others had made it in the past, and he ensured the flow of blood to hands and feet was not constricted before leaving me and setting himself into a very light sleeping bag.

It was chilly that night, and I shivered there in the dirt,

laying naked on my side. Yet despite that I managed to fall asleep with a degree of contentment I had not felt since leaving China.

Morning came, and he cut loose my ankles, while leaving my wrists bound behind my back. He raised me to my knees and pulled aside his robe, revealing his erection, and I immediately placed my lips around it, bobbing slowly up and down as I worked moisture into his dry flesh. As it became more slick I increased the length of my movements, and then, hoping it would surprise him, pushed forward to the base of his cock, taking the full length down my throat. I felt quite rewarded by a grunt of pleased surprise, and his strong hands coming down lightly upon my head. I held my position, my nose jammed against his abdomen, then slowly eased back, letting him slide back out of my throat and into my mouth.

I sucked and licked at the front of his erection for long seconds, then pushed deep once again, taking him all the way inside me. As before, I let my lips hold still against his groin for long seconds, then backed off to work on his head with my mouth again. His fingers began to comb through my hair, and I felt a little shiver of gladness at this sign of affection, redoubling my efforts.

No man, however strong, could resist such treatment for long, and soon he was spurting a prodigious amount of seed into my mouth. I swallowed quickly, working my lips and tongue as fast as I could around his fountaining cockhead so as to maximize the length and pleasure of his orgasm. Only when he softened did I pull back, licking lightly along his cock so as to clean him off.

He let his robe fall into place and moved away, leaving me on my knees. I sat back on my heels, feeling pleased, and watching as he set up his bowl for breakfast. As before, I joined him, kneeling in place, sitting on my heels as he fed himself, and then me. Neither of us spoke. It would have seemed wrong, somehow, even if we spoke each other's language.

He washed his things off himself, then saw to his horse. When it was saddled and ready to go he pulled me to my feet and led me over to it once again. At its side, however, he halted. His hand rose to my hair and pulled it back, firmly, but not cruelly, so as to raise my face and arch my back. His other hand slipped between my legs, and strong, rough, but knowing fingers slipped inside me. He must quickly have noted my heat and moisture, for he smiled ever so slightly. Then his fingers began to manipulate my sex, stroking quickly against my clitoris so that the heat fairly exploded within me.

In mere seconds I was panting and moaning, my legs spread apart, my hips grinding shamelessly against his fingers as I stared up into the sky above. I came quickly, explosively, bucking wildly against his fingers and crying out my pleasure.

He casually mounted then pulled me up before him where I rested my head against his shoulder and gulped in air.

We left the oasis and soon found ourselves back in the soft sand of the desert. We rode for an hour before the ground hardened again. This time there was no oasis, but long fields of scrubby grass, and then crops appeared, and soon after a narrow river. A light trail appeared, which turned into a well-used track, and then a dirt road. Small white houses appeared in the distance off to left and right.

We saw a few people, but none close enough to identify, and then after another hour or so of riding we turned onto a tree-lined road which led to an enormous structure. It was a palace. Long and beautiful and white, with towers at the corners and uncountable windows along its length. We rode around to one side, where stables and a garage lay, and he slipped gracefully down, then took my hips and lifted me down as well.

Two small, thin Arabs in dark robes hurried out, their

eyes widening at the sight of me. After only a few days back among 'polite society' I had already lost my casual acceptance of public nudity, and knew a fluttery little tremor of excitement at their reaction. They bowed their heads rapidly, though, and when he spoke to them bobbed up and down and quickly took the horse away while he led me into the palace.

The corridors were all wide and high enough to run a bus through. My bare feet stepped alternately atop polished marble and deep, soft carpeting. Paintings and sculptures were everywhere, and the richness of the place outshone anything in my experience. Whenever we passed someone in the hall their reaction would be to stare at me, then bow deeply, or sometimes, drop to their knees as we passed.

We turned a corner and came upon an immense carved wooden door. Two uniformed guards in white trousers and blouses stood framing it, each with an actual sword in his belt. They both bowed low to him and one opened the rightmost door. Neither gave me a second glance.

Now we were in a wide, low-roofed area, the floors and walls of dark gold stone, with many alternating patterns picked out in black and silver. Different areas were curtained off, sometimes by heavy curtains in red or gold, other times by sheer curtains through which we could see people moving about.

We halted before a woman of middle years. She was Arabian, with a full stomach and heavy breasts. Her dark hair was bound back, and her nose was quite large. He spoke to her as she bowed her head, then she looked at me and spoke back. He nodded as if satisfied, turned and left.

The woman stepped closer to me, then took my jaw in a strong hand, turning my head to the left, then to the right as she examined me. A heavy thumb pushed against my lower lip, forcing it down, and I opened my mouth as she examined my teeth. She muttered to herself, looked at my breasts and

226

sex, then took my arm and wordlessly led me through an opening in a long brown curtain into another part of the area.

Was this the harem, I wondered with some excitement. Was I to be a harem girl?

The purpose of the room seemed obvious, for a half dozen enormous golden marble tubs were placed about, each with gold fixtures. The wall was mirrored, the mirrors holding gold tracing. The floor was also marble, but in green. Lights were recessed in the ceiling, making the room fairly glow.

She ran a tub, and then released the rope binding my wrists. I stepped into the tub and sat, submissively allowing her to wash me and then shampoo my hair. Done, she sat me on a fine padded chair and spread my legs wide, then shaved my sex of the small bit of hair which had begun to grow back. She massaged sweet-smelling oils into my skin from toe to throat, then brushed out my hair until it was full and soft and seemed to shimmer around my head.

All of this done she led me back through the curtain and then through another. Now we were in an area with rack after rack of clothing, shelf after shelf of colourful silk, satin and lace fabrics.

She wound the top of a two inch wide T-shaped belt of sheerest white silk about my hips, bringing the vertical strip down between my legs and up between my buttocks before tying it off there with a thin string. On top of this went a loincloth of sorts, made of a bright blue satin fabric. It was perhaps a foot long and half that wide. A white halter so sheer as to be almost invisible was tied over my breasts so that it pressed in like a second skin. Then a kind of half vest in blue satin covered it, left open. Blue slippers followed and she nodded her satisfaction before taking my arm and leading me through several curtains to a wooden door. This she unlocked with a key kept on a chain around her neck.

The room inside was filled with jewellery of every imaginable kind, wealth beyond my imagining. I gaped at it as she examined boxes and trays set all around us. She picked up a stunning choker made of squared sapphires in deep blue mixed with glittering diamonds, and fixed it around my throat. Two matching bracelets went around my wrists, and then anklets of gold, with emeralds and diamonds completed my look.

She brought me to another room, one with bright lights and large mirrors, and left me there to admire myself.

Some five minutes later she returned accompanied by a tall white haired man wearing rich clothing.

"You look very pretty," he said.

"Thank you, master," I breathed, dropping my eyes demurely.

"Say that only to Prince Achmed," he said, frowning.

"Yes... sir," I said.

"This is how you will be adorned once you have shown you have earned it," he said, running a finger along the emerald choker. "This is how Prince Achmed's trusted concubines are rewarded. Each time you please him you will be so rewarded. Each time you fail to please him you will be punished."

I nodded. This, of course, was to be expected.

"You will remain here one year. At the end of that time you will be returned to your people, and may bring with you whatever of the Prince's pleasure you have earned. Do you understand?"

I nodded. I was to be a harem girl, a slave of his body, for a year. But at the end, there would be more change. I was sure I would be able to please him, and thought with a little shiver of delight, about the life ahead as a harem girl. It was, after all, the oldest of all desires to those who, like me, held the darkest of fantasies. Prince Achmed was a demanding man, and, I was sure, would be quite strict indeed with an English girl.

I had already learned discipline, the discipline of the

228

Chinese. Now I would learn what discipline Arabs expected of their slaves. I was no longer an ignorant girl, however, and was confident of my ability to please him and those he chose to gift me to.

It would be a time of learning for them, as well as me.

I smiled at the thought.

The end.

230

And now the beginning of next month's title "SLAVE SCHOOL: A Slaveworld Story" by Stephen Douglas.

CHAPTER ONE

The village lane was almost a dark tunnel, a thick high hedge on one side, the towering slab-sides of barns on the other. Only a single street-lamp at the lane's end provided illumination, but Susan, humming softly to herself as she made her way home from the pub could see well enough by moonlight. She was merry but sober enough. Her lover unexpectedly having had to work that evening, but knowing he'd be home and horny later, she'd just had a couple of halves.

It was a quiet little village, a nice place, so when the car cruised up behind her, following instead of just sweeping past, she felt more puzzlement than the heart-pounding apprehension that would have been her first reaction when still living in a big city. She stepped up onto the grass verge, further out of the way, waving the car past, sure the driver would have seen her as she'd sensibly worn a reflective yellow Sam Browne type belt and shoulder-strap. The car stopped, a powerful engine purring, harsh lights stretching her shadows away down the lane. Susan looked back, squinting in the glare, only to be further dazzled by flashing blue strobe lights. The police car was skewed slightly across the lane, pointing directly at her.

The driver's door opened. An arm across her eyes, she could just make out a peaked cap, the glint of a badge on the cap and on the uniformed man's shoulders, before the policeman's powerful torch stabbed into her eyes as well.

"Both hands up!" the policeman barked. "Above your head where I can see them. Name!"

"Uh... Susan Barncroft," she stammered, arms obediently raised, totally blinded now.

231

"Step down onto the road in front of the car. Turn around. Keep those hands up!"

"What's this all ab..."

"Quiet!" he barked. "Just do as you're told. You can tell it to the detectives when I get you to the station."

The blue lights danced here and there, bouncing off the high hedge and the towering side of the barn. In the headlights she had two shadows, an overlapping X, as she stood obediently in front of the car, hands on top of her head. The police car's radio crackled, but she couldn't quite make out what was being said.

"Okay, slowly. No sudden moves! Toss your handbag behind you."

"But I haven't done anything," Susan protested. "You've made a mistake!"

"Tell it to the judge. Do it!"

Susan obeyed.

"Good! Now the coat."

She heard the unseen man rummaging through her coat pockets, her handbag emptied across the car bonnet. Now in just blouse and skirt she felt far more vulnerable, goose bumps coming up on her skin even though it was a mild night.

"Okay, good. Now, before I can put the cuffs on you, I need you to show me you haven't got a knife or something hidden somewhere. I want you to run your hands over your skirt. That's it; pull it tight!"

Biting her lip, Susan grasped the sides of her skirt and pulled it taut over her buttocks.

"Good girl. Now stroke down the thighs. Hard!"

Breathless, she obeyed.

"Very good Susan. Now up the inner thighs. Pull your skirt up to show me."

Susan made a little pleading noise, more a gasp than a word, but was ignored.

"I once arrested a hooker with a flick-knife pushed down her stocking top," the police officer continued conversationally. "Not making that mistake again. Pull the skirt higher. Show me the tops of your stockings Susan."

Heart pounding, thudding in her chest, Susan felt cool night air on her backside.

"Good girl, you're doing fine. Now stroke around the waist. Good. Now squeeze between those ass-cheeks for me."

Flushed, almost panting, she obeyed. She could hardly think. This was so unexpected.

"Right, now turn and face me. Stroke down between your legs. Harder. Harder! Okay lift the skirt. Let's see what you've got hidden down your panties."

"But I can't," Susan stammered. "Not..."

"I told you to be quiet," the officer said menacingly. "Now be a good girl and I'll make sure you get a nice cell. The one covered by the entrance camera, so that the lads on night-shift can't come visiting."

Susan held up her skirt and then pirouetted to order, displaying her stockings and suspenders, the night air a strangely sensual caress on her bare flesh. She was very aware she was wearing a thong.

"Good girl. Now the tits."

Without resistance now, she obediently slid her hands over her breasts, fear and perverse excitement leaving nipples swollen hard.

"No, squeeze those tits properly!" he barked. "Harder! What's the matter? Got a razor-blade hidden in your bra? Just waiting for a chance to cut me?"

"No! I would never... I mean... No!" Susan stammered.

"Squeeeeeeze!" he ordered lasciviously, drawing the word out.

Susan obediently kneaded, pulled and squeezed her own flesh. Her nipples were aching hard now, breasts lust-swollen, heat stirring in her belly. God, this was making her hot! Finally the still unseen policeman called a halt.

"Okay, no weapons. Now let's find the drugs. Bend forward over the car. I'm going to search you."

Dreadfully aware she was wet, Susan obeyed.

"Arms wider, on the edge of the car. Legs wider. Wider!" the policeman barked.

Legs spread so wide her skirt was pulled halfway up her thighs, holding the edges of the police car's bonnet, Susan's body was bent forward from the waist, almost horizontal. The blue flashing lights were turned off, the headlights dimmed, but the engine still purred under her, vibrating through her hands. A long American-style police-baton was stroked under her chin, raising her head.

"Don't move an inch!" the uniformed man ordered her.

"Please!" she whispered, throat exposed and spine arched as the baton pushed her chin higher.

"Not an inch. I'm warning you!"

The lights dim now, and still dazzled, Susan could only make out his shape, a hint of uniform. He was tall; big!

Behind her now, a firm meaty hand closed around each ankle, and slowly, firmly, with a tight grip, stroked up her stockings. Bent sharply forward from the waist, she was quite helpless, could do nothing except fall forward onto the car. The sliding grip moved up her calves, over her knees, and up the outside of her thighs, pushing her skirt up over her hips. She quivered helplessly as fingers traced and then stroked under her suspenders, the bands pulled taut across her hips by her position.

Susan squeaked in outraged surprise as fingers stroked down between her legs, actually pushing the material of her panties between her sex-lips, and tried to rear up off the police car she was bent forward over. A handful of hair and one arm pushed up behind her back froze her into place.

"Do you think we're stupid in the police? Just because you stuff the drugs up your ass or snatch, you think I won't find them? That I won't dare search you properly? Twenty years ago, maybe, darling!"

"But I haven't..."

"Quiet!" he snapped.

With her legs spread wide, and bent forward, an arm pushed up behind her back, Susan couldn't support herself with one hand. Her uniformed tormentor pushed her forward and down, deliberately pushing her breasts down onto the police car's throbbing bonnet. She cried out in forced pleasure, vibration hitting her erect nipples with the shock of 240 volts. And then engine heat burned through blouse and bra with a delicious warmth.

The police officer allowed her up a moment, and then pushed her breasts back down onto the hot vibrating metal, the large mounds flattening under her, her tormentor ensuring maximum flesh in contact. Up, and then she was forced down again, totally helpless, pleasure and humiliation strangely intertwined, her cry a confused wail. He pushed her free hand back down onto the edge of the bonnet, his free hand now resting carelessly on a bare buttock.

"Going to be a good girl now?"

"Yes, yes," she stammered.

"I prefer members of the public to address me as Officer!"

"Yes Officer," Susan gasped obediently.

He stroked her behind, then reached under her to heft and knead a full breast. Susan groaned as a nipple was pinched.

"You've no objection to a body and internal search? You consent freely?"

"Yes Officer," she moaned.

Slowly, but firmly and deliberately, extracting the maximum humiliation from the situation as well as testing his power, the uniformed man hooked his fingers under her panties and pulled up, forcing the now sodden rope of material deeper between Susan's sex-lips. She squeaked when he yanked up, the thong cutting painfully deep into the soft flesh of her pussy, pulled up onto her toes. A palm between her shoulder blades - lightly, guiding not forcing - pushed her breasts back down onto the police car's bonnet again. Susan cried out helplessly in delight.

Vibration! Heat! And her poor pussy being cut in two! God, she was so wet!

The pressure on her sex was reduced, Susan allowed to come down off her toes and up off the throbbing, hot, bonnet. The officer stroked a buttock. Trained now, she made no move or word of protest when the sodden crotch-rope her thong panties had become was used to pull her to her toes again, big breasts obediently pushed down onto hot, vibrating metal; her only response a helpless moan. Ass up, breasts down, again and again, until she was gasping, close to sobbing, close to coming!

The search was long, slow and relentless. Standing up against her, his crotch pressing up against her, Susan could feel the police officer's erection. He reached up under her blouse, fingers sinking into her stomach, tracing the line of her rib-cage. Stroking over her shoulders and down under her, the big man's fingers ever so lightly caressed her collar-bones, stroked her throat; and then his breath hot on her neck, he reached inside her bra.

It was a fantasy come to life. Susan, obediently motionless, sighed in soft pleasure as her swollen nipples were rolled between thumb and forefinger, groaning as her breasts were pulled out of her bra, the full firm mounds roughly squeezed and twisted. It was even better than the submissive fantasies her lover had forced her to reveal to him, kneeling naked and bound at his feet, while he dripped candlewax onto her breasts. Perfectly docile, she was still as her breasts were handled, her sex-lips stroked and pinched, buttocks patted and stroked.

"Head up, keep your legs wide. Dip your back a bit more.

Present that ass!"

The still unseen man standing behind her had a hand between her legs, cupping her pouting sex in one palm, his flesh hot, burning, on Susan's. She gasped as he ripped open her blouse, buttons scattering across the police car's bonnet, and then tied the remnants out of the way behind her shoulders. The night air caressed her breasts, now pushed up and squeezed together by her bra under them, and was even more exciting than it had been on her bare behind. Being naked out of doors, the risk of discovery, had always been one of her turn-ons.

Up beside her now - she could see the uniformed man's rank badges; an Inspector - he cupped her chin with one hand, forcing her mouth open. Blunt, strong, fingers, tasting faintly of soap, probed around her teeth, under and over her tongue. Susan whined as a firm grip pulled her tongue right out of her open mouth, but it did no good.

He pushed her legs together long enough to pull her skirt and panties down her legs, contentedly patting her on the behind like an obedient domestic animal when Susan obediently spread her legs wide again without being told. Panties and ripped-off bra were bundled up into a ball and pushed into her mouth. Susan tasted her own juices!

To be continued...

The cover photograph for this book and many others are
available as limited edition prints.
Write to:-

Viewfinders Photography
PO Box 200,
Reepham
Norfolk
NR10 4SY

for details, or see,

www.viewfinders.org.uk

TITLES IN PRINT

Silver Mink

ISBN 1-897809-22-0   The Captive *Amber Jameson*
ISBN 1-897809-24-7   Dear Master *Terry Smith*
ISBN 1-897809-26-3   Sisters in Servitude *Nicole Dere*
ISBN 1-897809-28-X   Cradle of Pain *Krys Antarakis*
ISBN 1-897809-32-8   The Contract *Sarah Fisher*
ISBN 1-897809-33-6   Virgin for Sale *Nicole Dere*
ISBN 1-897809-39-5   Training Jenny *Rosetta Stone*
ISBN 1-897898-45-X   Dominating Obsession *Terry Smith*
ISBN 1-897809-49-2   The Penitent *Charles Arnold**
ISBN 1-897809-56-5   Please Save Me! *Dr. Gerald Rochelle**
ISBN 1-897809-58-1   Private Tuition *Jay Merson**
ISBN 1-897809-61-1   Little One *Rachel Hurst**
ISBN 1-897809-63-8   Naked Truth II *Nicole Dere**
ISBN 1-897809-67-0   Tales from the Lodge *Bridges/O'Kane**
ISBN 1-897809-68-9   Your Obedient Servant Charlotte *Anna Grant**
ISBN 1-897809-70-0   Bush Slave II *Lia Anderssen**
ISBN 1-897809-74-3   Further Private Tuition *Jay Merson**
ISBN 1-897809-75-1   The Connoisseur *Francine Whittaker**
ISBN 1-897809-77-8   Slave to her Desires *Samantha Austen**
ISBN 1-897809-79-4   The Girlspell *William Avon**
ISBN 1-897809-81-6   The Stonehurst Letters *J.L. Jones**
ISBN 1-903687-07-1   Punishment Bound *Francine Whittaker**
ISBN 1-903687-11-X   Naked Deliverance *Lia Anderssen**
ISBN 1-903687-13-6   Lani's Initiation *Danielle Richards**

*UK £4.99 except *£5.99 --USA $8.95 except *$9.95*

All titles, both in print and out of print, are
available as electronic downloads at:

http://www.adultbookshops.com

e-mail submissions to:
Editor@electronicbookshops.com

TITLES IN PRINT

Silver Moon

ISBN 1-897809-16-6   Rorigs Dawn *Ray Arneson*
ISBN 1-897809-17-4   Bikers Girl on the Run *Lia Anderssen*
ISBN 1-897809-23-9   Slave to the System *Rosetta Stone*
ISBN 1-897809-27-1   White Slavers *Jack Norman*
ISBN 1-897809-31-X   Slave to the State *Rosetta Stone*
ISBN 1-897809-38-7   Desert Discipline *Mark Stewart*
ISBN 1-897809-40-9   Voyage of Shame *Nicole Dere*
ISBN 1-897809-42-5   Naked Plunder *J.T. Pearce*
ISBN 1-897809-43-3   Selling Stephanie *Rosetta Stone*
ISBN 1-897809-46-8   Eliska *von Metchingen*
ISBN 1-897809-47-6   Hacienda, *Allan Aldiss*
ISBN 1-897809-48-4   Angel of Lust, *Lia Anderssen**
ISBN 1-897809-50-6   Naked Truth, *Nicole Dere**
ISBN 1-897809-51-4   I Confess!, *Dr Gerald Rochelle**
ISBN 1-897809-53-0   A Toy for Jay, *J.T. Pearce**
ISBN 1-897809-54-9   The Confessions of Amy Mansfield, *R. Hurst**
ISBN 1-897809-55-7   Gentleman's Club, *John Angus**
ISBN 1-897809-57-3   Sinfinder General *Johnathan Tate**
ISBN 1-897809-59-X   Slaves for the Sheik *Allan Aldiss**
ISBN 1-897809-60-3   Church of Chains *Sean O'Kane**
ISBN 1-897809-62-X   Slavegirl from Suburbia *Mark Slade**
ISBN 1-897809-64-6   Submission of a Clan Girl *Mark Stewart**
ISBN 1-897809-65-4   Taming the Brat *Sean O'Kane**
ISBN 1-897809-66-2   Slave for Sale *J.T. Pearce**
ISBN 1-897809-69-7   Caged! *Dr. Gerald Rochelle**
ISBN 1-897809-71-9   Rachel in servitude *J.L. Jones**
ISBN 1-897809-72-2   Beaucastel *Caroline Swift**
ISBN 1-897809-73-5   Slaveworld *Steven Douglas**
ISBN 1-897809-76-X   Sisters in Slavery *Charles Graham**
ISBN 1-897809-78-6   Eve in Eden *Stephen Rawlings**
ISBN 1-897809-80-8   Inside the Fortress *John Sternes**
ISBN 1-903687-00-4   The Brotherhood *Falconer Bridges**
ISBN 1-903687-01-2   Both Master and Slave *Martin Sharpe**
ISBN 1-903687-03-9   Slaves of the Girlspell *William Avon**
ISBN 1-903687-04-7   Royal Slave; Slaveworld Story *Stephen Douglas**
ISBN 1-903687-05-5   Castle of Torment *Caroline Swift**
ISBN 1-903687-08-X   The Art of Submission *Tessa Valmur**
ISBN 1-903687-09-8   Theatre of Slaves *Mark Stewart**
ISBN 1-903687-10-1   Painful Prize *Stephen Rawlings**
ISBN 1-903687-13-6   The Story of Emma *Sean O'Kane**

UK £4.99 except *£5.99 --USA $8.95 except *$9.95